THE CONNECTION

The Connection

Two Worlds. One Connection.

DANA CLAIRE

Chamberlain Publishing House

To my mother, whose death inspired me to live a hundred lives through the stories I write. Our dream of creating fiction together was not in vain. This one's for you, Mom! You are loved and missed but your legacy lives on with each turned page...

Chapter One

Cash

One week before

I sprinted through the corridor, adrenaline pumping, lights flickering above me, the DOAA's alarm piercing my eardrums. The others followed somewhere behind, my pace outmatching theirs. I was fast. Hell, the fastest on my planet. But right now, it was anger that fueled my speed, not ability. Seraphina was dead, and someone was going to pay, human or not.

Two guards rounded the bend just ahead of me. I laughed in their faces as they drew their weapons. Increasing my speed, I catapulted off the wall, grabbing the first guard's necktie, cradling it like a noose around his throat. More than anything, I wanted to kill him, but I'd settle for him passing out. I tightened my hold until he slumped to the ground. The second DOAA agent came at me with his Ferroan knife, the only weapon on Earth that could kill me or my kind. The long blade was forged with a sharply tapered point and the letters DOAA etched on the brown handle. I grinned as it shook in his hands.

"First time holding that, kid, or first time intending on using it?" I sneered. His reaction was warranted. Not many

1

DOAA agents had to fight us. We generally came in peace and in truth could overtake most humans without even batting an eye. Not that I thought this guy stood a chance at my demise. He was just a kid, most likely a new recruit, ordered to cross my lethal path. But part of me wanted to be put out of my misery, so I welcomed his effort.

He positioned his body, feet wide and knees bent.

"You sure about this?" I taunted him and gave a nod to the guard on the floor.

"Captain Kingston, the Director just wants to talk to you." His voice cracked like a prepubescent human.

I laughed. Director Dod wanted to talk. My girlfriend was murdered, and these humans wanted to talk. With a swift uppercut to the boy's jaw, he flipped backward, hitting his head on the wall before landing on his side.

The corridor filled with a deafening silence, soon interrupted by my sister's faint voice. "Cash," she called to me.

Steeling myself, I slowly approached the doors at the end of the corridor, waving my hands in front of them to release the locking mechanism. I stepped inside and came to a complete stop.

A lone metal table stood in the center of the dimly lit room. Strands of Seraphina's jet-black hair draped over its edge, her prone body covered by a white sheet. Wires strung from her arms to machines that towered over me. They were keeping her "fresh," as they called it on Earth. Her body was being preserved for transit back to Ferro.

I pulled back the cloth as energy crackled over my skin, settling into a steady hum as the source inside me coursed through my veins. It was Sera. Her last memory stretched out to me in sound waves, urging the energy source inside my chest to read her message before anyone else.

Alongside the pain I felt in losing her, I hoped she would tell me how she died. I would do anything in my power to find who was responsible. And when I did, I would make them—and anyone else who got in my way—suffer.

My pulse timed itself with the pounding footsteps in the outside corridor, leaving me with only seconds to connect to her energy source stored within her chest cavity. My sister's hitched breath from the other side of the room made me pause. I wanted to mourn the body beneath the sheet. I wanted to touch her one last time, but I couldn't allow my emotions to take hold of me.

I moved the sheet back a couple of inches, exposing our matching scars, and traced her skin. The ridge of a dia-mond-shaped marking grazed my touch, and I pressed my finger gently into her flesh. The memory flooded through me almost instantaneously, soaking my mind with Seraphina's last seconds on this planet.

She was lying on a metal table in what appeared to be a cave. Two deadly cuts lacerated her right ankle and right wrist—the rest of her body covered in dirt. Sweat sprinkled her brow. Blood dotted her lips—lips I had kissed a thousand times and would never kiss again. Along her jawline were traces of bruising in hues of deep purple. Seraphina suddenly gasped and expelled a voice foreign to hers. "My daughter—you need to protect my daughter. She holds the key. You need her, and she needs you. Remember the safehouse I told you about. Start there. Go now. There's little time. Find her, Cash, please. Crede Mihi."

The last bit of energy thrust me across the room, hurling me backward until my back slammed against the wall. I opened my eyes to find my sister kneeling above me. Tears fell from her cheeks, landing on my chest as she cupped her hands around my face.

I gasped for air, confusion hitting me all at once. "It wasn't her. It was Faye."

Chapter Two

Beatrice

Present Day

My friend Chris leaned his hip against the locker next to mine. His piercing blue eyes danced annoyingly between Darla and me. "So . . ." Chris lowered his voice to almost a whisper. "Have you heard who's back at Cartwright High School?"

Taking the bait, I answered, "No, who?" Not like I gave a rat's ass. This day was already throwing me off my game. Dad was acting like a freak this morning, asking me a hundred parental questions. *What time will you be home? How long is track practice? Have you gotten an oil change for your car recently? Maybe you should today after school. I don't like you driving that old thing if you don't keep her up to date on repairs.* I wanted to roll my eyes right out of my head.

I grabbed my English textbook and stuffed it into my messenger bag. An exposed safety pin snagged the skin on my hand, and I winced—Darla's handiwork. Twenty-five safety pins later and many prick marks, I was ready to kill her creative juices and forbid her from altering anything again, even in the name of fashion.

Darla sent an exaggerated huff into the air, expelling the same sentiment I was so desperately holding in toward both of my friends. "You're so annoying, Chris. Just tell us."

He glared at her but continued.

"The Kingstons and the Flannerys."

Darla's bag slipped through her hand and landed on the ground. Her books spilled onto the green-and-white checked floors. Welp, that got her attention. "No way! How do you know?"

"How do you think? The queen of gossip, Kathleen Butler, has been telling everyone," Chris said.

My gaze darted back and forth from Darla to Chris.

"Who are the Kingstons and the Flannerys? Why is that a big deal?" Blood bubbled in the wake of the puncture, and I sucked my hand to stop the minor cut from ruining my clothes.

Darla stared at me with a wild expression I, unfortunately, knew too well. Only two topics piqued Darla's interest like a bloodhound: hot boys and hotter boys. "Do you remember when we were paging through my junior yearbook, and you said, 'This guy's gorgeous. What's his deal?'"

"Maybe. He had a twin sister or something, right?"

"Yep, that was Cash Kingston and his sister, Tasha." Darla crossed her arms over her chest, covering the guitarist's lizard-like tongue depicted on her shirt. Her apple-red lips curled into a devilish grin. "Rumor has it a talent agency discovered them and the Flannery triplets before you moved back here, and they went to Los Angeles. Just picked up and left."

I'd only been back in town for two months since middle school. A tang of jealousy swam in my stomach at the mention of the time I had been away.

"I don't see why they didn't ask me." Chris gestured to his physique. "I could model. I'm blonde with blue eyes, tall, and the star of Cartwright's baseball team. Some have even called me dreamy." He bared his pearly white teeth and posed with an imaginary bat.

"Yeah, who? Your mother?" Darla laughed, pushing him out of his stance.

I rolled my eyes as I pulled another book from my locker. "So, why are they back, then? Who cares?" I avoided the death pins as I shoved the fat English book behind my science notebook.

Darla and Chris didn't even hear me. Instead, they froze, and stared over my head.

No, correction. Chris stared. Darla salivated. She looked like a hungry lion eying a raw steak. I had a feeling I knew what they were looking at, or should I say whom. I begged my body not to turn, but curiosity got the best of me.

Well damn. The yearbook did *not* do them justice. Did the Twilight Vampires with tans just walk in? Seriously, these five were beautiful. I recognized the boy in the middle right away from Darla's yearbook—Cash Kingston. His chest and arms were ripped. I'd like to get a hold of his workout plan. That boy had no body fat. I noticed his eyes, the closer he approached. Something about them were wrong. His irises appeared to be a mirage of deep purple, red, and green, circling against a dark sapphire blue. In a flash, a white core pulsed through the black pupil. I had seen eyes like this before. In my dreams. I blinked, and dark blue eyes appeared. I shook my head. Was I losing it?

Two blonde boys flanked Cash. They were just as tall and muscular, equally striking, but somehow boring, comparatively speaking. Not the boys you bring home to your parents by any means. At least not my dad. It'd be a cold day in hell before Dad let this crew into our home. But they didn't scream *hide your babies* like Cash did. He was straight-up terrifying.

The girl on the right looked exactly like Cash. That must have been his sister, Tasha. She had the same dark brown hair, wavy and thick, but much longer—down to her butt—and the same high cheekbones, yet hers were dusted with a light pink blush. Her face was stoic.

As they neared my locker, the gang broke up. The two on the left went into the adjacent classroom, the two on the right continued past us, but Cash stopped right in front of me. The world around me blurred except for him. I wanted to run—god, even hide if I could fit into my locker. But I couldn't. I was paralyzed.

My heartbeat picked up as he leaned into my personal space. His breath danced across my cheeks; we were so close. And his eyes—the rainbow colors swirling within each other, slithering around the white center—were back, toying with me. A feeling of familiarity tugged inside of me, drawing me into a memory too distant to recover. I reached deep into my mind, desperate for answers, but a current from my left breast shot through my blood, flooding it with an electric charge that caused me to lose focus.

A low growl seemed to come from him. At first I thought I misheard. But the hairs on my skin didn't. They stood at attention.

I stepped backward and knocked into the lockers. The cold metal stung my exposed skin. In a moment of clarity, I realized I looked like a dork. A clumsy freakazoid. The small distraction broke Cash's trance, causing his expression to harden. His eyes narrowed, darkening to a stormy blue, the brilliant colors dissipating to nothing. His mouth thinned into a straight line as he ran his hand through his thick dark hair. Tension rolled off his shoulders in waves. Things just got majorly weird.

"You're blocking my locker." Cash grinded his teeth.

My legs betrayed me. My body unable to submit to anything but a shudder.

"Move," he growled.

I begged my body to obey. Right or left. With a deep breath, I finally managed to shift left. Cash pounded his fist on the door once, and it popped open. He slipped a book out of the top shelf, closed it with a little more force than necessary, and then continued down the hall like nothing happened.

"Oh my god." Darla grabbed me by the shoulders, her fingers hot against my skin. She shoved her face so close to mine I could smell her coffee breath. "What the hell was that?"

My thoughts exactly. He had looked at me with such hatred. It's not like I knew that was his locker. And his eyes . . . I shuddered.

Chris waved his hand in front of me. A trace of his cologne followed in their wake. "Earth to Bea. You in there?" When I didn't answer, he turned to Darla. His nose crinkled. "I think he stunned her. Do the Kingstons have magical powers now? I wouldn't be surprised."

Fire ignited in my core. No matter what Cash's reasons were, he didn't have to be such a . . .

"Douchebag!" I finished my thought aloud.

"Oh, good. She's alive." Chris rolled his eyes. "We could have told you that. They aren't the friendliness crew. It's probably best if you stay away from them and refrain from ogling like a boy band fan."

But that's the thing. Cash was gorgeous, and yes, I'd be lying if I said I wasn't attracted to him—worse was I feared him. And I had no idea why.

Darla looped her arm through mine and grabbed both our bags from the ground. "Come on. Let's get you to class before you combust." Darla spun me around and then waggled her fingers over my shoulder. "See you later, Chris."

By the time we reached English, I'd calmed down. We hurried to our seats just as the bell rang. But my momentary contentment came to a screeching halt as I witnessed the dismayed expression on Darla's face. Her eyes traveled over my head as I mouthed to her, "What's wrong?"

Before she answered, a shock rippled through my chest and my body jerked. I turned around impulsively, and my mouth dropped open for the second time that day. My gaping stare fluctuated between shock and disbelief.

Could I have had worse luck?

"You following me?" Cash cocked his brow with disdain. "Do I have to get a restraining order on my first day back?" His arms crossed his chest, stretching the t-shirt he wore and accentuating the ripples underneath it.

Heat rushed to my cheeks, but my traitorous voice never found a way to my mouth. Instead, I turned around, gripping the sides of my desk for support. Darla cringed sympathetically before turning her focus to Mr. Mack, our English teacher.

Not even a minute passed and the acid reflux burning in my chest returned. Again, I had the urge to twist in my seat. I turned and found Cash staring at me as if I was some rare wildlife. He hated me. That was obvious.

"What?" I scowled, massaging my chest.

Cash's eyes followed my movement. "I was concerned you were mute. Now that we have that cleared up, what's your name?"

Words caught in my throat. My name?

Cash uncrossed his arms and leaned forward, closing the space between us. The heat of his breath grazed my skin for the second time today, warming the chill splintering through my body. His lips were suddenly too close to mine.

"Your name? I'm starting simple." His voice was deep and throaty. Both his eyebrows were raised to his dark brown hairline.

Frustration swelled in my chest. I choked out. "Why?"

Cash smiled. His eyes connected with mine while his expression turned annoyingly smug.

"Well, I'll need it for the restraining order." He tipped his head sideways, waiting for a reaction.

The blonde-haired girl next to Cash, Kathleen, the famous Cartwright busybody, snickered at our conversation. My cheeks were probably a permanent dark pink—they'd be scarred for life.

"You . . . you're an . . ." The words tangled around my tongue, strangling my speech. Finally, I managed to spit them out. "Ass!"

Cash threw his hands over his heart melodramatically and leaned back on his chair, pretending to be offended. "Aw, don't get your panties in a bunch over me. I've been called a lot worse." He winked.

I could only imagine. In my mind, a list of detention-worthy names reared their ugly heads, but I bit my lip and turned back around.

By some terrible twist of fate, we shared the same schedule. Cash's glare continued throughout the day. By the end of last period, my stomach twisted in so many knots, I felt like a wrung-out washcloth. I positioned myself far away from him in all our other classes after English, but the heat of his eyes always seemed to find me. And even though I tried not to care, every hate-filled glance singed me to my core. The strange low hum in my chest was persistent. It was as if my body had picked up a static radio station. At lunch, Chris asked me if I had done something to piss Cash off; by the end of the day, Darla was convinced I had.

I left Coach Barb a message that I'd miss track practice after school. I never missed track. I was the best. Coach Barb said she never saw a human run as fast. She didn't know it was because feeling the ground under my feet and the cool air against my cheeks comforted me. I hadn't had a lot of relief since my mom died.

But holy crap on a cookie, the burning in my chest was so severe I didn't think I could make it around the course without vomiting. Maybe I was coming down with something.

After the final bell, I walked out to the parking lot. The late fall breeze cooled the boiling blood inside my veins. The reflection from the setting sun shone on my rusted yellow Beetle convertible, causing me to stop dead in my tracks. Strange honey-like goo covered the ground and my car. *What the hell?* I searched for a nearby tree, thinking it might be sap. Nope. Nothing. The closest bundle of vegetation was a row of bushes outlining the lot entrance, and it was nowhere near my car. I shook my head. My car might not be brand-new, but she didn't deserve to be a garbage disposal. Someone must have thrown remaining contents of food or liquid on my car instead of a trash can. I opened the door, careful to avoid the gook, and slipped into the driver's seat, silently thanking the defacer for missing my windshield. I shoved the keys into good ol' Betsey and threw her into reverse, taking out all my anger, frustration, and embarrassment on the gas pedal, and floored it down the highway toward home.

As I pulled into the pebbled driveway, I noticed two unfamiliar cars: a black SUV and a black sedan. Both license plates were unmarked, and both cars had tinted windows. Anxious memories flashed in my mind, shooting a chill across my skin. The only time I had ever seen cars like this was after my mother died. Strange detectives showed up, questioning my father. I say strange because they had no identification, asked questions unrelated to the accident, and did a search of our house, leaving it in complete disarray. The next day, Dad announced we were moving back to Pennsylvania.

Panic squeezed at my chest, restricting my breath as that familiar sense of melancholy swelled into an overwhelming feeling of dread. Leaving the keys dangling from the ignition, I swung Betsey's door open and flew up the driveway toward the front door. My feet barely touched the gravel.

Inside, I slowed my pace. Multiple voices trickled out from the living room. I clutched my chest. Did something happen to Dad? The acidic feeling had returned to my chest and singed my lungs. I was going to invest in Tums after this. I swallowed in an attempt to alleviate it while extending my right ear so I could hear better.

"Are you sure?" My dad's voice was low—fierce. He was here. He was okay.

"Yes. I think I'd know her," a male answered bitterly. His voice instinctively sent goose bumps to my arms.

"I'm sorry, Robert, but it's true. It's inside her." This time it was a female's voice, young sounding and laced with concern and sympathy.

"But how? Why?"

"I have no idea. But good thing you ran. The whole agency is looking for you," the unfamiliar male spoke again. "I'm lucky I knew about your safehouse. Have you figured out where they went? Has she said anything to you? Are you pressing her enough for answers?"

His questions sent heat to my cheeks. Who was he referring to? Did I know him?

"She knows nothing." There was a bitter edge to my father's reply, and the words that followed sent a chill through my heart. "Her memory was completely erased. And remember, you were the only one who received a message. I know less than you. Clearly, a lot less than you. I've been against her being in this world since the day she was born. Why do you think we lived in a No Zone for so many years? It was not my choice to go to California in the first place."

What was going on? I sucked in a deep breath and rounded the corner into the living room. My eyes found my father right away. He paced in front of our electric fireplace with its artificial coals. A faded baseball cap covered his light brown hair, which had recently begun to gray. He wore a jogging suit. His headphones dangled from his phone, which snugly fitted in the armband around his bicep. It actually annoyed me that he refused to wear the AirPods I gave him last year for his birthday. He was super anti-technology.

"Beatrice Ann," my father exclaimed, stopping abruptly. "I thought you were at track practice until five." Sweat glistened along his hairline as his gaze quickly diverted across the room to the long L-shaped couch.

My body stiffened the instant I followed his gaze.

Cash Kingston sat on the sofa like he owned the place.

Chapter Three

Beatrice

I held my breath until I began to see spots. Cash Kingston. In my home. On my couch. With my father. What the hell!

His guttural voice interrupted my internal meltdown. "Robert, I thought you said *she* wouldn't be home." His body leaned forward while his shoulders constricted. His muscles bulged with peaks and valleys.

How did Cash know my dad, especially by his first name? The room started to spin like the teacup ride. I was going to vomit.

"You met her already?" My father's hands went to his hips. His curious tone lowered to a paternal growl. Cash shrugged, then glared at me like *I* was the intruder. My father shifted his focus to the girl leaning against the adjacent wall and asked, "I thought you landed yesterday when Bea was at school."

I hadn't even taken notice of her, but sure enough, it was Tasha, Cash's sister. She had changed into black dress slacks, a white button-down shirt, and a black suit jacket; a look completely different than school attire. Her wavy locks were pulled into a bun with loose tresses framing her face. What were they feeding that girl? She seemed so much older than her twin.

"We did," she said, addressing my dad. "No one was supposed to engage with the subject today; just observe." She closed in on the space behind Cash, eyeing him with suspicion before smacking him on the back of the head.

I jumped, startled by her response.

"Hey, what was that for?" Cash twisted in his seat while rubbing his head. His muscles relaxed as he threw her a sheepish smirk. It was good to see that he didn't treat everyone as awful as he had me. Remind me to never stand in front of his locker again.

Tasha shot him an expression that said: *You know what that was for.*

"We haven't been formally introduced. I'm Tasha Kingston." Her voice was polite but far from warm.

I glared at my father for an explanation. He stared back at me like I had ten heads, then glanced at Cash.

"I can't guard her!" Cash rose from the couch. His fists clenched and unclenched. The muscles in his forearms rippled in a domino effect up to his elbows. "Your planet is on my last nerve, Robert." His stormy eyes blustered with menace. Did he say *planet*?

"Cash, stop," his sister warned, placing her hand on his shoulder. He eyed me like a bull staring at a red cape. If I had any understanding of self-preservation, this was when I should have run.

Tasha turned her attention to my father. "Maybe you should talk to your daughter in private. We can come back later. When things—"

"What's he gonna say to her?" Cash interrupted her with a venomous tone. "Don't sweat your new bodyguard? You know she can't stay away from me!" He jerked his shoulder away from Tasha's hand.

My hands flew to my hips. "Is this some type of joke? I do *not* sweat you and I do *not* need a bodyguard. And I don't even want to be near you!" That last part might have been a lie. My body was such a traitor. It called to him since the second I saw him in the hallway today. He might have petrified me, but he also had this alluring draw.

"Your body is the last thing I want to guard," Cash assured me.

"You're an ass!"

"Yeah, you said that already. Remember?" Cash rolled his eyes. "Seriously, your kind has such limited vocabulary. It's really embarrassing." Stepping forward, he motioned at the coffee table with his hand, and it moved out of his way. Just like that, the metal table moved. Freaking moved on its own. Across the room!

Your planet? Your kind? The coffee table . . . Oh my god. Oh my god. My throat closed suddenly. A suppressed scream burned my esophagus, threatening to claw its way out. I clenched my jaw and started retreating backward with no idea where I was headed.

"Bea," my father said softly. My questioning eyes shot to him. Why was he not freaking out? "Calm down. They are not here to hurt you."

They? The signs were there but I was having trouble connecting the dots. Maybe I just didn't want to. I tried to breathe, but damn my lungs . . . I needed to sit.

Cash snapped his fingers and the folding chair resting against the wall opened. With the wave of his hand, it flew across the room, landing under me as I almost fainted. My butt pressed into the cold seat as my hands gripped the sides, desperately clutching onto something real. This can't be happening. They weren't human. Cash wasn't human.

My breathing picked up. "What are they?" I couldn't form words beyond that. My heart pounded against my rib cage, threatening to break a bone. Part of my brain, the realistic part, didn't want to believe what I saw, but the other half— this nagging memory—knew that this was really happening. An overwhelming feeling of *déjà vu tugged at the back of my mind.*

"Is this necessary? You're scaring her half to death." The creases around Dad's eyes furrowed. He inched closer, a hand outstretched as if to console me, but he must have thought better of it, crossing his arms over his chest instead.

Cash shrugged.

"Beatrice, we need to talk. Cash and the others . . ." Dad paused as if unsure how much my mind could take, ". . . are not human, but they are our friends. I've invited them here. They were Mom's friends, too," Dad said with a sympathetic voice. He shot a look at Cash and Tasha. "Why don't you give us a minute?"

"Does that mean we should leave, too?" a male voice called from the adjoining room that I hadn't even noticed was occupied. Three people sat at the dining room table where computers, papers, and other technology had replaced our fake floral centerpiece. They were the Flannery triplets.

"Yes, you guys, too," Dad said, his expression quickly becoming vexed. "Cash, stay close. We'll have to assign people to guard Bea, and I need you here to give out orders."

Wetting my lips and smacking them together, I tried to speak. "Guard? Why do I need a guard?"

"People are after you; probably will kill you," Cash said bluntly. "Not that I blame them." The last part he grumbled.

"Cash," Dad warned.

"What? It's true!" Cash shrugged his right shoulder and leaned against the couch arm.

My insides coiled like a barbed wire. Kill me? I pinched the skin on my forearm. Maybe I was dreaming. Maybe I could wake myself up out of this insane night terror. I pinched myself again. Nope. Real. This was stinking real.

"You can thank your mom for this mess." Cash's words snapped me back to the conversation. His eyes pierced me. My mom? An unexpected surge rippled through me. I shot up from my chair, marched right up to him, and stepped into his personal space. He didn't move. In fact, the crook of his mouth tilted up in an arrogant smile. I raised my hand to slap him across the face. No one spoke about my mother. No one. Before I knew what had happened, he held my wrist in a grip so tight, my bones ached. My arm dangled from his grasp.

"Let her go." Tasha's heels clicked toward us. Cash held up the palm of his other hand, warning her to back off.

"This is a ridiculous waste of time," she hissed, yet she had stopped in her tracks.

Cash towered over me, glaring. The intensity of his gaze sent shivers down my spine. My heart rate sped up, connecting with the charge running through my body. I swore it was audible.

"You have no idea what I know or what I can do. For example, every thought you had about me today, good and bad, I heard," he spoke in a voice so low I must have been the only person to hear him. Suddenly, he was the only noise. It was like everyone else had vanished.

Still holding my wrist, he stepped closer.

"You're wrong." My voice was a mere whisper.

I held my ground, refusing to be bullied backward. The space between our bodies diminished. His heat wrapped around me like a python. I hated how good it felt to be near him, and I wondered if he sensed it, too, because for a split second, his eyes softened. He shook his head and blinked. All too soon his glare returned, and his eyes were deadly.

He leaned in so our cheeks touched. His mouth brushed against my ear, doing stupid girly things to the inside of my stomach. "I'm not wrong. I know everything inside your head. I know more about you than you know about yourself."

Anger grew within me, hot and electric. I wanted to pull away, but he tightened his fingers around my wrist, jerking me into submission. He inched forward another step. This time, I retreated backward. Objects flew past me as if he beckoned them out of our way. He matched my movements until he pinned me against the wall. His grip loosened.

"Why did Faye do this?" He shook his head as if he were battling an internal tug of war.

My chest constricted. My pulse spiked. Mom. What did my mom have to do with this? I looked to my father for the answer. How could he let Cash treat me this way? But Dad was frozen in the spot I last saw him. His right arm rested on the mantel, his head against the wall behind him, and his left hand cupped the back of his neck dangling his elbow in the air. His eyes were glazed over. Fear flooded my insides, drowning me with panic.

"What are you?" My voice wavered. "How are you doing this?" The idea of Cash as an extraterrestrial slammed around in my brain, reverberating, echoing, punctuating my reality. He could freeze people. Literally.

Cash ignored my question. "Your mother took an awful risk, gambling with your life and everyone else's. All for what?" He shook his head. "And this . . ." He placed his palm on my chest. My freaking chest. But not in a *let's get to second base way*. A heat like no other collected in my chest, as if my blood had rushed to his hand, dancing under my skin as if it belonged to him and wanted to break free of me. "This! This isn't yours." His words hovered between us, an insane jigsaw puzzle.

"I don't understand." My legs shook. If he had not been holding me, I doubt I would have been able to stand.

"Of course, you don't understand, but your mother did." I watched his teeth clench so hard, I wondered if they might break. He threw down my arm. Unable to hold my body weight, I slid to the floor, clutching my knees into my buzzing chest.

"How could she?"

Successive waves of rage threatened to level me, crushing me into the wall with invisible pressure. Heated words burst out of my mouth before I even processed them. "Screw you. Don't talk about my mother! Ever. EVER! I don't care what you are!"

Hot tears stung my eyes and released down my cheeks. My lungs expanded, and I sucked in a sharp breath causing my lower lip to tremble.

Cash's jaw twitched, as if the sight of me pained him.

The others in the room started to move as though the private moment between Cash and me had never happened. My dad's eyes flickered to Cash, and then searched the room for me.

"So, it is true."

"Yeah, because that's something I would make up," Cash spit out at my father. "Your daughter is my own personal hell."

Whoa. If that's not the most insulting thing a person . . . well, non-person could say to someone. And even worse: Dad never defended me.

Cash shook his head several times before nodding to my father in what seemed to be a private thought between the two. "We need to set up some ground rules. Both of you must lay low. That means do not draw attention to yourselves." He looked at me with contempt.

My father nodded, releasing a breath he'd been holding for some time. I worried more about the unspoken words between them. Dad walked over to me and lowered himself to the ground, wrapping me in his arms. I soaked up their warmth, clinging to them like I had my whole life. Arms I always believed could and would protect me. But now I was filled with uncertainty and distrust.

"It's okay, honey. We'll be okay," he said as my tears absorbed into his sweatshirt. His words contradicted his rapid heartbeat, which thudded against my cheek.

Clearly, Cash was in control and began barking orders left and right. "Paul and Mark, stay the night in Robert's guest room. Someone must remain here at all times. We will switch on and off. Sammie, Tasha, and I will set up back at the house. Contact all informants. Go through Faye's notes, her work computer, her personal computer, books, laptop . . . hell, go through everything. I want to know when Faye did this and why. I want to account for every second of her life before she died."

Cash turned to me and paused. At first, I thought he might say something. His lips parted, and the whisper of a breath slipped through. Then the curtains swayed in the living room, and he was gone.

Chapter Four

Cash

Back at the safe house, I threw a kitchen chair against the wall and roared. Splintered wood rained down onto the tile. I hadn't been inside these four walls since Seraphina was killed. Nothing had been touched, just abandoned. When the news of her death arrived, the five of us jumped on the first flight out to California. Returning to this house was excruciating. Every nook and cranny reminded me of Sera—our memories, the moments we shared together. There wasn't a place you could sit that we hadn't christened. I envisioned her eyes dark with passion, her hair mussed, her cheeks red from my unshaven face, and her lips swollen from my kisses. The thought of going up to the bedroom we shared made me want to tear this planet apart for answers, sparing no human in the process. And now after all these months, I find Faye's daughter only to realize Faye screwed me.

"Calm down," Tasha's voice resounded from the hallway.

"Calm down. You want me to calm down?" My tone rose, taking all my anger out on my sister. Faye took my girlfriend's energy source and harbored it in her daughter like a womb. Her last wish was that I would protect her, knowing it would be devastating for me—and dangerous. And my sister wanted me to calm down. Hell no!

Tasha placed the kettle on the stove, heating up water for her tea like we were having a normal sibling conversation. One thing about my sister—she was never dramatic. She was my anchor. But now that Sera had been murdered, with Faye robbing her memory as well as my answers, I wasn't sure anyone could keep me in check.

"Yes, I'd like you to get it together and be the leader you were trained to be. The leader you are destined to be." Tasha's calm voice filled my ears. "Because right now, you're acting like an asshat and we don't have time for this. So, get it together, dear brother, because our planet and Earth doesn't have time for your meltdown. The clock is ticking. You know what will happen."

Of course, I knew. It's all anyone ever talked about in my presence.

"Don't go throwing that in my face. I am well aware of the prediction."

I waved the refrigerator door open and willed a can of soda to my hands. I popped the tab and gulped the fizzed beverage until the can was empty, then threw it toward the back door. Tasha used her powers to stop the can midair and guided it into the recycle bin.

I rolled my eyes. Even amid a crisis, my sister cared about Earth. Sometimes I wondered if she cared more for this planet than ours.

She walked over to the refrigerator and opened it like a human, retrieving the milk for her tea. I used my powers for everything. Tasha conserved them like she did water when California was in a drought.

"Do you think she knows more than she's admitting?" I settled in a chair and leaned my head back against the wall. Beatrice's responses to everything today didn't feel like she was hiding something. It was more like she was being impaled by information, blow after blow. And I didn't go easy on her. Why would I? After what her mother did to me . . . did to all of us.

The kettle whistled.

"No," Tasha said thoughtfully. "I think Faye erased Bea's memory and, even if there's a hint of recall, it would take a very strong energy connection or assimilation scientist to bring it back. I don't even know if it's possible without causing damage to her human heart and brain. And as long as she is the womb for one of Ferro's opposing energy sources, we need Beatrice to stay safe . . . and that means alive." Her pointed glare wasn't lost on me. Tasha needed me to get my act together and not do something stupid—like when I attacked the DOAA headquarters after learning of Sera's death.

The scent of Tasha's tea was beginning to calm me, allowing me to get a grip on my emotions. I desperately wanted to know what happened to Sera, and the answers could only be found in the energy source stolen from Sera's chest cavity and surgically placed in Bea's. Even if Bea's presence made me want to rip her head off, I would do everything in my power to keep her safe. Nothing would happen to her. I guess Faye was getting exactly what she wanted.

"Faye would never harm her daughter," Tasha insisted as if reading my thoughts.

"A daughter we didn't know existed until now." I shot a glare at my sister. Faye, our longest human friend, never told us she had a daughter, and this was how we found out. She not only hid her from us for the last four years but had her assimilated as a safe haven for one of the two most sought-after energy sources of our lifetime.

Tasha sighed a long breath before taking a sip of her tea. "I don't know why Beatrice was a secret. But there must be a reason. I trust Faye, and I know somewhere beneath your anger, you do too." Maybe Tasha was right but, in this moment, betrayal had a stronger hold on me than my faith in her.

Warm hands grazed my shoulders as Sammie walked through the kitchen. Vanilla scent wafted in her wake, and she took a seat at the table. She kicked her pink heels across the room.

"I don't like her, Tash." She glared at me like I had something to do with this pesky human being in our lives.

"You don't have to like her. You have to help her," Tasha reasoned.

Sammie's eyes never left mine. "And what do you think?"

"Don't start with me, Sammie. I'm not in the mood." I stood to leave. I was done with this conversation. I needed space. Sammie shot up from her chair, positioning herself right in front of me in seconds. Anger emitted from her emerald eyes. The swirling around her pupils was a typical Ferroean reaction to uncontrollable emotions. Part of me was proud of her tenacity; the exhausted part of me didn't have time for her jealous antics. "I'm serious. Don't!"

Her shoulders dropped as she leaned in, pressing her hands gently on my chest. She pushed up on her toes and brushed her lips against mine.

"I'm not above teaching her a lesson," she whispered, drawing her mouth across my cheek to my ear. "Fix this."

The corner of my mouth lifted. "What would you like me to do? Kill the human who holds Sera's energy source inside of her—and do what with the source? You know our mission. Opposing energy sources are only born when there's an imminent threat to our world, or the universe. We were put on Earth to observe until we are called back to Ferro, and I'll be damned if we do anything less than our jobs."

Sammie pushed my chest. Frustration radiated off her. I grabbed her wrist and swung her around, pinning her arms down. She fought for a second and then slouched in my hold. Her blonde hair tangled against me. We were all mourning in different ways. I knew that. But I didn't have time to contest anyone else when I was already hurting for all the things I should have done. It's my fault Sera was dead. It was my job to fix it. But getting rid of Bea wasn't the answer.

"I want her back." Sammie's voice mirrored a child's temper tantrum. My grip tightened around her not to cause pain but to comfort her better than any words I could conjure. Words were not my specialty. There was nothing I could do, and that helplessness would be the death of me if I didn't guide this team to redemption. Tasha was right. I needed to lead.

The front door flung open, crashing into the wall. I released Sammie and went for the weapon in my ankle strap. Tasha dropped the teacup she was cleaning. Porcelain cracked and scattered the ground. She positioned her body, feet wide and knees bent. Her hands slipped into her seamless pockets to retrieve the Ferro knives from her thigh belts. She flipped them around in her grasp, the blades glinting off the kitchen lights. Sammie somersaulted toward the fake pantry, pressed the button underneath, and caught the weapon that dropped into her hands. We postured, ready for battle.

Honey-colored goo dripped on our floor as dress shoes clacked against the tile. I didn't need to see his face to know who he was.

"Welcome back, Cash, dear boy. Oh, how I've missed you!"

It was Grouper, and this day just got a hell of a lot worse.

Chapter Five

Beatrice

After Cash, Tasha, and Samantha left, Mark and Paul retreated to the basement, where we had stacked the boxes containing my mother's possessions. I hadn't been down there since we moved back to Grandma's house, the home I lived in until we moved out west. I wasn't ready to face the memories. For me, it was hard to believe she died. It was even harder knowing I was there when it happened. When I woke in the hospital, my dad told me Mom and I were in a hiking accident while on our camping trip. Although the authorities weren't exactly sure on the details, they had assumed we slipped and fell down a canyon. When a park ranger found me, I was suffering from dehydration, lacerations, and exhaustion. But Mom was found miles away from me, torn up at the wrists and ankles, even a large cut to her chest. The police believed she was attacked by rabid animals.

When I came to at the hospital, the doctors diagnosed me with post-traumatic amnesia. They said my memory might come back, or I may never remember what happened. No matter how hard I tried, nothing jolted any recollections, and after a few weeks, I was okay with the emptiness of my mind. The idea that I could have saved her or was the reason she died was too suffocating to bear. So instead, we just buried her memories. Her name. Everything.

My dad showered and changed while the others began to pick through my mother's things. When he came back downstairs, his hair was messy and damp. He poured a bowl of cereal and sat across from me at the kitchen table, where I sulked in front of a frozen pizza that I'd warmed in the toaster oven.

Thirty minutes passed without my father or me exchanging a word. By the time he broke the silence, I had just finished mutilating my third slice by flinging all the toppings, one by one, into the garbage.

"Are you going to eat any of it or just play hoops?"

I glanced at the waste can. Scraps of pizza lay on the pale blue ceramic floor, some clinging to the sides of the garbage bag like a family of slugs.

"I am sorry. I know you have questions, and I know how hard this must be for you—"

"You think?" Hard was an understatement. My whole world was freaking rocked! Everything aliens did in the movies was confirmed by an annoyingly good-looking guy in my high school who apparently hated my dead mother—and me. I wanted to scream, hit something. I also wanted to crawl under the covers and pretend it wasn't happening.

Dad sighed. "Honey, your mother and I worked for an agency called the DOAA. It stands for Department of Alien Affairs."

I slowly raised my head as a prickle rippled down my spine. My skin puckered, sending the hairs on my limbs to attention. Well, that didn't sound creepy at all; totally normal. Dad put his hand over mine, yet it did nothing to comfort me. I was speechless, numb . . . I was downright frozen.

"Your mom and I were trained agents in combat, intelligence, and protection. Our main assignment was the DOAA's assimilation department. We guarded Earth's scientists who performed, perfected, and studied the assimilation of aliens like Cash and Tasha." His grip tightened around my hand as if I might run. Truthfully, running sounded like a great idea if I could get my muscles to coordinate with my brain. Not happening.

"It's why we traveled so often. Cash and the others are agents for their planet, Ferro. Our planets have an understanding allowing access to study one another. Cash's team was assigned to an Earth assimilator, Dr. X, who helped them take human shells. Mom and I were the doctor's guards at the time of the assimilation. That's how we all met."

What was I supposed to say? How does someone react to news like this? In one afternoon, I went from being an average high school student to a girl who had an alien bodyguard—and parents who were kickass Earth defenders.

"So . . . you're not a traveling salesman?" My lips curved into a forced grin. I know it sounded like I was naïve. There must have been signs my parents worked with aliens—heck, even a space program—but nothing I can remember. There was nothing out of the ordinary until today.

My father's expression turned grim. "No, we are not traveling salesmen."

"Why do I need *them* as bodyguards?" If my dad was an agent, trained in combat and all, why the alien guards? Couldn't he protect me?

"Cash and the others are more capable against the threat. They possess skill sets surpassing humans."

A nervous laugh escaped me. Cash was more capable? Of what, torturing me to death with his lethal stares, sarcastic comments, and nasty mom remarks?

But my dad's face remained stoic. He was dead serious.

"What threat?"

"People are looking for you. It's why we moved back to Cartwright."

I had to force myself to breathe. Dad told me we moved here to get away from bad memories. I thought he meant the haunting reminder of my mother's death, not because we were on the run. Hell, I was excited to move back to Cartwright, where my two best friends since kindergarten resided. The only two friends I kept in touch with after our move. Grandma's house reminded me of Mom and happier times. I was damn near delirious when he suggested the idea of moving back. I never thought to question it further.

"I'm sorry your mother and I never told you. I believed it was safer this way. Truthfully, I never wanted this life for you. Moving you out to California was a mistake. And now, we need Cash and his team's help to keep you safe. I can't do it alone."

Fear bubbled back to the surface. "Why are people after us—after me?"

"Go on about your life as normal and let Cash and the others handle the rest. Your safety is all that's important."

His words hit me sharply in the chest. Is he insane? After all this, he wanted me to act like nothing happened. My entire world had shifted. Hell, I wasn't even sure my brain had caught up. Part of it was still firing denial signals out while the other was slowly accepting my father's words as truth.

But to stay silent and pretend like nothing has happened . . . Was he nuts?

"Don't I have a right to know what the hell is going on?" I pushed the plate of mutilated pizza away from me. Does my father not know me at all? I've never sat on the sidelines. It's not like Dad was telling me Santa didn't exist. It was more like he *did.* How did he expect me to believe in something that sounded so fictional and not ask questions? I deserved more of an explanation. I deserved the truth.

I grabbed for the soda next to my plate. My hand trembled against the cold condensation of the glass, but I forced it to my mouth and drank so fast that the bubbles tingled inside my nose, and my eyes watered.

When I finally spoke, my voice faltered. "Well, Mom's dead. Who protected her?"

My father's jaw contracted, and I knew my words had hit home. My shoulders recoiled with regret. I hadn't really wanted to hurt him. I was trying to prove a point.

"I didn't know what she was doing, or I would have intervened. Your mother and I didn't agree on your involvement in this world, and without my knowledge she took you camping to do who knows what. If I had known, I would never have let her . . ." He abruptly stopped and paused.

Wait. What?

"Known what? Mom didn't tell you we were going camping? She . . ." I took a deep breath. "Kidnapped me?" My voice was low and breathy. "Did I really fall and get amnesia?"

My dad shook his head. It was as if the floor was moving. I couldn't take in air. Spots clouded my vision while my fingers gripped the kitchen table for support. If I didn't fall and bump my head, then what happened and why can't I remember? Before I could ask, my dad interrupted.

"Cash and I feel it's important that you continue on like nothing has happened. The less you know, the better we can protect you. The details in all of this are not important. Keeping you safe now is."

I stared at my dad as if he were speaking Latin. Up until today, I didn't even know Cash existed. Now, he and my father were collaborating like old friends about what was in my best interest? Was he not even going to address what happened?

"I'm sorry, honey. I wish things were different but that's final. This is not up for discussion. You are already in over your head because I failed you, and it's my job to protect you. We are doing this my way." Dad rubbed the back of his neck.

I'd heard enough. I stood and threw my napkin on the table and walked out of the room.

When I grabbed the railing to the stairs, I paused and turned to look at my dad. His chin rested in his hands; his eyes closed. Part of me wanted to run back and throw my arms around him. Losing Mom was hard enough; losing him would kill me. But my stubbornness won, and I continued up to my room, leaving my father alone with his thoughts.

In my bedroom, I changed, and then turned to my favorite hobby—scrapbooking. My parents never allowed me to post internet pictures or sign up for social media. "Crede Mihi," Mom said when I pouted and pleaded for an account. In fact, that was her answer to everything when she didn't want to justify her responses. Now I wondered if there was more to her protective behavior than her love for the Latin term. I reached under my bed and pulled out the box of unused memorabilia, postcards, and photos, mostly consisting of landmarks, scenery, historical sites, and architecture. It was my mom's idea at first but once I started, I loved it. She even brought back pictures from their sales trips, which I now know were missions. It was how I was able to be with them without physically being there. I used to treasure those photos the most. Now they symbolized all the lies my parents told me. Stuck in the pile, I found a photo of my mother standing in front of the Welcome to Fabulous Las Vegas sign. It was taken three years ago, and she posed like I would have—hands on her hip with one knee bent. I look a lot like her: hazel eyes, long, wavy brown hair, and legs that went on for days.

Flipping through the pictures increased the aching in my heart and pressure in my chest. I hated my mom for dying, and now I hated her for lying to me. Anger festered in me like termites in wood. I replayed over and over again the events of today, pausing at the same spot: when Cash asked me what my mother had done. Wouldn't I like to know?

By midnight, I climbed into bed under the security of my goose down comforter and allowed my body to relax. My muscles were knotted and sore—it was worse than after track practice. Without realizing it, I started to cry. Tears streaked my face and dissolved into my pillow. The strength and resolve I had shown earlier had run dry, and my stomach twisted with raw ache.

"Why are you crying?" a low voice said.

I jackknifed up in bed and switched on the lamp on my nightstand. My eyes followed the voice to my desk, where Cash's broad shoulders peeked up above a tall stack of my schoolbooks as he straddled my computer chair.

"What the hell are you doing in here? In my. . . my room!" My voice cracked and that damn burning in my chest returned.

I held the blanket over the simple, and slightly see-through, white tank top I'd worn to bed. Cash grinned at me, his expression exasperatingly smug.

"Don't worry. It's nothing I haven't seen before."

"Really? You are in my bedroom in the middle of the night and that's what you have to say? Are you mentally unstable?"

His brow arched while a smile danced on his lips. "I'm not sure, actually. I don't think your planet really cares if I'm mentally stable or not, so long as I'm on their side."

I shook my head. "How long have you been in here?"

"Long enough to wonder when you would stop crying. Trust me, tears don't change anything."

"Ya think?" Were all aliens a pain in the ass, or just this one? And what would he know about tears? I doubt he's ever felt like his world has been ripped out from under him.

"You have no idea," he mumbled so quietly I almost thought I misheard him.

We sat in awkward silence for several moments while Cash's eyes studied every inch of me. The clicking of my alarm clock and the gentle hum of my ceiling fan filled the room. I gripped the covers fiercely, digging my nails into the goose feathers. My throat was tight and dry. Did he really need to be in my room to keep me safe?

Finally, I broke the awkward quietness. "I realize you have no boundaries and god knows there's nothing you won't say, but maybe we could make a deal," I offered, hoping to set some of those ground rules he'd mentioned earlier.

My computer chair rolled forward on its own, closer to the bed. How did he do that? My pulse raced in response. As he moved toward the circle of soft light surrounding my bedside lamp, I could see that he wore gray sweatpants and a white undershirt that hugged his arms like spandex. I hated my traitorous mind for its wandering and my double-crossing heart for its jumpy pace.

"I'm listening. Tell me about this deal." He arched his perfect half-moon brow.

Stay focused, Bea. I took a deep breath. "If I'm not allowed to know what you're doing here and why you're protecting me, then you have to pretend to be normal around me." He laughed. "Fine. Somewhat normal. You can't freeze the room or whatever you did earlier; no sneaking in and out of places, especially my bedroom, and . . ." I paused. "My friends aren't to be harmed."

"Hmmm, that's interesting and all but what do I get out of this?" He folded his arms over the back of the chair and leaned closer.

"In return, I won't keep asking what the hell is going on and what you are doing."

"Fine," he said without protest.

Too easy. What had I missed?

"Okay, now that our deal is settled—why are you in my room?" I crossed my arms over my chest mirroring him.

"You said you wouldn't ask me any questions." He smiled. Cash moved the chair closer. His knees bumped the bedframe and brushed against my leg, which barely peeked out from the sheets. I scooted back, pressing myself against the wall to keep distance between us. Even though I couldn't stand him, my body pulled to him like toying with two magnets.

"No, I said I wouldn't ask you why I need protection or what you're doing here."

"Being in your bedroom is what I am doing. You humans complicate everything, don't you?"

"Oh my god!" I threw my hands up in the air. "You are so frustrating. Forget the people after me; you literally might kill me by aggravation."

His lips curled into a grin. "Can human death even occur from that? I'm no doctor, but I doubt it."

"That's it." I stood on my bed. "You need to leave, or I am going to scream. I doubt my father would condone you sneaking into his daughter's bedroom." I pointed to the door. "I mean it—get out. Now!"

Cash ogled me from head to toe. The electric pull toward him amplified and buzzed through my body, snapping like a rubber band against my rib cage. Standing in only my boy shorts and a tank top, I suddenly felt chilled. I dropped to the bed, scrabbling under the pink-and-yellow striped sheets and cocooning myself in their shelter.

"See you tomorrow, Beatrice," he deadpanned. He stood and, with the wave of his hand, the chair slid back into place under the desk.

"Wait," I called after him. He turned his head, running his fingers through his thick locks. His other hand remained fastened to the doorknob. "You're using the door!"

At first, his brows scrunched together, but then the crook of his mouth lifted. "Isn't that the exit?"

I gaped at him and nodded. It's not like that's how he came in.

"You humans are weird."

Irritation found me again, and I grabbed the closest pillow to chuck at him, but Cash vanished before it even launched into the air. The pillow bounced off the door and landed on the floor.

When I woke, my head hurt like a woodpecker had mistaken me for a tree. My mouth was dry. A quick vision of my mother popped into my head. She was wearing combat gear and black boots. Her clothes were torn and tattered. Sweat and grime speckled her pale face.

"Bea, baby, run . . ."

I blinked and whatever I thought I heard and saw disappeared, leaving me with a splitting headache, cotton mouth, and more questions.

Chapter Six

Beatrice

The next day at school, I pawed at my books in my locker and sent them tumbling into my backpack. I felt like a zombie. My reflection in the mirror hanging above a picture of Mom and me revealed that dark circles had formed under my lashes. My lids hung heavy. Bloodshot lines of red crossed the white parts of my eyes.

After Cash had left my bedroom last night, I'd tossed and turned. How could my parents work with aliens? What type of aliens were the Kingstons and the Flannerys? But the most maddening question of all repeated like a shriek every time I managed to relax: *How could the most annoying, frustrating, obnoxious, and downright terrifying being in the universe also be the one to protect me?*

"Hey!" Darla tugged my hair. "You look like crap."

She opened her locker, throwing her bright yellow zip-up inside, leaving her in a white, racerback tank. It popped against her olive skin and jet-black hair.

I shrugged.

"Still not feeling well?"

I assumed Coach Barb had told Darla's mom I skipped practice. Those women blathered more than teenaged girls and yet they barely knew each other. Coach Barb was new to our school but befriended Darla's mom, Alice, right away. Alice, being the busybody she was, enjoyed having an inside ear at Cartwright.

"I didn't sleep much," I admitted, closing my locker door. I turned around and rested the back of my head against it. My eyes closed for a second, taking in a moment of peace.

It's not as if I could tell Darla my dad worked for a secret agency dealing with extraterrestrials, and five teenage aliens from another planet were here protecting us.

"You ready for English with Mr. Kingston?" Darla laughed as my eyes shot open. "Is that why you're not feeling well—Cash? Can't say that I blame you. Did you see the way he looked at you yesterday? Everyone was talking about it. It's like you ran over his puppy with your car." She paused. "And then backed up over it for kicks."

I threw her a nasty glance and zipped my book bag before flinging it over my shoulder.

"You didn't kill his puppy . . . did you?" she said grinning.

"No," I groaned.

"Ignore him. He's only pestering you because you let him. Maybe he likes you or something."

"What?" Seriously? He had threatened me, talked shit about my mom, secretly snuck into my bedroom, and chastised me for crying. If that was "being liked" by Cash Kingston, I was afraid to ask what dislike would be.

Darla lifted her palms into the air. "I'm kidding. Wow—calm down. You're wound a little tight today." She gave me a quizzical look. "You're acting like a virgin on prom night. Relax. Don't let him get to you. Okay? That's all I was saying."

"Sorry. I'm really tired."

During English, I completely ignored Cash. I tried to pretend the last time we had seen each other was yesterday in school—not in my bedroom. Half-clothed. My cheeks flushed as I remembered the look on his face when he saw me in booty shorts.

Psst, sounded in my head. No that's impossible. He must have said it aloud. I took Darla's advice and ignored him. Seconds later, I heard, *You can't ignore me forever.* How was it no one else seemed to notice Cash annoying me? I turned, questioning whether I was losing my mind or not.

"What do you want?"

"You look awful."

"Thanks for the compliment." I turned back around, trying to focus on Mr. Mack. Could I tell Cash about my vision from this morning? Should I even? Part of me felt like I was concealing something of importance, and the other part of me felt like a freak for having a deceased mother hallucination.

His breath grazed my neck. I scooted my chair up until my rib cage pressed against the desk, hoping the distance would ward him off. It did for about two minutes, until my chair moved backward on its own. I turned to see a wicked grin plastered on his face as he twirled a ruler in between his fingers.

"Seriously? Is there anything in particular you want, or are you planning to torment me for the entire period?"

"I think you are hiding something." He arched his brow.

"Oh, do you," I grumbled. "And what, pray tell, could that be? I'm pretty sure my disdain for you is clearly written all over my face. But if not, let me tell you out loud. I think you suck."

I turned my head back around not even waiting for Cash to respond.

Cash's desk slid forward. The chair legs screeched along the tiled floor. Several students turned and stared. I felt his warm breath through the strands of my hair. The scent of mint, pine, and honey filled the air around me. Oh god, I wished he'd leave me alone.

"I think you remember somewhere deep down what happened on your camping trip with your mom."

White hot anger rose inside of me, and I whipped my head around. If he thought for one second . . .

My nose smacked right into him. Pain exploded in my face as if I had smashed into a brick wall. Blood poured out of my nose in a cascade around my mouth and chin until it dripped down to my t-shirt. My hands flew up, trying to staunch the crimson fluid.

At first Cash looked shocked, and then apologetic—and for a moment I thought I had gone crazy, because Cash didn't seem the remorseful type. But what he said. How could he make such a claim?

Darla screamed, alerting the class to my injury.

"You're bleeding. Oh my god. What happened? Did he hit you?" She jumped to her feet in no time rushing over to my desk.

Cash balked. "Really? You think I hit her?" He handed me fast-food napkins from his pocket. "What type of reputation do I have?"

"Clearly not a good one," I huffed, reluctantly accepting his help. My head tilted back while I pinched my swollen nose at the arch. The brown recycled napkin quickly immersed to a dark red.

"Don't lean back. You could choke! How did this happen?" Darla fussed over me like a mother goose. I tilted forward, putting more pressure at the bend in my nose. "Does anyone have any more tissues?" She lobbed her head back and forth.

"Miss Walker, I think you should go to the infirmary," Mr. Mack said, motioning toward the door.

"I'll take her," Cash responded. His fingers squeezed my flesh as he lifted me by the elbow.

"I'm not going anywhere with you!" I attempted to pull away. Fail. Damn alien strength.

"You're going," he said with a commanding tone. I rolled my eyes. If this was his idea of guarding, I would be hospitalized by week's end.

"Mr. Kingston, make sure you don't break her leg on the way out," Mr. Mack warned.

The classroom giggled, but Darla shot Cash a death stare. I silently thanked her for her solidarity. Cash lowered his face next to hers, so only the three of us could hear. "I would never hurt her. Ever."

Her jaw fell, and she nodded.

"Can you please take me to the nurse?" I pushed him forward and stumbled until I remembered to tilt my head back. He held the door open for me. As we entered the empty hall, I turned left toward the infirmary. Cash grabbed my hand, sending an electric current up my arm and an unwanted thrill to my core. Quickly, I tried to retract from his grip, but he tightened his fingers around me.

"I don't think so. This is definitely a job for someone more qualified than a school nurse. Come here."

He wrapped his arm across my shoulder blades and scooped up my legs, cradling me in his arms like a baby.

My head snapped at the sudden movement, and cerise fluid gushed from my nostrils, overwhelming my hands and seeping onto his shirt. I groaned and leaned my head back in defeat.

"Where are you taking me?" I asked as we approached the front doors of the school. They whooshed open, seemingly of their own accord like the automatic ones at the mall, but these weren't electric. Another fun extraterrestrial power.

"To my car." He strode toward the student parking lot carrying me as lightly as a stack of books.

"What? Why?" I kicked my legs. It was childish, but his car? No thanks.

"Stop moving. I'm taking you to my car so I can heal you without anyone seeing. Trust me."

"What do you mean, heal me?" My tone dripped with suspicion while my leg tantrum ended.

"One of the many perks of being me."

I ignored the cocky response and instead wondered how many more so-called "perks" Cash had.

"There won't be permanent effects from your healing me, right?" I thought I should probably call my father before letting Cash play doctor with me.

Cash smiled that sexy I-know-what-you're-thinking smile. "You'll be fine. Don't be such a human."

The passenger door to his black SUV opened with a wave of his hand, and he gently placed me inside. I eased myself over and removed a pair of large brown flip-flops from under my butt while he came around to the driver's side. The floor was littered with trash from fast-food restaurants and an open Gatorade bottle was lodged in the cup holder. Apparently, tidiness wasn't one of his superpowers. I lowered the sun visor and slid the mirror open to look at the dam-

age. I screamed. Black and blues had already formed a mot-
tled pattern over my face, while the swelling disfigured my
once small button nose into a throbbing red ball. Blood continued to pour out of my nostrils.

"Your thick brick head broke my nose! We need to get to
a hospital."

"Simmer down. You rammed your head into me, remember? It's not my fault I'm not as soft as you. Our kind may
look like yours but under our shell runs a liquid alloy which
automatically hardens when we are attacked." He smiled
wickedly. "Impressive, huh?"

"This isn't funny." My fingers lightly approached my for-
eign-looking face. "I'm hurt."

"Are you?" He raised his brow. "You screamed at the ini-
tial blow and when you saw yourself, but you haven't said
anything about the pain."

He was right. Sure, my face resembled uncooked meat,
but I felt nothing—no pain, throbbing, or any other indica-
tion that my nose was shattered. How was that possible?

I crossed my arms over my chest. "What did you do to
me?"

"I'm trying to heal you, but I need to touch you." He
swallowed hard, leaning over the center console. "Can I
touch your face, please?"

My mouth dropped.

"Now what is it?"

"You said, 'please.'"

He rolled his eyes. "Why are you always pointing out the
obvious? Is this going to be something you do all the time?
It's annoying."

I shook my head and sighed. Me, annoying? "Fine, you can touch me. Whatever." I put my hand up in the air. "Only to heal me," I clarified. After he nodded, I dropped my arm. Cash placed his hands on my shoulders and then began to move them slowly up my neck. Slight pressure from his fingertips sent tingling sensations throughout my veins and traveled with his hands until they cupped my face. Heat penetrated off his fingers like steam from a kettle, and then a bright white glow appeared in my peripheral vision.

"Close your eyes," Cash ordered, his voice soft and low, void of annoyance, anger, or cockiness.

I shut my lids and inhaled, deep breaths expanding my rib cage with air. At first, the darkness unnerved me, but warmth slowly crept in, soothing my skin like a hot bath. My shoulders loosened into the supple leather seats. Soft, butterfly kisses danced on my skin while my insides turned to jelly. A small sigh leaked from my mouth. I had never felt so relaxed, so rejuvenated. How long were we locked like this? When I opened my eyes, it had only been minutes.

Cash leaned against the opposite side of the car, as far away from me as possible. He stared off in the distance like he was lost in thought. Slight disappointment settled in my stomach at his coldness. But when I eyed the mirror and saw nothing except for the dried blood covering my face, neck, and clothes, relief filled me. My button nose was once again its adorable old self.

"How did you do it?" I swiveled toward him, but the driver's seat was empty. I jumped out of the passenger side and rounded the car, where I found Cash shirtless.

"What are you doing?" My brain cauterized all thought with a mighty scream—*holy hell, you are hot!* Cash's muscular chest was golden tan, as if he had spent days in the sun.

He was solid. Lean. Perfect. His stomach showed each rippling abdominal muscle, which ended in the beginning of a sexy "v" shape.

And then my eyes stopped on his right pectoral muscle. He had a scar, a diamond-shaped scar like mine but on the opposite side of his body. It was so identical; I touched my own chest, confirming mine was still there. How could it be?

"What?" His lips thinned into a tight line.

"Your chest. . ." I sucked in a deep breath and asked, "That scar on your chest . . ." I pointed to the rhombus shape. "How did you get it?"

"Same way you got yours," he said in a monotone voice.

My hands flew to my hips. "That's how you are going to answer? Mind providing me some details?"

"You should ask your mom."

I ground my teeth. Sure, let's ask my dearly departed mother who Cash conveniently loves to blame. Like that's an option.

He held his stained t-shirt in the air. It was dripping wet. "Take this." He motioned to the blood on my face and neck. "You can't go back into school looking like a crime scene. Our English class is undergoing Influence now. No one will remember how badly you looked before, so clean up."

"Influence?" I did not like where this was going. How could he make an entire class of teenagers and a teacher forget something that had happened moments ago?

"Well," he shrugged. "Not only am I devilishly handsome and can heal poor humans with crooked noses, I can also use the power of Influence to recreate what the mind thinks it saw."

I couldn't fathom the thought. With the powers he and his friends shared, Earth was lucky to still be standing in one piece. We could all have been turned into slaves by now.

"Our planet couldn't care less about you." He took the thoughts right out of my head. Insult and disgust threaded his voice. "Trust me—ruling over your kind would be more of a hassle than it's worth."

"That's comforting," I said drily. "Can you explain how you are using this 'Influence' in our classroom?"

"Sammie and Tasha recreated the scene in our class's mind. I texted them for assistance after your little friend accused me of hitting you."

"Have you ever used Influence on me?" If that was why my heart flipped like a gymnast each time I saw him, I would kick his butt all the way back to whatever planet he came from. Although it would be comforting to know my magnetism to him was fabricated, and not at all real. I was starting to question my hormones.

"No. It won't work on you." He glared.

"Why won't it work on me?" I leaned against his car, threading the damp t-shirt through my hands. Knowing my bizarre luck, there was something wrong with me.

"You said no questions. Remember our deal?" Cash opened the back door of his SUV. Of course, he would use the deal against me when it worked in his favor. Even when he answered, he never really clarified my questions. God, he was frustrating. "I have extra clothes in here somewhere." He pulled out a faded pink cropped t-shirt, which was probably Tasha's. He eyed the size of the tee and then eyed my body, sending shivers down my limbs. I wrapped my arms around my waist, suddenly feeling exposed under his scrutiny. "This will have to do." He threw the shirt at me, knowing I couldn't fill it out the way his sister could. He reached back into the vehicle and pulled out another t-shirt for himself. It looked identical to the one he had worn earlier, except this one was maroon. There must have been a sale on formfitting t-shirts and he bought every damn color.

Cash moved closer to me. "Hurry up or I will put it on you myself."

"Give me a freaking second." I dipped my face toward the damp shirt.

He mumbled something about humans under his breath and slipped his clean shirt over his head. I changed on the other side of the car after making him promise not to look and noticed how he rolled his eyes.

My mind raced with new revelations. Cash and I had the same scar. These aliens could move objects, heal, and Influence. What else they could control or create? I hoped the answer would be nothing.

By lunchtime, everyone but Darla had forgotten about our nose collision. Chris, Darla, and I sat toward the back of the cafeteria by the windows, while Cash and his crew assembled at a table in the middle of the room. Cliques were most conspicuous in the cafeteria because the tables automatically formed us into groups. It was like the school was designed to break us all up into neat little stereotypes.

"I can't believe your nose looks like that." Darla studied my face. I avoided eye contact, afraid of her investigation. "How did it heal so fast?"

"What do you mean?" Chris asked before biting into his peanut butter and jelly sandwich. Strawberry jelly caught in the crook of his mouth, reminding me of the blood that had covered mine. He wiped the jelly away with his forearm.

"Bea and Cash collided in English. He nearly took her nose off." At that moment, I realized Cash and his friends didn't Influence Darla.

"You didn't hear about it?" Darla continued as she opened her pudding snack. I remained quiet. The less I said, the better.

"Kathleen Butler said some girl got a bloody nose in English class today because she picked it." Chris guffawed. "That was you?" He pointed at me and broke into wheezing gasps of laughter.

"Oh my god, no! I wish Kathleen would mind her own freaking business. Why would someone say that?" I leaped to my feet and practically sprung across the cafeteria, feeling as wired as a cheetah. It was bad enough Cash broke my face this morning, but now they were telling everyone I was a violent nose picker?

"Can I talk to you?" I barked, standing above Cash. He bit into his turkey sandwich without giving me a glance. Mayonnaise squeezed out the sides, landing on his plate.

"I'm serious. We need to talk." My tone sank into the stern voice my mother had used when she wanted to make a point.

"Sounds like your little admirer is mad at you," Samantha grinned. "Bet she tried to make a move and you turned her down. Or maybe you think her nose-picking habit is gross?" So, *she* was the one conjuring the lies.

"What's your problem?" I snapped, having our first conversation be one of the worse ones I've ever had. The gleam in her eyes flared with hatred. She and Cash had something in common.

"You!" she spat at me. "You're my problem."

I really hoped she didn't have the power to shoot rays of fire from her eyes, or else I was about to get charred.

"Okay . . . Could you be any more vague?"

"First of all, you're wearing my shirt and I want it back." She glared at Cash, who shrugged. Ah, so it hadn't been his sister's shirt. I wondered why Samantha's shirt was in the back of Cash's car, and then felt myself beginning to blush. "Secondly, everything about you is my problem now—your life, your friends, your humanness. Because of you and your family, we are all at risk. And I'm not supposed to have a problem with that?" She threw her blonde hair over her shoulders and batted her black, mink-like lashes. "Enlightening enough for you?"

"You think I *like* having you in my life? You think I asked for this? I don't even know what any of *this* is about."

The lunch table started to shake as Samantha dug her nails into it—like, her nails literally slid through the metal slab like it was butter. *Holy shit.*

Tasha whispered, "Sammie, calm down. This isn't the place."

Sammie retracted her catlike claws from the table and stood up to face me. Our eyes leveled. The glint in her gaze was like the blade of a sword, deadly and sharp.

"Oh please. I don't buy the victim card. You want to know what I think? I think you love all the attention Cash has been giving you. But you know what? He doesn't give a shit about you."

Before I knew what was happening, the anger rolled off my tongue in a stream of words so rapid and smooth it seemed like I had memorized them ages ago. My voice resonated at twice her pitch.

"Listen here, Cash is hot. I'm admitting this because everyone knows it. But there is something you don't know about *me*—I'm not shallow. I don't care that he's good-looking. He's also an ass and definitely not someone I even want in my life. I can see how that would be confusing for a mean girl like you." My voice thickened with sarcastic pity. "But I don't think you have a clue what Cash thinks about me. Last night when we were in my bedroom, he couldn't stop staring at me." My hands quivered, and I crossed my arms over my chest and pressed my trembling hands into my sides. My palms moistened against her shirt. Then, I turned my attention to Cash, who looked like a deer in headlights. His hands, frozen in the air, still gripped his sandwich. "From now on, stay out of my bedroom."

I stalked back over to my table. My heart pounded in my chest. Darla and Chris gaped at me like a herd of pigs flew circles above my head.

"Bea," Darla whispered. Speechless, Chris continued gawking, jelly lingering on his lips. God, he ate like an animal.

"What?" I fired back, only then realizing the entire cafeteria was quiet. I surveyed the room. Students were either staring or whispering. *Oh my god. What did I just do?*

I thought I might die. Bile rose to my throat.

I ran straight to the girl's bathroom.

Chapter Seven

Beatrice

Darla crashed into the girl's bathroom behind me a moment later. She dead-bolted the bathroom door and threw her small body against it as though an angry mob was on the other side. Standing at the sink, I splashed cold water on my face, attempting to cool my flaming red cheeks. What was wrong with me? It's like I went all "Regina George" on Samantha. That wasn't my style. And why couldn't I stop thinking about her shirt in the back of Cash's car?

"What was that about?" Darla's chest heaved, and I wondered if she was hyperventilating as badly as I was. I threw more water on my face, attempting to subdue my anger-fueled adrenaline rush. Cash was going to kill me for implying anything. He hated me just as much as Sammie and I led the school into believing . . .

I splashed more water across my face, wishing I could drown in it.

"Well, it's safe to say we might have to stay in here for a while," Darla continued. "I don't know who might fight you first—Tasha, who looked like she might puke when you mentioned her brother, or Cash's girlfriend."

I gawked at Darla's reflection in the mirror. Drops of water cascaded from my jaw and into the sink. Did I hear her correctly? Girlfriend? *Oh hell no.*

"Now, she looks like a girl who might actually commit murder," Darla prattled on.

"Wait, what?"

"I said she looks like someone who—"

"No, no, no!" I waved my hand in the air. My pulse raced. "What was that about Cash having a girlfriend?"

Darla's head tilted to the side. "Samantha. They're dating. You didn't know that? Why aren't you on any social media again? Seriously, I don't know anyone who's more anti-technology than your family."

My breath caught in my throat and my knees started to wobble. *Oh my god, oh my god.* I gripped the edges of the porcelain sink, trying to hold myself upright. When I didn't speak, she continued. "Did Cash really come over last night? Why? He totally hated you yesterday."

"Darla, stop. Please." I needed to think. When I managed to suck in a breath, the weight of the situation crashed into me like a pile of bricks. Samantha Flannery was going to kill me for implying her boyfriend was in my room ogling me last night. It straight-up sounded like he cheated.

"This is bad. This is really bad," I muttered.

Darla's reflection nodded at me vigorously. "It's not great."

We sat on the cold tiled floor of the girl's bathroom, our backs to the door. It was unsanitary, yes, but also unavoidable. I wasn't ready to leave our safe haven just yet. I explained everything to Darla. Well, not everything. I couldn't very well tell her that Cash was an extraterrestrial, could I? I explained that my father was friends with the Kingstons, and when I got home from school yesterday, they were there. Then I told her Cash was in my bedroom last night, but he was only there for a second, confusing my door for the bathroom.

"Oh, this is bad. You totally stretched the truth in front of the whole cafeteria."

"Yeah." I sighed. The truth . . . She had no idea. "What should I do?" I rested my head in my hands while my knees shook.

"Is changing schools an option?" Darla snorted.

Our friendship had been solidified from the moment we met in kindergarten when a boy pulled my ponytail and Darla tripped him for it. I loved her immediately and never stopped. Even when my parents put three thousand miles between us, Darla never made me feel far away. And now, when I felt embarrassed and overwhelmed, she knew exactly what to say. I threw my arms around her, gripping her tightly into a hug.

Finally letting her go, I said, "Wanna do something tonight? I could use the distraction."

"Sure. I'll come over after school. Should we head back to class or do you think the Barbie bitches will be waiting for us?"

"Well, I can't stay in here forever. Eventually, I'll have to face them."

Slowly, we opened the bathroom door. We looked right and left. To my surprise, the halls were empty. We went to our lockers and gathered our books for class. Detention was unavoidable now, but it was better than Samantha flaying me alive with lasers from her eyes.

As we turned around, Tasha Kingston stood in our path. Her dark hair swept over her shoulders, spilling across her olive top. Her features were perfect, like Cash's. They even shared the same impatient expression: sunken brows, stormy eyes, and tight jaw. Her arms were folded under her chest—as if she needed the lift—reminding me how very different our body types were. "Darla, I need to speak with Bea alone."

"No way!" Darla's petite frame stood in front of me like a bodyguard.

"I'm not going to hurt her. It's important and has nothing to do with the childish fight she and Sammie had in the cafeteria."

I grabbed Darla's arm and gently pulled her out of the way. "It's okay. Like I said, our families are friends. I'll be fine."

"Are you sure?" Darla's voice hesitated.

"Yeah, get going. I'll see you later."

Darla nodded and headed down the hall, glancing over her shoulder one last time before she turned the corner.

Once Darla was out of sight, Tasha's expression turned cold fast. My stomach sank. This wasn't good.

"You are going home." She pointed her French-manicured finger at me and motioned toward the exit.

"Umm, but—"

She stepped closer; inches stood between us. "I called your dad and told him about the display at lunch. We're protecting you, but the door swings both ways. You are supposed to be laying low, not drawing attention to yourself and making our job harder."

"Hey, I was provoked!"

She held up a finger. "Before you say anything more, Sammie's been dealt with. I'm not excusing her, but you can't go around throwing a temper tantrum when something doesn't go your way. You will get us all killed if you don't take this seriously."

I stared at her, frozen. Everything bubbled up inside of me, and I wanted to scream, but Tasha didn't look like she wanted to hear it or even cared.

"Let's go!"

When I got home, my father yelled for an hour, pacing the kitchen in circles. He wasn't only mad about my nose, which I couldn't believe anyone blamed me for, he was mad I missed classes and made a scene in the cafeteria. He was especially furious that I'd told Darla he was family friends with the Kingstons. I tried to explain, but every time I spoke, he cut me off with a barking rebuttal. He even chastised *me* for Cash being in my room. It's not like I invited him in.

Eventually I stopped talking. I rested my head in my hands and let my dad vent. Maybe he needed this. I couldn't be the only one feeling the exhaustion of the last two days.

Thankfully, the doorbell interrupted dad's lecture.

"I'll get it," he scowled, pointing at me to stay seated. Not like I had any intention of running to the door to see who was on the opposite side. Knowing my luck, it was probably a zombie coming to eat my brains for dinner.

A bubbly voice sounded through the halls. Nope. Not a zombie. I heard my dad's loud steps follow behind it.

"You never came back to school. Coach Barb is pissed." Darla walked into the kitchen. She went straight to the cabinet and picked out the plastic "I Love New York" cup my mom had brought back from one of their trips. Dad grabbed a seat at the breakfast bar and riffled noisily through a sports magazine. His frustration was evident in each dramatic page turn.

"Barb called my mom. She even called Chris's house and spoke to his mom. Peggy freaked out—thought your picture was going to end up on a milk carton or something. What's wrong with Barb? Hello, stalker." Darla grabbed a coke bottle from the refrigerator. As she twisted the cap, it fizzed. "Where did you go, anyway?"

"Tasha took me home." My father's head whipped around, glaring at me. I winced. What was I supposed to say?

"Home? Why? What is it with you and the Kingstons and Flannerys? Cash practically breaks your nose; Sammie goes all overprotective girlfriend on your ass; and Tasha takes you home? How creepy is that? Mr. Walker, how do you know these guys?" Darla's head was deep inside the freezer. I was tempted to shut her in there for her overactive mouth.

My dad glowered at me. "They're originally from California. I knew their parents from when we lived out west." Not a bad lie for spur-of-the-moment fibbing. I wondered how many lies my father had told because of his secret job.

"Well, I think their kids have it out for Bea." She dumped a handful of cubes in her soda. She walked over to the table and took the seat across from me.

"Even the teachers are starting to gossip." Darla took a long, satisfied-sounding sip.

"What are they saying?" I asked slowly, watching Dad's back stiffen. The fact that I was school gossip was not a good thing.

"Coach Barb said Mr. Mack talked about Cash and you in the teachers' lounge. Barb asked my mom to ask me if I could find out what was going on between the two of you.

Asked if you've been hanging out in his circle. She wants to make sure you stay focused on your track career." Darla rolled her eyes. "My mom really needs to get a new friend. Barb's totally obsessed with you, always asking my mom about you. It's freaking weird."

I crumpled up a napkin and threw it at her. "Thanks a lot."

"Bea is quitting track anyway," my dad interjected, not even lifting his head out of the magazine. He's the only human I know who still has subscriptions.

"What?" Darla and I exclaimed in unison. I gaped at my dad. What was he talking about? Track meant everything to me.

"Dad, you can't be serious. I love track. You know I'm trying to get a scholarship for college. I'm the best on the team. I'm not quitting."

My father swiveled in his seat. "This is not up for discussion. Send Coach Barb an email tonight letting her know. Do you understand?" His voice grew in intensity.

"Dad, please! I love track." Moisture welled in my eyes while Darla's widened. Her jaw lowered a good two inches.

But before I could protest further, the doorbell rang again.

"Apparently, we're hosting a party this afternoon," my father grumbled, throwing down the magazine and stalking out of the kitchen.

"What's going on?" Darla whispered.

I shrugged. If I tried to talk, the tears would shed, and it would be a cold day in hell before I let these aliens get the best of me.

Two male voices bantered down the hall, and a hearty chuckle exploded as they entered the kitchen. I didn't even have to turn around to know it was Chris. His laughter was distinct like an old man with a belly—deep and growly.

"I even checked the lost-and-found in the janitor's office." He patted my dad on the back when they came into view. "There you are!" His baby blue eyes connected with mine and he smiled. There was a glimmer of humor in them but also a sigh of relief.

"Senior year at Cartwright and you are already causing trouble. My mother called me today, hyperventilating because Coach Barb told her you were missing, like you were an escaped animal from the zoo." Chris looked at my dad, who threw him a box of Cheez-Its from the pantry.

"Nice." Chris caught the box. He plopped down next to me at the table and dug his hand inside.

"You know my mom. She freaked." Chris frowned a little. His father and only sibling died when he was a toddler, leaving him alone with his overprotective, overbearing mother, Peggy. Now that woman was a trip. A car alarm could have her calling 911. I could only imagine how Coach Barb's call affected her.

"I can't believe Coach Barb called so many people. Shouldn't that be against school policy?" I huffed. "Apparently, I'm more important than I thought."

Chris leaned over and kissed the top of my head. "You're important to us."

Darla rolled her eyes while I smiled at him.

"Now that we know Bea is alive and well, anyone wanna update me on what's been going on?" He flipped a cracker in the air and tried to catch it in his mouth. It bounced off his forehead and landed on the floor, but he picked it up and ate it anyway.

"Ewww," Darla murmured.

I threw my head into my folded arms as the reality set in that I would have to quit track.

"Nothing." My lips blew hot air against my skin. "Other than the fact that my dad is making me quit track."

"It's not that bad," a deep male voice said, sending the hairs on my neck to attention.

My head shot up. Cash leaned his hip against the doorframe of the kitchen, his arms crossed over his chest so that his biceps and pectorals bulged. His lips twitched like he was fighting a smile.

"Nice of you to knock, Cash," Dad growled.

Darla mouthed, "What's he doing here?"

I shook my head. I had no idea.

Chapter Eight

Cash

Robert escorted Chris and Darla out of the house and then followed me to the front porch. We had unfinished business from yesterday, and I wasn't about to let another day go by without addressing it. Bea's unexpected arrival home cut us short from a very important question, one I feared from the moment I met Beatrice Walker: what was she really?. And after my conversation with Grouper yesterday, I was beginning to wonder if she was who I've been looking for these last several years.

I leaned my hip against the railing, glaring in Robert's direction. He lowered into the white wicker chair and crossed his shin over his thigh. In the past, I liked Robert. He and Faye had been integral during our transition to Earth. But he was different than Faye. He followed orders, didn't complain or fuss, and got the job done; robotic-like. It was Faye who stood out. Her skills were second to none. She crossed boundaries, asked the hard questions, and refused to take no for an answer. I not only respected her, I idolized her. But now, my perception of both humans had changed.

I crossed my arms at my chest, feeling my muscles pull against my shirt. The same strain I felt in my brain every time I went over Beatrice's true identity in my head. "Anything you'd like to tell me about your daughter?" I emphasized the word *daughter* with my voice. My patience was at an all-time low. With the fate of two planets hanging in the balance, you'd think these humans would want to do the right thing for the masses.

Robert stared into the afternoon sky without meeting my gaze. "Ask me the real question you want answered."

"Is Beatrice your biological daughter?" The words were a courtesy. The second I realized Bea had Sera's energy source, I knew the truth. We all did. No human could hold an energy source in their chest. They would die immediately. The source would burn right through them. And since Beatrice was Faye's twin in most physical aspects, I knew they were related.

Robert shook his head. "No."

"Who is her father?"

Robert's eyes glistened. "I honestly do not know for certain, but I have an idea. An ex-Ferroean seat member, one with high powers and status; someone Faye was once involved with. She never answered me when I questioned her, and after several years, I stopped asking. What did it really change knowing who Faye had an affair with? The pain was all the same. But as far as the definition of a father, I am the only father Beatrice has ever had. She is, for all intents and purposes, my daughter."

Robert uncrossed his legs and leaned forward, resting his elbows on his thighs. "There's no reason to tell her. So much has happened so fast. It would crush her to hear another lie, one we kept from her all these years and one of this magnitude. She's already lost her mother. Don't take me, too."

I squatted down to Robert's eye level, placing my hand on his shoulder. I may be angry, but I'm not callous. I knew only too well what a broken family felt like. Tasha was all I had left.

"I'm not here to hurt your daughter, or you. I understand this isn't the life you wanted for Bea, but Faye threw her into the middle of it, and now there's no choice." I tried to ease his own remorse, something I was far too familiar with. "I'm here for answers and I will not allow for your resistance to get in the way of the truth. We are running out of time. If the two energy sources are not fully connected, we could lose both our planets. Every day is a day closer to our deaths, and that includes your daughter's."

I removed my hand from his shoulder. "Bea is a Blood-Light, half human and half Ferroean. She's obviously a viable womb for energy sources. But it's difficult for me to believe Faye would allow for her daughter to harbor an energy source, knowing many half breeds die when the energy source is removed. Even if she survived the removal process, the DOAA would find out and take her into custody. She'd be their prisoner." I shook my head. "We are missing something. Faye always had a plan."

Robert nodded.

"Can you think of anything else about Beatrice we should know? Anything useful? Anything that happened before they disappeared? Anything Faye had mentioned to you?" I was desperate for a lead, a direction to follow instead of a web of questions.

"Faye and I had been fighting a lot. I wanted to move us back to Cartwright when your mission was up. I never wanted to leave a No Zone. I wanted to keep Beatrice far away from the DOAA. Knowing what she is and keeping her so close to the DOAA was a recipe for disaster."

"And Faye? Did she think it was a disaster?" I asked.

Robert shook his head. "Faye wanted Bea involved in this world. She believed Bea was more to the DOAA than someone who was both human and Ferroean. She believed some of them would end up protecting her."

"Protect her? But they are the ones who imprison half breeds. Why would they protect her? And from whom?" I questioned.

"She had been hanging around Dr. X a lot. And you know that old kook had many radical theories about humans and Ferroeans. I think he was poisoning Faye's mind. He could even be linked to Faye and Seraphina's deaths."

I shook my head in disbelief. "I agree he's a little out there, but you can't believe that old man could commit murder, could you?"

Dr. X, one of Earth's lead assimilation scientists, was Faye's mentor and longtime friend. They were so close, they were like family. Dr. X was an odd, weird-looking guy but not a killer or coconspirator. He had white hair, big thick glasses, and always wore a red and brown bow tie with his white collared shirt. Sera once asked him how many bow ties he owned, and his reply was, "*How many pairs of underwear do you own?*" Like I said, weird but not a murderer.

"He may not be the one who caused their deaths," Robert said, "but I'd bet my life he knows something about it and why Faye put the energy source in Beatrice. I think we need to find the best doctor we can, remove the energy source, and go on the run from the DOAA." He looked at me with urgency in his eyes. "Beatrice isn't safe anywhere."

In theory, I understood Robert's desperate plea to rewind and proceed with Beatrice as he planned before Faye intervened, but there was no going back. I didn't have an answer, at least not one that would comfort Robert. Energy wombs are like bank deposit boxes, they hold something safe until it's needed again. The problem is the removal process isn't always successful and can cause death to the half human. I couldn't guarantee the surgery would be successful even if we tried.

"We can't remove the source until we have more answers. I'm not exactly sure she is strong enough to even recover from the removal process. It's dangerous." I raked my hand through my hair at the thought of it. So many things could go wrong. "The good news is she cannot fully connect to her opposing source and be weaponized the way Sera was intended. No human heart can survive that. Which means, eventually, the source will have to be removed for us to use it against the threat. But I'm hoping we can figure out why Faye did this before then."

Robert let out a long, audible sigh. "The question that keeps me up at night is why *would* Faye do this? If there was the slightest chance Bea could die, why would she take the risk?" He wasn't asking for my response, but simply voicing the shock that Faye would put her own flesh and blood in harm's way. I didn't blame him. That was one of my many questions as well.

"I don't know, but the answer to saving Earth and Ferro lies in your daughter's chest cavity. I fear you will pay for your crimes against your government; but until I understand Faye's strategy, my team and I will protect Bea with our lives and keep her safe," I promised. "As far as the DOAA and my planet are concerned, we are back in Cartwright for our original mission: disguised as high school students to observe humans and their interactions. We will continue to send our reports back to our planet so no one will be the wiser. In the meantime, keep a low profile."

"I know you are doing this for Sera's source but for what it's worth, thank you." Robert shook his head. "I don't care what happens to me as long as Beatrice isn't harmed."

I turned and walked down the porch steps. The second-floor light caught my eye, and I looked up to see Beatrice's outline pass in front of the window. I couldn't help but stare. For the first time in all this mess, I realized how innocent she was. A human girl with no understanding of the power inside of her. She turned and faced the window, gazing out toward the sunset like Robert had earlier. She looked so much like Faye. I used to joke with Faye that she hung out with us too much and was becoming a Ferroean. Her eyes always changed with the reflection of her clothes. Bea had her mom's long, thick brown hair that cascaded into waves. I watched as she pulled it up into a ponytail and then wrapped the strands into a braid just like Faye did on missions. Sera had copied her, too. I'd pull on the tresses as I'd walked by. Anything to provoke Sera's smile.

Bea slipped her shirt off, and I hastily turned my head. We'd have a discussion later about her closing the blinds. I looked back at Robert and asked curiously, "Why did you protect them all these years, keeping Beatrice a secret?"

It was a known fact that all Blood-Lights were required by federal law to live in DOAA-monitored dormitories called BLH, Blood-Light Housing. Years ago, the DOAA tested complete assimilation on these humans, trying to give them Ferroean powers. All subjects died within twenty-four hours; 100% failure rate. The trial was shut down. After that, the DOAA concluded it would be illegal to mate with one another. No interplanetary fraternizing, they called it. There are currently less than twenty-five Blood-Lights still in existence and the only reason they weren't killed was to provide backups energy wombs like Bea.

Robert sighed.

"Faye might not have been in love with me, but I was with her, and that little girl is my daughter in every sense of the word. Without the two of them, I have no world." Pain was etched in his face as if the human years that aged him carried the lines he had to cross in his wrinkles. The more I looked at him, the more I saw the lengths he was willing to go for Bea.

"I hope you know what you are doing," I warned something I imagined Tasha would say to me if this were her and me.

"I don't." Robert opened the door to the house and slipped inside.

I looked up at Bea's window again. Her back was toward the outside. She slipped her sports bra over her head, pulling her braided hair out from underneath and then did the same with her tank top.

Damn it. This girl was going for a run. Why couldn't she stay in one place. In less than two minutes, I was changed and waiting for her to come out onto the pavement. I might not like her, but after today I did empathize with her. Yesterday, she was a normal high school girl. Today she was a puzzle piece in her planet's quest for survival and a victim of her parents' actions. Unfortunately, I knew all too well what that felt like.

In my peripheral vision, I spotted a black sedan with dark tinted windows like the ones we were issued from the

DOAA. This street was quiet. Not one car until now. When I turned to get a better look, it drove off. I tried to catch the license plate but couldn't.

Chapter Nine

Beatrice

Something was up. I could tell by the way Cash eyed my father and by the look of concern etched across my father's face. In just two days, my dad had aged. His eyes held permanent creases while his face appeared pale and withdrawn. His shoulders were constantly slouched, where before they had always seemed to hold confidence and strength.

After minutes of whispers back and forth between the two, my dad called out to me, "Cash and I will be back shortly."

As soon as the door closed, I ran up to my room. My dad may have decided I had to quit track, but that didn't mean I had to quit running. I wrote a short email alerting Coach Barb to my temporary lapse from the team due to family issues and pressed send. As soon as these beings were out of my life, I would beg her to let me back on the team. Until then, I'd practice on my own. And honestly, I needed some alone time with the pavement, my running sneakers, and my mind.

I pulled my hair up into a ponytail braid like the way my mom used to wear hers when she worked out. I threw on my sports bra and spandex tank top, stepped into running shorts, and tied my kicks. I flew down the steps and walked swiftly to the edge of the driveway. I turned right on the sidewalk, ready to break into a jog . . . only to stop dead in my tracks.

My hands balled at my sides. "What do you think you are doing?"

Cash smiled wickedly as he stretched. He was wearing royal blue basketball shorts, and a tight white t-shirt. "Getting ready for my evening run. You?" His eyes scanned my body, bringing heat to my cheeks. He had a way of looking at me that simultaneously irritated and ignited me. How was it possible to be attracted to someone you loathed?

"How convenient." My voice was thick with sarcasm while my arms folded over my chest. His lips twitched as if he was fighting back a smile.

"It is, isn't it?" He practically hummed as he stretched down to his toes. His back muscles pressed against his shirt, alerting me to each ripple.

I huffed out a determined breath. I was over this battle of wits. "I'm not running with you."

Cash arched his back in the opposite direction. "I'm not thrilled about guarding you, either, but I have no choice in the matter." He straightened and gave me a pointed look. "I'm protecting you and that's final."

"Fine," I said, turning on my heel and taking off in the opposite direction. I had to modify my route to steer clear of Darla and Chris's houses. If they witnessed this, I would never live it down.

"Try to keep up," I called sweetly over my shoulder.

Cash fell behind me, and suddenly I was acutely aware of every single thing—from my braid swinging back and forth, to the sweat trickling down my back, to my shorts riding up my legs, to my jiggling butt. I was about to ask him to match his stride with mine when he grabbed my arm and pulled me back. I stumbled and almost fell, but he steadied me. "Do not move," he whispered in my ear. "Do everything I say. Got it?" His hot breath sent chills along my flesh. Goose pimples rippled like dominos across my limbs while the buzzing in my chest jumped like a heart monitor. I nodded breathlessly.

I followed Cash's gaze across the street, where two men leaned against an unmarked car. They both wore black suits, white button-down shirts, and skinny, dark gray ties. Did they just jump out of a *Men in Black* movie or what?

"Captain Kingston, isn't this interesting?" the salt-and-pepper-haired man said, crossing the street. His strides were long and swift. His partner's eyes darted from side to side before he followed.

"Hey, Dominic," Cash smiled. If he hadn't told me not to move and wasn't gripping my elbow so hard, I would have assumed this a friendly encounter. But the pressure of Cash's fingers against my skin confirmed this wasn't a social call.

Both men stood only a couple feet away. "Who's your friend? She looks familiar." Dominic scanned my face while I inspected his. He didn't remind me of anyone I knew yet something about him, his clothes, his mannerisms, his gait . . . something seemed familiar. He slowly pulled his jacket back, revealing more of his white shirt and a black chest holster with a pistol. His partner did the same thing. *Holy shit!*

My heart slammed against my rib cage. My knees trembled. But Cash only laughed. He actually laughed. Two men with guns stood in front of us, and he thought it was funny. "She's not my friend," Cash said. Dominic placed his hand on his gun, emphasizing its existence. I wanted to let him know I saw it the first time, but I think the threat was targeted at Cash and his cavalier response. I sure as hell had fright written all over my face like a neon freaking sign.

Cash chuckled, pulling me into his side with one hand. The warmth from his body seemed to calm me. He had such a strange effect on me. I watched as he raised his other hand into the air. His fingers balled as he twisted his wrist, like he was turning an invisible doorknob. He summoned the gun. My eye diverted from his hand to Dominic. The tip of his gun melted and reformed around the leather sheath like a rope into a knot. Unbelievably, Cash had just microwaved the man's gun into a pretzel shape. Dominic ripped at the holster, tearing it off his body. The white shirt he wore under the jacket blackened and sizzled from the heat, exposing his flesh, which appeared bright red like raw meat.

"Damn it, Cash," he shrieked. "Was that necessary?" He pressed his other hand into the wound.

Cash shrugged. "As necessary as you flaunting the hunk of metal under your jacket. Seriously, are you showing off your toys? Because if so, I have a much larger toy I could—"

"Cash," I hissed.

"We don't want to hurt her," the short and stocky man said, bringing the conversation back on track. "We need her to come back to DOAA headquarters and speak with Director Dod."

DOAA? My father was part of that agency . . . and my mother. Wait, me? Why would they need to speak to me?

Cash turned to me, interrupting my internal questions. "Bea, would you like to be escorted to DOAA headquarters with these two fine gentlemen or would you like to stay with me?" His tone was playful. These men were threatening us, yet he was acting like this was some sort of game.

I shifted closer to Cash, my eyes searching for any sign of alarm. Nope. Nothing.

Great! This cocky bastard was going to get us killed.

"She seems perfectly happy here, boys," Cash answered on my behalf.

"Can't do that. We have orders. Does your father know what you are doing? I don't think he would approve. I can't imagine you are under his orders right now." Cash stiffened at Dominic's mention of his father, and I wondered who *was* his father. "You have my word we won't hurt her," the younger man insisted. He puffed his chest out as a show of confidence, but the sweat forming on his brow spoke volumes to his uneasiness.

Cash pushed me behind him. His fists clenched and unclenched. I watched as the muscles in his arms rippled like waves from his wrist to his forearms, up past his biceps and triceps, expelling into the air in the form of invisible energy. The doors of the unmarked car flew off their hinges and veered across the street, the setting sun gleaming orange against the metal sheen. The doors crashed into the two men and toppled them over.

I gasped. It's not every day you see two grown men attacked by car doors with an alien's temper.

Cash leaned over their prone bodies, finally detaching himself from my side. "How did you find her?" he growled. The edge of his tone sent a shiver to my spine.

"Hey," Dominic groaned, struggling out from under the door. He stood slowly and brushed the dirt off his pants. He gave a hesitant look to the other guy and nodded. They both reached into their back pockets and pulled out daggers. Strangely familiar daggers . . . They were long blades with sharply-tapered points. The brown handles were etched with the letters DOAA inside the shape of a diamond. I've seen this before, but it was different. The letters . . . they were different. I squeezed my memories, searching for what they reminded me of, but I couldn't pull the thread of knowledge from my brain. It was like when a word is on the tip of your tongue, and you couldn't bring yourself to vocalize it. The memory was too far away, out of reach.

The men started to cage us in, and I lost my train of thought, focusing back to the perilous moment. Cash. My god—they were going to kill Cash. These weapons could kill him. I don't know how I knew, but I did.

"No, I'll go with you. Don't hurt him!" I found myself standing in front of Cash, my arms flung out.

Cash grabbed my wrist and jerked me back. "What the hell do you think you are doing?" Panic and fear choked me. I couldn't let him die because they wanted to question me. They were with the government—with my parents' agency.

Out of the corner of my eye, I saw Dominic slash at Cash with his dagger. Cash blocked him and grabbed his arm, swinging it under Dominic's body and twisting it an unnatural way until his shoulder bone cracked.

But by the time he had him pinned to the ground it was too late.

The other guy's knife was at my neck, while his remaining arm secured me under my chest. My heart dropped to my stomach. Fear tangled with confusion. Why did these men need me to go to DOAA? And why were they using force to get me there?

"I wouldn't do that, Claude," Cash warned, his look menacing. Panic flooded my veins as the blade pressed in. It was ice cold against my skin. If I breathed, the sharp edge might begin to slice . . .

"It wasn't supposed to happen like this. There are protocols." I could feel Claude's pulse beat against my back. He held onto me so tightly, I felt ill from the closeness. "We know Faye did this and we know why. But do you?"

Mom? It always came back to my mom. What *had* she done? And what the hell did it have to do with me?

Cash ignored the question. "For the record, Claude, I warned you." Cash held Dominic with one hand and raised his other in the air, calling Claude's gun from his holster. The shiny black weapon moved past my body and flipped in flight so that the front of the pistol pointed to Claude's head, inches to the right of mine. Great, I had two weapons that could kill me, all near a very important extremity. My head.

"I will ask again, but there will be no third time. How did you find her?"

Sweat dripped down from Claude's face and landed on my shoulder.

"How?" The vibration of Cash's voice shuddered down the boulevard. The streetlights flickered wildly like strobe lights, but this was no party. Cash's anger festered with each waiting second, rattling the metal poles around us.

"We received a scrambled message from a Ferroean who sensed her energy in the area. It didn't take long to put the pieces together. Faye's disappearance and death, the child's scar, this town," Claude answered. His hand trembled, sending the tip of the blade closer to my throat. I sucked in a breath, hoping to create a larger distance between me and the weapon.

"Who else in the DOAA knows?" Cash demanded.

"Just Dominic and I—we didn't report back in. Dom wanted to confirm the lead first."

"If I let you go, will you go back to the DOAA with what you have learned?" Cash asked.

"No, I promise we won't." I felt a slight nod. Claude's chin barely touched my head, but it was enough of a motion to make me survey my surroundings. I realized whom he was signaling to.

"Cash, look out!" I screamed, forgetting about the blade pressing against my neck.

Dominic held the dagger to Cash's wrist, but Cash was lightning fast. He drove his fist into Dominic's face and flicked the knife away with a twist of Dominic's forearm. He rolled onto the ground and reached for the knife. With grace and speed I'd never seen before, he stood and lodged it in Dominic's chest. The agent stumbled back as Cash stalked forward. He kicked high, driving the knife's hilt deeper into the man's torso. Dominic crashed to the pavement. Cash twirled around. His eyes held mine as I heard his voice. I was so panicked I didn't even see his lips move. *Close your eyes, Beatrice. Now!*

As I squeezed my lids closed, I heard the loudest pop imaginable. My ears rung from the closeness, confirming exactly what happened. Cash had shot Claude.

Chapter Ten

Beatrice

Silence. For moments after the gun went off, all that existed was silence. By the time I opened my eyes, the others had arrived. I watched as if the world moved in slow motion. Cash's mouth opened and closed in a ringing roar, explaining to the others what transpired.

I was frozen with fear but also with something else: a nagging memory of the knife. It could kill Cash—somehow, I knew that. I shook my head. He was so powerful. Hell, he shook the streetlights, pulled off two car doors, and melted a metal gun—surely a knife wouldn't cause any lasting damage. But I knew better. The knife *could* kill him.

At some point Tasha guided me home. She closed the front door behind us. Then she laced her fingers through mine and led me up the stairs and into the bathroom across from my bedroom. No one had said anything to me on the street. Not even my father. They were all in cover-up mode, quickly conversing then dispensing orders. I stood numbly. So numb, I didn't react when Samantha melted the unmarked vehicle into a pile of metal; or when Mark and Paul dragged the bodies off the sidewalk and disappeared from sight with incredible speed. I didn't react when my father and Cash cleaned up the blood left behind. I was too numb to react to any of it. I simply let Tasha steer me back to the house, thankful to have someone else in control.

It wasn't until she closed the bathroom door and turned the shower on, that she spoke. "I'm not going to ask if you're okay because it's expected for you not to be." She pulled at the hem of my shirt. I automatically lifted my arms like a child being undressed by their mother. The tank top weighed heavily with blood and sweat. I sucked in a deep breath as she pulled the wet shirt over my head. I had no idea if the fluid was mine, Claude's, or a mixture of both, and the sickening thought swirled around in the pit of my stomach like water into a drain.

Tasha wrapped the soiled shirt into a ball and stuffed it into a small garbage bag from under the counter. My gaze lifted to my reflection in the mirror. Crimson dots formed under my neck from the dagger. I traced my fingers over the spots, dragging the blood into a fine line.

Tasha eyed my throat. "It's barely a scratch." She grabbed my hand, sending heat throughout my body, and the tiny marks disappeared. Steam blurred the edges of the glass, closing in on our images. Within seconds, we disappeared into a white fog.

"Can I get you anything?" She moved toward the door.

"No, thank you." My voice was hoarse.

She grabbed the handle to the door and paused. Never turning around, she said, "Sometimes we have to endure sacrifices of few for the survival of many. It's a burden you will have to get used to. It is the burden *your* destiny could end up bearing."

And with that she was gone.

My hands trembled as I removed my shorts and undergarments, tossing them on top of the toilet seat. I stepped into the shower. The beads of water rolled down my back as I rested my head against the wall. My dripping hair framed my face while my palms pressed into my eyes. An overload of emotions slithered through my stomach, up my torso, and into my throat. I couldn't breathe. I was feeling too much pain, anger, hurt, loss, confusion, sadness, and everything else caused by the last mind-blowing couple of days. My reality had been shaken like a snow globe, and instead of beautiful snowflakes falling, it was hail. Each hit impacted me harder until I felt broken inside.

I don't know how long I stayed in the shower working my mind, but it was long enough for the water to run cold and send prickly goose bumps to my skin. My flesh was puckered at my fingertips and toes. No matter how badly I didn't want to face the world, I knew it was time to move forward. I turned off the water, stepped out, and wrapped a towel around my body. I peered out into the hallway to make sure the coast was clear and walked across into my room.

My computer screen was illuminated with several emails, bold and unread. I pulled out my chair and sat down. Coach Barb had sent five emails but the subject line of the last one made my heart plummet in my chest.

RE: Your mother

Dear Beatrice,
I've left several messages for you. It's important we speak. Your email mentioned family issues. I'm sure you are mourning the loss of your mother still. If so, I think I may have some information you'd like to hear. I knew your mother well. I was

hesitant to divulge that information when I first saw that you signed up for track, and since I do not know Robert. At the time, I felt it would be inappropriate to disclose my relationship with your mother. I do hope you will reconsider your track career, but regardless, please meet me in the gym tomorrow morning. I'm sure Faye would be upset you are giving up on your dreams. Your mother was quite the athlete herself. In fact, I've never met a girl with such grit. Looking forward to sharing my memories with you. I will see you tomorrow.

Coach Barb

Coach Barb knew my mother and she waited until now to tell me. My fingers curled into fists. I was really tired of people withholding information about my mom. It was time for answers . . . from everyone.

Chapter Eleven

Cash

After killing two men, I was hungry and pissed. Super pissed. I had no choice but to kill Claude and Dominic after I'd tapped into their minds. They had orders to bring Beatrice in by any means necessary but to make sure she was still alive. The funny thing was they were instructed to do the same with me. However, in my case it was dead or alive. What they'd failed to do was block my mind from this information, which they could have easily done. DOAA has extensive defense education against our powers.

Robert ordered six large pizzas, and I crushed one all by myself. I was about to open another box when Paul interrupted me.

"Are you sure DOAA got a message from a Ferroean?" From the kitchen, Paul launched a purple soda can at me. I caught it midair. Grape soda? Who would drink that?

"That's what Claude said, and I believe him. What I can't understand is *why* one of our own went to Earth's government and not the Ferro council." I flipped the tab and fizz sputtered on the rim. I slurped the foam before it rained down the sides. Damn, grape soda *was* good.

Paul plopped down next to Tasha on the long side of the couch. "The fact that they went around the council and straight to DOAA means their allegiance is with Earth, or they have a serious ax to grind with our leadership. You got a plan, captain? Because this ain't good."

"I'm working on it." Truth was, I had no plan. This shit-storm was not adding up. Even though the DOAA said they wanted Beatrice, they also wanted me, and not because of the bullshit I caused at their headquarters. Without even trying to block me, they'd loudly thought of their plan inside their heads. Why would they be so careless or deliberate? They were trying to secure both Sera's source in Beatrice and mine, but they are under the impression mine isn't needed to save Earth.

Beatrice dragged her feet into the room like she was moving through molasses, distracting me from my thoughts. She looked like crap. Her face was pale, her eyes puffy, and someone should get her a comb for her wet hair. But who could blame her? The first time seeing someone killed affected you. To me it was another day as a Ferroean guard. Back on our planet, many tried to overthrow the government, and thus many died before me. I was known for leaving my opponents injured but alive. Not all of my guards felt the same way. My father regarded this as a weakness of mine, while I considered it a strength. I'd rather leave them to the jails than to the afterlife. But regardless of my personal feelings toward my father and the council, it was my duty to protect their reign, even if it meant taking out one of my own or disowning my flesh and source. The mission always came first.

Bea curled up into the corner of the couch. She grabbed a pillow and hugged it to her chest.

We agreed to answer her questions. At least Tasha and Robert agreed. I grumbled. Bea had been thrust into this situation because of her boundary-pushing momma. Part of me wanted to protect her from it. The other part was uncertain of how I felt toward her. Damn humans. They made everything more complicated.

"Mark, throw me your thermo dagger." I dropped the slice back onto my plate next to the incredibly delicious grape soda which would be on Tasha's next shopping list.

"Why?" Mark tilted his head to the side while reaching for his hidden blade in his ankle strap. He tossed the hilt toward me and I caught it. In one quick motion, I sliced my wrist.

Bea screamed as light poured into the room, and honey-like glue dripped onto the floor. Imagine the sun shooting rays into the sky. Such a freaking cool trick. I loved my powers.

"Are you out of your ever-loving mind?" Tasha rushed to my side, threaded her hands in mine, and healed me. She dabbed at the goo on my wrist, wiping it clean. Of course, cutting our wrists and ankles with a blade fashioned from our own planet was the only way we could die, but I felt pretty safe in my team's company, and it was the easiest way to show Bea the source. "Thank the council you didn't burn anyone."

I laughed. Tasha was the most overprotective sibling to ever exist. "I was demonstrating the source. Thought you wanted to give her answers."

"Answers Cash, not scare her to death." Tasha smacked the back of my head. I laughed. "Seriously, how are you the one in charge?"

Beatrice's knees were at her chest and she was shaking. Alright, so it might not have been the best way to start, but it was still cool. "Could you possibly talk me through it rather than whatever the hell that was?" Bea gestured to the where the light waves had shone. But her eyes remained fixated where the goo had been like she hungered for it.

"Boring, but ok."

Her eyes diverted from my wrist to my face. "Wait!" She held up the palm of her hand in my direction. "Tasha, can you tell me? Can you start with why the DOAA is after me?" Clearly Bea didn't appreciate my Ferroean display of awesomeness. Her loss. I'm much more entertaining than my sister.

"You have something they need that has the ability to protect Earth." Tasha released my hand and threw the napkin into the trash. Bea's eyes followed the linen's descent.

Tasha returned to the couch next to Paul, lowered herself, and crossed her ankles. "Hey, we need it, too." Paul said, elbowing Tasha's side. "And technically it belongs to us."

"What could I possibly have?" Bea's eyes returned to Tasha's.

"Faye extracted part of a Ferroean and put it inside of you to keep it safe. It's why another Ferroean sensed you, or rather it detected what's inside of you," Tasha said while grabbing another slice of pizza.

Bea's brows scrunched together. "My mom put an alien part in me?"

"Yep. Your mom's a real genius. And of course, she didn't leave any explanation," I groaned. Leave it to Faye to create more questions than answers.

Bea frowned. Tasha eyed me as if to say, *Back the hell off.* I waved my hand for her to proceed. If we had college on Ferro, Tasha would major in history or psychology. She loved explaining Ferroean antiquity. "Might as well get comfy. We're gonna be a while," I grumbled.

"You see, Ferroeans are very similar to humans in makeup, except our blood is liquid metal alloy that connects to an energy source inside our chest." She dabbed the grease off her hands onto her napkin.

"The white light Cash recklessly showed you is the source. This allows our power to manipulate electromagnetic fields, which achieves a wide variety of effects." Tasha lifted her hand, and the lamps on the end tables rose with her motion. She flicked her wrists back and forth, making the lamps dance. Then she lowered her hands, and the lamps settled back down on the table. "We can control magnetism and the manipulation of ferrous and nonferrous metal. Since we can manipulate at a subatomic level, we can control chemical structures and rearrange matter." Tasha lifted her hands again, and the remote control dangled in the air. She curled her hand into a fist and the remote burst.

"Really, Tash? How are we supposed to watch TV now?" Paul spat, throwing his hands up in the air. Robert retrieved the broken pieces and placed them into a garbage bag, shaking his head at Tasha's display.

"Oops! Well, Bea, you get the picture at least. All of our powers come from the energy source inside our chest." Tasha placed her hand over her right breast. Bea mimicked her and the same horrified expression graced her face as when she saw my assimilation scar.

Tasha's eyes followed her hand, causing her brow to pucker. My bleeding heart of a sister felt sorry for her.

"You're what we call a Blood-Light. You have Ferroean lineage but were born human. Blood-Lights can only be used as an energy womb. There aren't many humans capable of being one. Your kind was outlawed long ago."

"My kind? Outlawed?"

"Yes. It's not as bad as it sounds," Tasha said with a weak smile.

No, it's exactly how it sounded and my sweet-talking sis forgot to mention it was also punishable by death. Faye's little affair could have gotten her killed, but her love child . . . damn, the DOAA would take her into custody for the rest of her life. Blood-Lights were DOAA prisoners.

"Wait." Bea turned her body to her father. Man, I did not wish to be him right now. "Which one of you is part alien, Mom or you?"

Robert hesitated, so I blurted it out. "Faye." It wasn't a necessary truth, and now that it was out, Bea could blame me for the deceit. Robert's eyes blinked as if he was uncertain to be thankful or pissed. I picked up where Tasha left off. "We've been searching for Dr. X, an Earth assimilation scientist who was very close with Faye. We believe he might have some information that could shed light on why Faye used you as an energy source womb and how she came into contact with the Ferroean's source you have inside of you."

Bea relaxed on the couch no longer looking like a scared little human. Her fists balled. "Let me get this straight. My mom, who has alien ancestry, essentially kidnapped me, drugged me, conspired with Dr. X, then implanted an alien power source in me, and then what? Just died? What *really* happened to her?"

"We don't know." I stretched my legs. Even as we told Bea the truth, I realized how many questions we also needed answered and wished this session went both ways. If we could jolt her memory, we might be able to find out what the hell Faye was up to. "We were hoping Dr. X could fill in the blanks, but we can't find him. We don't even know where Faye brought you the week you went missing. Faye asked me to protect her daughter—a daughter I didn't even know existed until I got her message." The irony of Faye entrusting me with her daughter's life, but also keeping her a secret from me for almost four years, was not lost on me. What reason did she have to hide Bea?

"Why you?" Bea sounded ticked off that I was dear mommy's number one choice in protection detail. Get in line, Bea. I was pissed, too.

"I'm the best. What mother wouldn't want the best?" I winked.

She rolled her eyes, making the tips of my lips curl. Pissing Bea off was as pleasurable as grape soda. Not sure it would make Tasha's grocery list, but it would definitely be on my To Do list from now on.

"How did the DOAA know what my mom did?" Bea asked.

Robert stood from the fireplace and walked toward the windows. The clouds had rolled in. Perfect timing for Mother Nature to clean what remnants were left on the street from our encounter with Claude and Dominic. Rain danced on the glass as he gazed out across the street. He had been exceptionally quiet up until now. "When you ended up in the hospital, the DOAA got suspicious. They saw your scar. It's the same one all Ferroeans have after assimilation. I needed to get you out of there, so I brought you home."

"Wouldn't they look for us here?" Bea's gaze roamed around the room. "Our old home seems like an obvious place."

Robert closed the shades, darkening the room and turned on a floor lamp before taking the recliner next to Bea. "Faye and I concealed this home. The DOAA never knew about you. It was set up as a safe house in case your mother or I ever needed to go into hiding. No place is safe from a Ferroean with the source inside of you, but this town is called a No Zone. Ferroeans are not allowed to live here, so I thought it would be the most secure option. Without a Ferroean present, no one could sense you."

"Why's it called a No Zone?"

Thunder struck, and Bea jumped. Tasha moved next to her on the couch. "Cartwright was set up by the Ferro Council and the DOAA as a mission territory, but it wasn't put into use until four years ago when we came to Earth." Tasha placed her hand on Bea's jittery knee. "Mission territories are not allowed to be inhabited by our kind so that they don't taint the research we do on humans."

"Why is the DOAA after the energy source?" Bea touched her chest again, and I swear I heard a zap.

"The source Faye stole is of importance to planet Ferro and Earth," Mark answered from the love seat, where he was sitting next to his sister. He leaned forward, resting his forearms on his knees. Sammie barely looked at Bea, but I knew better. The more we sat here explaining the DOAA, the council, and what Bea really was, the more Sammie's resentment grew. Which in turn was more for *me* to worry about.

Bea took a deep breath as if absorbing all of the information we were finally giving her. Then asked, "What's the importance?"

Tears welled up in Bea's eyes. "We could all die?"

Tasha removed her hand from Bea's knee. "Yes, but we are doing everything we can to prevent that. It's why what's inside of you is so important. It's why this is so serious."

"Do I have powers?" Bea pulled at her flesh on her arm, watching it snap back into place. "Like you guys?"

I laughed. Bea with our powers would be my nightmare. Thank the Council, Blood-Lights weren't strong enough. Although thinking back to our run together, her speed was faster than it should have been for a human. I made a mental note to have Tasha investigate hereditary traits for a Blood-Light from a Ferroean.

"No. The energy source has to be fully assimilated into your bloodstream. Right now, it's hanging out in your chest. That's why you are called an energy womb," Tasha explained.

"Can't we remove it?"

"That's the idea but we were hoping to learn more about why Faye did this before we took any measures. Until then, our job is to protect you." Tasha closed the last pizza box and threw it on top of the other empties.

"After what happened today, we need to come up with a plan. Bea can't be alone at all." Robert tapped his fingers on his knee and rocked back on the recliner.

"And no more runs," I barked. I didn't want to kill people every time Bea wanted to get some exercise.

"We need an explanation, so no one questions why our group is hanging out with her. It's not like she fits in with us." Sammie smiled, the dimple she shared with Mark and Paul popped on her right cheek.

"Cash has made an obvious public interest in her," Tasha butted in with a pointed glare. She cut off the crust of her veggie slice and piled it on a new plate. She offered it to Mark. He retrieved it from her with a dopey smile plastered on his face. What was up with those two?

"It's worked before," Paul answered Tasha's telepathic idea, "and would be an easy transition after today."

"No way," Samantha squealed, moving to the edge of the love seat.

Robert and Bea glanced from one to the other. Clearly, they couldn't read my team's mind. But I could. "You think Bea and I should start dating?"

Chapter Twelve

Cash

"You all think Cash and I should start dating?" Bea exploded from the couch like a loose spring. Her pizza toppled to the ground. Waste of a good slice. And I was still hungry.

Robert scratched his head as if struggling with the fact that I wasn't his first choice in male suitors for his daughter. "Bea isn't old enough to date." Yep. Definitely not a fan.

"It's a perfect plan," Mark interjected, smiling at me. "It would explain why they're always biting each other's heads off, why they're always together, and why she quit the track team."

"Plus, rumors about it are already all over school since Sammie and Bea basically fought over Cash today at lunch." Paul's dimples danced as he spoke. I wanted to punch them back into his face. Noticing Sammie's dark crimson cheeks, I was sure she did too.

Robert cleared his throat and shifted uncomfortably. His menacing glare matched his tense jaw. Damn, Robert. I wasn't that bad.

"Anyone care what I think?" Bea rose from the couch with her arms crossed over her chest. She looked cute all flustered. Did I think cute? Thank the Council, my team couldn't read my thoughts.

"What do *you* think?" I said as I leaned against the arm of the couch, interested. Why not hear Bea's opinion? At this point, she knows she's in danger. Claude and Dominic were perfect examples of that. Let's see if she will take this seriously and realize there's a lot more at stake than her ego.

She hesitated so I tapped into her mind.

Is this a trap? Why does he care what I think? It's not like he won't overrule whatever I end up saying. Ugh, and Sammie! She's still pissed at me; every available moment, she glares in my direction. The last thing I want to do is to pretend to date her boyfriend. Who knows where her rampant hatred will lead? I could wake up missing an eye with that girl. Dating, even pretend dating, Cash is out of the question.

My lips twitched.

"Well?"

She huffed. "Is it really necessary?"

"You could always pretend to date Mark or Paul. It doesn't matter to me." Her eyes widened. Well, that threw her off. "Would you rather Paul or Mark?" I looked over to Paul who had pizza grease slathered on his lips and chin. Then to Mark who was staring oddly at Tasha. Bea followed my gaze.

Her face burned with humiliation. She threw her head back and released all the air from her inflamed cheeks. I was enjoying this a little too much.

"Fine. I will pretend date you."

Samantha rose from her chair and with her powers threw one of the end tables across the room. It smashed and crumpled to the ground. The second one she lifted and willed it to hit me. I ducked, and it crashed into the floor lamp. With lightning speed, I moved in front of her. I pushed her back until she pressed against the wall. My forearm at her throat.

"You do something like that again and I swear I will send you back to Ferro."

Her eyes welled up. "I can't believe you're okay with this. She's nothing but a human and she's carrying her, our . . ."

I pressed harder, cutting off her windpipe and causing her to stop. We told Bea the truth but the hell if I was going to tell her about Sera. Sammie looked back and forth between Tasha and me. Tears streamed down her cheek. I released her and with a poof she was gone.

When I turned around, Mark and Paul's inflamed faces confronted me. "You didn't have to do that." Mark stalked toward me, Paul at his side. They stopped inches away from me. Mark lowered his voice. "She misses Sera, too. We all do. You're not the only one hurting. You can be a real asshole sometimes."

He was right, but I'd never admit it.

I looked around the room for Bea. She was gone.

"She's upstairs." Robert motioned with his eyes. "I'd ask you to not go up there, but I'd be wasting my breath." And with that Robert left the room as disappointed in me as the others.

I knocked on Bea's door, a courtesy I was not used to giving.

"Come in."

"Hey." I walked over to her desk, rolled the chair out from under and straddled it.

She said nothing as she focused on the book in her hand, even though I was positive she wasn't reading. After a prolonged silence, she put the book down. "What do you want?"

"I'm sorry." She glared. I continued, "I'm sorry you feel like your life is being overrun. . ." I raised my brow and caught her eyes with mine, "even if it is for your protection."

"Save your lame apologies for Sammie. She deserves them more than I do." She looked back down at her book. Her knuckles whitened around the hard cover. Okay, so she wasn't exactly happy with me. I could live with that if that kept her safe. But the Sammie thing was driving me nuts.

"Sammie and I are not together. She is not my girlfriend."

Her head snapped up. "What? But everyone at school thinks—"

I didn't let her finish. "Fake relationships work in missions because it explains to humans why we're all attached at the . . ." I looked up at the ceiling and snapped. What's that human saying?

"Hip," she finished.

"Yes, hip. It helps create an illusion necessary for our missions as teenagers. I'm trying to apologize for what you went through today and explain that Sammie's dislike for you stems from other reasons . . . but you make it so hard."

She quieted so I tapped into her thoughts. *Why pretend to date Sammie? She's awful. Her temper is almost as terrifying as yours.*

"Sammie's not that bad. She's been through a lot. If the two of you got to know each other . . ."

Bea's eyes went wide as she scooted back up against the wall. Her face paled. Shit. I answered her thought out loud. A rookie mistake I hadn't made in years.

I stayed tapped into her head.

Cash read my mind, like exact words read my mind. Oh my god. His words from the first day we met: Every thought you had about me today, good and bad, I heard. He hadn't been trying to scare me—he was telling the truth. All of the times I'd gawked at him, hated him, been upset by him. Everything. Oh my god. Oh my god.

"Bea." I stood from the desk chair and held up my hands.

"Get out!" She threw a pillow at me. "Get out of my room. Now!"

"Let's talk about this. It's not that bad."

"I'm serious, get out. Get the hell out of my room."

She stood and threw anything she could get her hands on: shoes, pillows, books. I dodged every item, freezing some midair and dropping them to the ground.

Finally, to stop this ridiculousness, I bear hugged her. She fell off-balance from the surprise embrace and ended up pulling me down with her. She was feisty, I'd give her that. When she tried to clock me with a shoe she found at her side, I pinned her arms over her head with one hand, and then lowered my body to restrain her flailing legs. And that's when it happened. I didn't even realize how much I needed to feed until that moment.

She clawed and kicked, making it even harder to control both my urges and her thrashing.

"Stop it." She bucked under me like a wild animal. My source thumped as her exertion continued. "This isn't helping anyone. Stop fighting me, Bea, and I will let you up." I had to let her up soon or . . .

Our eyes locked and I felt my eyes circle in my sockets. The atmosphere around us transformed. The electricity between us snapped and pulled like a rubber band. Wild and desperate hunger rushed through my veins until I was flooded with an inborn pull. Her lips parted as if she were about to speak, but words never came. We both stilled. The only noise came from our synchronized sharp intakes of breath.

She lifted her head closing the space between us. Misreading the situation, she kissed me.

I froze trying desperately not to give in to impulse. I hadn't fed in weeks, and the aching thirst was palpable. With the limited power I had, I pulled a millimeter away. Her irises flickered, and a dark rainbow of colors peeked through the hazel hue, circling like prey around the white core. The source was running through her veins. Impossible! Freaking impossible.

Her lips found mine for the second time. Everything inside of me wanted to take from her. Needed to.

I pressed my mouth to hers, catching her bottom lip between mine and breathed ethereal energy in. I took and took. Our kiss deepened, and I took more. My mouth devoured her with a vengeance. Light flowed out of her and throughout me. I was getting stronger. Much stronger. I could take on an army with this much power. She pushed the source into me, harder than Sera ever did. I tightened my grip around her wrists. The rush of emotions igniting inside of me was maddening. Just as it felt right and natural, it was wrong and inconceivable. I wasn't sure I could stop.

Then the bedroom door burst open and slammed against the wall, breaking the bond.

Chapter Thirteen

Beatrice

The door crashed through sheetrock and I screamed. Dad and Tasha were at my bedroom entrance, their mouths agape at the sight of Cash and me on the floor.

"What the hell!" Tasha leaned up against my dresser.

My dad's horror exploded next. "Get off my daughter!" His shoulders took up most of the entryway. His face was inflamed.

Cash pushed off his hands, moving in one fluid, unbelievably quick motion. He stood, blocking me from view.

"Want to explain what's going on?" Tasha's foot tapped rapidly against the floor. Her eyes pierced Cash's with pointed accusation. An expression she tossed at him frequently.

Dad mirrored Tasha's position—crossing his arms over his chest like he needed to restrain his hands from throwing a punch at Cash. "Explain!"

"It was nothing. Bea kissed me."

Oh my god, I had kissed him! I scooted back on the floor until my spine hit the wall. My hands flew up to my face, which burned with mortification. He didn't even kiss me back at first—I had practically forced myself on him. Oh man, I had *forced* myself on him!

Cash turned to me. "No, you didn't, but that's not the point."

My face blushed. Hell, my whole body blushed, especially all the parts that still remembered him on top of me.

Dad took a bold step forward. Cash met his step with one of his own, closing the space between them. Cash and my dad both towered over six feet and were in great shape, but my dad's angry presence seemed to tower over Cash.

"Kissing Bea back was a mistake, Robert." He shook his head. "Don't for one minute forget what position Faye has put me in."

"She's still my daughter." My dad countered with another step forward. His arms unfolded and his fists clenched and unclenched at his side. What the hell were they talking about?

"Then you should be pissed, too." Cash matched my father's step.

"I am!" My dad took one last stride toward Cash, until barely a foot stood between them. Tasha's face paled as her eyes darted from Cash to my father and back again. My father's face softened ever so slightly as he sighed.

"I think it's safe to say I would like you to stay out of my daughter's room. I understand your . . . position. But I'm not okay with this." My dad waved at Cash and me.

"There is nothing between us." I fought back tears and an overwhelming sensation of humiliation.

"This is my house and my rules. I'm still your father. So, if this," he gestured again between me and Cash, "is nothing, you won't be allowed to do nothing until you are thirty."

My head thumped into my hands. "Can everyone please get out of my room?"

"Cash and I are leaving." Tasha gave Cash a stern look. He shook his head and followed her out of the room.

I could feel the weight of my dad's stare. "Dad, please . . . go." Tears threatened my eyes and if my father didn't leave soon, I didn't know if I would be able to hold them back.

"I'd like to talk about this." His voice softened.

"Please leave." It would be one thing to have this conversation with mom, but dad? That was too awkward for me. I barely looked up.

"Okay." He glanced at the hole he created in the wall from the doorknob. "No more boys in your room." And with that he closed the door much more gently than he'd opened it.

I woke up the next day with Cash's minty pine and honey scent still lingering on my skin. It was a wicked reminder that the night before had been real. I showered and dressed in record time, and flew out of my house, avoiding my father and the occupants of the guest room. Since my dad had made me quit track, I was back to carpooling with Darla and Chris. As much as I loved my old vintage Beetle, I was happy to be a passenger in Chris's backseat, where I didn't have to pay attention to the road.

"You okay?" Darla loosened her seatbelt and twisted around to face me. Her eyes scanned my body.

"Yeah, I guess." I shrugged.

Her face knotted up in curiosity. "You gonna tell us why Cash Kingston showed up at your house and then your dad practically threw us out?"

Chris smiled and caught my eye in his rearview mirror. He gave me a supportive wink. We both knew Darla would never surrender until she had gleaned every last drop of drama.

"It's complicated," I mumbled.

Darla's eyes widened. "You like him!" She unbuckled her seatbelt and frantically climbed over the center console of Chris's Nissan.

"Whoa. What are you doing?" Chris bobbed to avoid a foot to the face. The car swerved ever so slightly.

"Tell me everything." Darla's hands shook my knees while Chris adjusted his rearview mirror to see me better. His face had paled.

"You have to tell me something. I'm going to die—literally die—if you don't give me details!"

"I doubt that." Not liking my response, she squeezed my knee tighter. "Okay, okay, we kissed. I don't want to talk about it." I turned my head away from Darla.

"Ooh, that bad, huh?" Chris's reflection grinned at me with false satisfaction. "He might be good-looking, but you know it takes more than a pretty face to know how to kiss." Although a part of me wanted to defend Cash, another part felt guilty admitting to Chris that Cash's kiss was the perfect combination of lips, tongue, and touch so I responded with a weak smile.

"Wait, what about Sammie?" Darla raised her brow.

"Umm . . . they broke up?" Why hadn't we all discussed what I was supposed to say?

"So, where did you guys leave it?" Darla released my knees. I probably had Darla-sized fingerprints under my jeans.

"My dad caught us so . . . well, I haven't really said anything to him yet," I admitted.

"Hot damn, Bea! This is one hell of a senior year."

As the three of us walked into school, Darla broke off to meet with a teacher about after-school help. Chris promised to escort me to homeroom and first period. Afterward, he stopped to grab a baseball mitt he had loaned one of his friends, but then came straight to get me at my locker.

"Ready?" Chris switched his bag to his other shoulder.

"Yeah, one second." I fidgeted with the tag in my pants. It was in the perfect spot scratching the crap out of my lower back. "Hey, can you get the tag in my jeans?" I pulled the label. I had meant to cut it out this morning but was too distracted by my desire to escape.

Chris laughed, shook his head, and then leaned over to assess the tag. "Bend over a little. You want me to rip it out or do you want me to cut it? I think I have scissors in my backpack."

"Rip it." I pressed my hands against the wall and jutted out the seat of my jeans.

"Wha—grhc!" Chris exclaimed as something slammed against metal. I whirled around to see Cash's fist wrapped around the collar of Chris's black shirt, pinning him to the wall of the lockers. His feet dangled above the ground. A muscle in Cash's forearm pulsed rapidly.

"What are you doing?" I dropped my bag to the floor and tugged on Cash's arm. Not like it moved an inch from my efforts.

"Why does *he* have his hands down your pants?" Cash's voice was a deep, throaty growl.

My face flushed with anger.

"Yo man, I was getting her tag like she asked me. I'm Chris, one of her best friends." Chris held up his hands, but Cash ignored the gesture.

"Put him down. Now Cash!"

Cash lowered Chris, slowly releasing his grip, one finger at a time. Chris straightened his shirt and inched back a step.

"What the hell do you think you're doing, attacking one of my friends?" I slid in between them.

The hall filled with students, gathering around the impending fight.

"What do you think *you're* doing?" Cash's face burned with anger. The curve of his strong jaw pulsated.

"Me? Don't you dare turn this around on me," I yelled getting up in his face.

Cash wrapped his arm around my waist and pulled me closer. My eyes widened with shock as he lowered his lips within inches of mine. He grazed them across my cheek leaving moisture in their wake as he positioned them over my ear. His voice was low but void of his previous anger. "We are supposed to be pretend dating, remember?"

Full of frustration and flooded with rage, my fingers dug into his arms. "Yeah, I remember." My adrenaline recoiled into sweet torture. His hand gripped my lower back, pulling our bodies flush. My breathing labored. His lips dragged back and hovered over my lips.

The warning bell rang foggily through my daze and Cash released me. For a moment, we locked eyes. He seemed so uncertain—almost as confused as I was. He leaned in and whispered, "I'm sure everyone will find it easier to believe we are together if the only hands on you are mine." He pulled away and winked at me. In one quick second, I went from overwhelmed to furious. My face burned.

"Nice meeting you, Kyle." Cash threw the incorrect name over his shoulder as he walked down the hall.

My entire body trembled. I sucked in two deep breaths and threaded my arm through Chris's. "I don't want to talk about this." I ushered him toward class.

"You don't want to talk about what just happened?" Chris fanned his notebook to his face and then elbowed me. "What the hell was that and what happened to my best friend?"

I didn't have an answer, but I'm pretty sure that girl died the moment these extraterrestrial beings came into my life.

As we hurried to first period, Coach Barb stood in our path. She had on a navy blue and white track suit and her red curly hair was pulled into a high ponytail. Her lips and face were void of makeup. Sometimes I imagined if Coach Barb dressed up, she'd be really good-looking.

"Beatrice, I'm surprised I didn't hear from you." Her email last night was overshadowed by the team's information dump and the kiss. I completely forgot about meeting her in the gym this morning before school and about her knowing my mom.

"I'm sorry, Coach Barb. It's been kinda crazy at home." Coach Barb's arms were crossed at her chest. Her unpolished nails tapped incessantly against her elbows. Her bright blue eyes were full of disappointment.

"You mentioned knowing my mom in the email." I squeezed Chris's arm, clinging to security. Having the why-I-quit-track discussion was last on my list for the day. But the how-you-know-my-mother conversation was clawing its way back up to the top.

"I did." Just then, Coach Barb did the unexpected and placed her palm over my assimilation scar. Her fingertips rested on my shoulders. My heart stopped when the same sensation the day Cash touched me there bubbled beneath the skin. "I think it's a mistake to quit track." My stomach rolled violently as my hands trembled at my sides. Something wasn't right. She dropped her hand and the acid-like feeling in my chest recoiled.

She turned to Chris and said, "You will stay quiet while I speak and not utter your first words until I am out of sight."

Chris looked stunned as my mouth dropped a good two inches. What was wrong with Coach Barb?

"Is there a reason you decided to quit?" she asked refocusing on me.

I swallowed hard. "I can't commit to a team right now. There's a lot going on at home," I said. My voice was low. "How do you know my mom?"

Her eyes narrowed on me. "Faye and I had similar interests growing up. In fact, we were in the same classes at this very school and received the same extracurricular education. She would be very disheartened you quit. You wouldn't want to disappoint her, would you?" Her lips curled.

I released Chris's arm. "No, but at this time I need to focus on my studies, and I know that is what she would have wanted." Obviously, this wasn't the truth, but any normal adult would accept that as a responsible reason and stop the interrogation.

Coach Barb unzipped her fanny pack and pulled out a Think Watch Band, which monitors heart rate, speed, distance, and calories burned; used most often with professional athletes. "Here, take this. A gift from me to you to use until you can come back to the team." She grabbed my arm and latched the watch onto my wrist. "This way you won't give up your dream. Your mother wouldn't let anything go, especially when she believed in it. I can promise you, she and I shared that bravado. Something I hope to see in you one day."

Her shoulders tensed. "I must go." She looked around frantically. "Don't take the watch off. It's important you keep tracking your progress. Promise me!"

And before I could answer, she bolted down the hallway.

I released the breath I didn't even realize I was holding as I saw Sammie round the bend. She strutted toward us. Her heels clacked loudly against the tile. Her lips held a tight line. She stopped two feet in front of me and glared at Chris.

"Guess that's my cue. Good luck," he murmured, not even acknowledging my conversation with Couch Barb. He hurried down the hallway, leaving me there with Satan Sammie.

"I don't like you." She tossed her blonde curls over her shoulder. They bounced like they nodded in agreement to her salty comment. "But you do have something we need, so I'm giving you another try. Tonight at 8 p.m.; the movies. Girls do that together, right?"

Speechless, I nodded.

"You say one thing that pisses me off, and I swear I will chop your stupid hair off while you sleep." She pivoted on her heels and clickety-clacked down the hallway toward class, hips sashaying side to side.

"Wait, Sammie." I ran after her. She ignored me. "Please, please. Wait!" She turned and glared at me, her arms crossed tightly against her chest. "Why can't we remove the source right now?"

Her eyes swirled with strands of colors like a whirly pop as her jaw strained. "Cash trusts Faye, and she said to protect you. If she wanted the source removed, she would have said it."

"What does that mean?"

Sammie took a deep breath, and with her release, she relaxed her arms down by her sides.

"Cash is giving Faye time."

"Why?"

She shook her head and turned in the opposite direction. Fear inched its way up my throat. As if she could sense my overwhelming emotions, she pivoted back around. "Removing the source would most likely kill you."

Chapter Fourteen

Cash

After school, I ordered everyone back to the safe house. Darla and Robert were with Beatrice at home. I felt confident we could get to her in time if she needed us, especially on the heels of all the ethereal power I had digested. I was stronger than ever before even after I accidentally fed too much from when Sera held the source. Something wasn't right about this Blood-Light. Her assimilation to the source should be impossible.

Mark and Paul sat on the edge of the couch playing video games, squealing with every kill shot. I couldn't be bothered with human games. In my reality, weapons didn't pretend-fire. Sammie paced in the kitchen, blathering to Tasha about all of Bea's annoying traits. My eyes tracked each arm flail that accompanied her disdainful words. She was a loose cannon when she was upset. Right now, I needed her focused. Thankfully, my sister was the voice of reason.

Tasha opened a bottle of wine and poured herself and me a glass. We weren't habitual drinkers, but after this week, our human wine collection had suffered. And after I let myself cave to the source's connection, I needed to take the edge off all the ethereal power I'd absorbed. I had lost control feeding from Bea's energy source like a drunkard. It was different with Sera. We had known each other our whole lives and the source's connection contributed to our relationship. From the time we were kids until our years on earth, we were never apart. Our romantic relationship had merely developed in the last four years, and it had started slow, gradually building to an epic bond. The elders had given us a measuring device Sera wore around her neck to keep us both balanced, but after she was killed, it couldn't be found.

With Bea the connection was raw and compulsive, something completely different. I drank her kiss in and couldn't stop, much like a vampire feeding off its prey. I hated myself for it and hated myself even more for letting her think it was her fault. And then today, when her human friend, Chris, put his hands on her, I lost my mind as if she were Sera. I would have shattered every bone in that human's body if Bea hadn't broken me from my own spell. Rage washed over me. It's not always fun reading human minds, and Chris's thoughts were full of loud Bea compliments. He couldn't stop internally blathering about how beautiful she was, and how he wanted to kiss her.

"I hate that I have to go to the movies with her," Sammie snarled, grabbing my glass from my hand and taking a sip. "Tasha should come."

"No, you need to do this on your own. Get to know her as Beatrice, not Sera's source thief," I said while drinking straight from the bottle. That should gross her out enough to give me my glass back.

"You're an asshat," she said as she slid my glass toward me. So predictable.

Sera was Sammie's best friend. Knowing a piece of Sera was harbored inside this foreign human shell felt in many ways like Sera was robbed. It's how I found myself first looking at Bea until recently, until I fed from her and realized it's not her fault. I hoped this girl bonding crap would help ease the tension. Maybe Sammie can see another side to this Blood-Light and get her blonde head out of her butt and focus on our mission.

"You both are," Tasha said, responding to Sammie. She pulled a chair out at the table and sat. "This girl's been through hell, and all you two can think of is yourselves." She gulped the rest of her glass back. "She witnessed two humans killed in defense to her life and feels guilty about it. Maybe we should give her a little more credit. I think she's handling everything pretty well for having her world rocked and rattled."

Screams in the background alerted us to Mark winning whatever stupid video game they were playing. The controls crashed against the wall and arguing between the brothers got louder as they neared the kitchen.

A hand slapped my shoulder. "Dickhead won, or so he thinks. I let him win," Paul said. He took the seat next to me, motioning to Mark to grab a glass from the cabinet.

Mark grabbed three more wine goblets and sat down. He slid one toward his sister and the other to his brother. "We've got bigger problems than Bea's emotional state. We need to find out who sensed her and tattled to the DOAA. Don't you think it's a little weird another Ferroean sensed Sera's source and told DOAA agents instead of its own council? Since this is supposed to be a No Zone for Ferroeans, I think we need to visit other possibilities. Someone with an ax to grind against our planet's been living in a No

Zone and now they are siding with the DOAA instead of their own."

"What do we know right now?" I said, frustrated with all the *what we don't know, what we cannot do.*"

Sammie kicked her legs onto my lap, and I threw them off. She flung them back up, and I let them stay. Small victories for her made life easier for me. "Here are the facts. Beatrice is a Blood-Light with Sera's energy source inside of her. As long as she's safe, Sera's source is safe. The DOAA is after both Beatrice's and Cash's sources and are ordered to bring them back to HQ. We have until the end of the year to join the sources to save . . ." Sammie paused. "Wait, which planet are we trying to save?"

"Both!" Tasha interjected. "The goal is and always was both."

Sammie shook her head. "That's right! Oh, and Robert isn't Bea's dad, but Cash has a theory as to who her daddy is but won't share that information, or what he's intending to do about it." She stuck her tongue out at me. "We're not stupid. We know you have something up your sleeve." She turned to the rest of the group. "I guess that's all we know."

Mark poured half his glass into Tasha's wine, motioning for her to have it. "We also know that the Ferro council is torn. Half of the members want both sources back in Ferro regardless of the prophecy, and the other members are scared of what will happen if we don't listen to the elders. The DOAA is desperate to keep them here for obvious reasons. So literally anyone has motive to try and steal Sera's source and use it for their cause."

Paul interjected while rubbing his head. "I'm with the council members who want to bring both sources back to Ferro. Earth isn't our responsibility. Why not remove the sources from this planet and bring them back to their rightful place? Let's save our people! That's the oath we have taken as guards."

I waved my hand toward my sister. "Go ahead, you love this crap. Explain the prophecy to Paul for the umpteenth time so he understands why he and those idiotic council members should give a rat's ass about Earth."

Tasha sat up straighter. Her eyes lit up. Sometimes I wondered how we were related. We were nothing alike. Ferroan history or legend, as I like to call it, was not my wheelhouse. But for Tasha it was her ultimate high.

"Every few thousand years, opposing energy sources are born from an original's bloodline. There are only five descendants: the Sayer, Kingston, Malloy, Laylan, and the Flannery families. Only one of these bloodlines can carry opposing sources. Both Seraphina Laylan's and Cash Kingston's sources set the prophecy in motion—both born with sources of a unique color. It's when a source emits a purple shimmer at its base rather than yellow that we know there is an imminent threat of destruction. The prophecy says that two worlds will be in danger, and if you choose to save one, they will both perish. Hence why, when we found out about Earth's asteroid hitting before ours, we were sent here to 'observe humans' while we tried to find a way to save both worlds, Council forbid they hit at the same time." Tasha held her two pointer fingers up to show human quotes.

"Yeah, yeah, I kinda remember all that. But why two opposing sources? Why can't one of them save the planets? Then one stays here, and one goes back to Ferro?" Paul asked.

Tasha smacked her forehead. "Really, Paul? Did you sleep in training? It's their combined power that will kill the asteroids. They aren't powerful enough on their own. Cash needs to feed, and Sera needs her source absorbed as they become one. The universe created this balance so that no Ferroean could ever make the decision without its counterpart to protect or destroy."

Mark crossed his arms over his chest and leaned back on two chair legs. "I'm pretty sure Mom and Dad would lose their shit if they heard how lame you are. Did you pay any attention in Guard school at all?" He shook his head. "Literally this is in our exams. Who'd you pay off to get a passing grade?"

Paul smiled stupidly at Mark. "I think the teacher had a crush on me." He turned to Tasha. "It's not like I was asleep the whole time. I know that it's impossible to kill the opposing sources. I got that question right on the test."

Sammie snarled. "You're an idiot! If they couldn't be killed, then my best friend wouldn't be six feet under." She stood, curling her hands at her sides. I scooted my chair closer to Sammie and placed my hand on her arm, dragging her back down to sit.

"Sera's not buried. Don't be dramatic," I said while squeezing her hand in a comforting way. Deep down I wanted to growl, too. I shouldn't have let Sera go to California without me. We were warned to never be apart and I failed her. "Paul is an idiot. He meant the sources inside us. Everyone knows our shells can be killed."

Mark sighed, then tried to ease the tension. "Switching gears a little, but has anyone wondered why Faye would use her own daughter? I know Blood-Lights are rare, but Faye could have found another. She had access to the list in California, and at least a dozen of them would have volunteered just to get out of the prison they are in."

I had theories but I wasn't sure what I should or shouldn't share with the team. Everyone was already on edge. I didn't want them to worry about one more thing. Part of being their leader was taking care of them—not just physically. If they knew everything I was considering, it could be harmful to the mission. We needed to keep the energy source safe and viable for complete connection at the end of the year. Only then could we save any planet. If Faye cared about the mission as much as I think she did, then the theory I was holding back—the only answer to this insane jigsaw puzzle—was that Beatrice could ignite the source and connect to me. And if that was possible, then everything I was ever told about Blood-Lights was wrong and no planet was safe. Beatrice could kill us all.

Chapter Fifteen

Beatrice

Darla and I stepped out of Betsey at the Reddington Theater and waited for Sammie to show up. The crisp air smelled like fall, while the wind sent goose bumps to my skin. After my encounter with Coach Barb today, the chill wasn't only in the air but in an unsettling atmosphere impossible for me to shake. I rubbed my arms, trying to put warmth back into my body. After the day we'd had at school, I was looking forward to a night with the girls. Even if Sammie was part of it.

Darla sighed. "I still can't believe we are hanging out with Samantha Flannery. When did you and Barbie become friends? Just yesterday, her claws were out in the cafeteria, and you were her scratching post." She crossed her arms over her chest in protest. She'd huffed and puffed the whole thirty-minute ride until her persisting snorts became impossible to ignore.

Cash had ordered Sammie and I to get to know each other better, and it was his suggestion to go to this old crappy theater to connect. It's not like I hadn't put up a fight, but my dad agreed, saying it would make things easier on all of them if the two of us could get along. I had already planned to spend the night with Darla, so I dragged her with me for the bonding experience. Let's just say she was as thrilled about it as me, but she was much more vocal. Her first words were, 'I'd rather be a thirty-year-old virgin than hang out with Samantha Flannery.'

"Cash and my dad told me I had to play nice, so you do, too." I popped open the trunk.

"Your new boyfriend and your father, who is acting like a weirdo lately, gave you a list of approved friends?" Darla's voice rose while she followed me to the back of the car. I didn't blame her suspicion. "Did Chris and I make this list?" She leaned against Betsey's side. Her nose crinkled like the words had left a bitter taste on her tongue.

"Barely," I joked, hoping to lighten the mood.

"That's not funny." Clearly, she was not going to let this go.

I lowered my head into the trunk and rummaged through the hordes of clothes. Nothing I could say to Darla would make her understand, so I decided to ignore her questions altogether. "I have a zip-up hoodie in here somewhere." I pulled out my track sneakers—god, I didn't miss track anymore. A pair of sweatpants, a bathing suit top—where were the bottoms? A Frisbee and two of Chris's baseball bats. How many bats did he own?

"Hey." A voice came from the side of my car.

I glanced up, avoiding the lid of the trunk, and saw a dressed-down Sammie. She wore jeans, a pink zip-up, no makeup, and her hair pulled back. Very un-Sammie-like.

"You look different." Darla eyed Sammie, starting from her flat shoes to her casual hairdo.

"Yeah, whatever." She frowned, playing with the ends of the strings dangling from her hoodie.

I returned to the scavenger hunt that was my trunk. Who cared what Sammie was wearing? I had bigger problems; finding my hoodie was at the top of that list.

"Bea . . . Bea, get out of the trunk."

"Hold on, I'm trying to find my zip-up. I don't even know how some of this stuff got in my car," I mumbled.

"You do not have time. Get out of the trunk!" Sammie yelled.

A thunderous sound echoed in my ear as an arm around my waist drew me back from my car. A bright flash flickered in the sky as lightning struck Betsey, tearing her in half. Part of the car rolled onto its side, while the other half wobbled back and forth until it settled flat. The smell of burnt metal flowed through the air, reminding me of the inside of a mechanic's shop. The passenger car door wavered with a metallic scrape, hanging on by its last hinge. Little flames ignited along the edges of the door, until a gust of wind extinguished them, leaving it to thunk onto the asphalt.

My blue zip-up fluttered in the air, landing in the middle of the rubbish.

"Oh my god," I screamed, still wrapped in Sammie's arms. I clung to her elbows, my nails sinking into her flesh. My eyes followed a stray tire that rolled down the hill, toward the highway. The hubcap separated right before the tire faced oncoming traffic. I cringed, unable to look, as cars screeched below.

"You okay?" Sammie whispered in my ear. I couldn't answer, unable to process what had just happened. My car was obliterated. Goo dripped down off its limbs, which reminded me of something . . . familiar. Then the fear of an absent Darla filled my mind and I screamed for her. I pushed out of Sammie's embrace and spun. Had the bolt of electricity hit her?

"I'm right here." My eyes searched the parking lot, and found Darla pinned under Cash, in a heap of leaves. When had he gotten here? He grabbed her by the elbow and helped her to her feet.

"Causing trouble, again?"

He smiled that devilish grin, which spread across his lips and reached his eyes with a twinkle. I wanted to smack it off his face. Darla ran over and patted me down, making sure I was in one piece.

Cash looked up at the darkening sky. The clouds rolled in, resounding like a stampede of horses. My bones rattled from the noise.

"We have to get them out of here." Sammie eyed Darla and me.

"Not yet." Cash leaned up against a tree. His arms crossed at his chest, while his foot rested against the trunk roots. Whatever was coming, Cash didn't look concerned. But Sammie sure as hell did, which was enough to scare the crap out of me.

"What are they talking about?" Darla wiped the foliage off her clothes. I leaned over, plucking leaves from her hair. She resembled a forest nymph.

"My, my, my . . . Look who's here," a garbled voice said from atop my destroyed vehicle. A bald-headed man, probably about seven feet tall, with white glowing bulbs as eyes, perched himself on the overturned car. His long legs dangled in white linen pants over the door, displaying his calf-high, periwinkle socks and shiny brown dress shoes. His skin appeared stretched, with a bluish tint. Definitely an alien.

"Cash Kingston. Twice in one week. It must be my lucky life," the man sneered. His white irises blazed in the direction of Cash. It was as if two light bulbs were stuck in a human eye socket and lit up. I instinctively backed up as my breath ceased and my throat spasmed.

"Ah. You sought me out the first time. I only thought to repay the courtesy and visit your stomping grounds. It's good to see you are still a fan of the arts." Cash motioned toward the cinema's large illuminated vertical sign, and the triangular marquee below which was lined with tiny blinking light bulbs.

"The arts and pretty shells, my boy." One bulb eye flickered. I think it was a freaky wink.

"Are you flirting with me, Grouper? Because I'm flattered, really. I don't go both ways, but I appreciate the compliment, even if it's coming from you." Cash pushed away from the tree and neared the dismembered vehicle. His muscular body moved with grace.

"One day you might change your mind. But today's not the day for frisky banter."

"You made quite an entrance. Again! Ya know my door still needs fixing. Can you think of any handymen in the area I could call?" Cash circled his pointer finger.

"Stay together and behind us, you understand?" Sammie whispered to Darla and me. I nodded, grabbing Darla's arm and linking it with mine.

Sammie positioned herself next to Cash. "You know how charming Cash can be." She slid her hand into Cash's, trying to block us from the alien they called Grouper. "He's always forgetting his manners. Are you trying to hit on my boyfriend, or do you have important business to discuss, like maybe why there are other Ferroeans in a No Zone? We got word a Ferroean reached out to DOAA. Any idea who that could be? Anyone who runs in your rogue circle?"

"Is this girl nuts?" Darla turned toward me. I'm sure she was expecting an equally annoyed response from me, but all I did was put my finger to my mouth.

The hideous extraterrestrial life-form ignored Sammie and looked curiously around Cash to find Darla and me. "What do we have here?" His hairy brows lifted while his bald head scrunched like a bulldog's face.

"They're just pets," Sammie said nonchalantly.

"Pets! Did she just call me a pet? Oh, hell no," Darla shouted. Cash turned toward Darla, who was glowering at Sammie. His darkening eyes appeared black, while his shoulders tensed under his shirt. The material strained against his muscles.

"Speak," Grouper commanded. I held Darla's hand and tugged her back, but she pulled away, shooting me a look of disdain. She marched passed Sammie and Cash, eyeing down Grouper.

"I don't know who you are and what funky contacts you are wearing, but I am not her pet, and this isn't her boyfriend. They broke up. This is Bea's boyfriend." Darla gestured to me.

The alien reared his head back, and goo flung across the grass. "Cash, you're with a human? Now I think I've seen it all. You've been a naughty boy this year."

Darla didn't even flinch. "I think you escaped from the institute down the street." Shady Oaks was a mental institution several blocks away. But I was pretty sure Grouper wasn't from there. "We can help you get back, if you come down from the car. Or I could call someone for you? Do you have family?" Darla held out her phone. In an instant,

Grouper's eyes singed it like my car, blowing it up with one strike. Only pieces of charbroiled plastic remained in Darla's hands. She stared at these for a moment, and then dusted her hands together.

"First of all, weird eye the science guy, that was a brand-new iPhone! And second. . ." Darla froze, and the blood drained from her face. All her rambling finally caught up with her. She might not have known what Grouper was—hell, I didn't know what he was—but by the paleness of her face, she'd realized he was dangerous.

"Darla, this is Grouper," Cash said calmly. "He is not a human and not interested in human things. In fact, I'm pretty sure he's not familiar with any of Apple's products. So, if you could kindly move back next to Bea and let Sammie and I handle this, we would really appreciate it." Cash's fists clenched at his sides, creating ripples in his massive forearms.

I reached for Darla's hand and yanked her next to me. Her fingers trembled inside mine. I gave her a supportive squeeze but kept my focus straight ahead. My heart bounced around in my chest like my rib cage was made of rubber.

Grouper let out a roar of laughter, or what I think was laughter. "She's feisty. I like her. But the other one, she's got a pull to her—an electric energy. And she smells." Well, that was rude! I leaned my head toward my shoulder and took a quick whiff. I smelled like strawberries and cream, my shampoo. He tilted his head curiously. Before anyone spoke, a whoosh of stale air whirled around me. Sticky fingers latched around my throat.

Up close, I saw his unearthly toned skin, his sunken cheeks, his serrated yellow teeth. He looked like something out of a horror film . . . something that liked to eat people. His breath smelled of formaldehyde and stung my eyes to tears.

My hand fell from Darla's as Grouper's grip tightened and he lifted me from the ground. My legs dangled, while my toes barely skimmed the hardtop. Grouper's hold sealed off the flow of oxygen, closing my pipes. Panic clawed slowly up from my gut as I pulled at his grasp, desperately trying to alleviate the pressure bearing down on my neck. The skin on his fingers felt scaled, rough and edgy. As I pulled at them, a warm liquid excreted, sticky like honey. Oh my god, my car. I immediately remembered the guck from last week that had dripped from my door. It felt just like—

"Grouper, you have two seconds to put her down before I kill you. And I *will* kill you," Cash warned, his voice menacing.

Grouper ignored Cash's threat and continued to stare at me with what I could only describe as confusion. His nostrils flared while the small brown hairs that covered his nose stood straight up, at attention. "Why do you have such a familiar smell, little human?" Grouper asked, squeezing tighter. His bulbs for eyes burned brighter, and my gaze narrowed on him. Sweat formed on the back of my neck. "What are you? It's more than familiar . . . it's Gabe?" He gasped. His mouth opened wide, exposing web-like strands coated in brown goo. Oh man, he didn't even have a human tongue! His looked more like a lizard's tongue, forked at the end. Bile rose from my stomach. Fear, panic, and Grouper's alien grip held it down.

In my peripheral vision, I saw multiple blurs coming toward us.

"No. You can't be," Grouper hissed as he tossed me up into the air. I desperately dragged oxygen into my bruised throat while the cool wind whirled around my body. I soared, crashing into something hard and cold. The impact sent a sharp spike of pain through me, unlike anything I had felt before. My eyes fluttered. I found the impact of my fall—a car dashboard. A stabbing blaze of heat impaled my flesh as shards of glass pierced my back. I screamed—really screamed, like I'd never known I could. My lungs contracted until all their air deflated into the night. Pain erupted like a volcano inside of me. Darla's cries sounded in the distance. I wanted to help her, to make sure she was all right, but my body refused to move. A wet substance leaked through my mouth, tasting like copper.

Two strong arms wrapped around me, and the smell of mint, honey, and pine fueled my senses. Cash. He whispered, "Crede Mihi." Words my mother used all my life. Why would Cash say that? But before I could muster the energy to ask, the background noise faded like the end of a song. My world went dark.

Chapter Sixteen

Beatrice

Voices garbled like static on a radio. I couldn't see them, but I could hear them. There were several hushed conversations filling the air, but none on which I could focus.

"She's awake," a male voice exclaimed. His heartbeat thumped in my ear; he was so close. "Beatrice, can you hear me?"

I tried to speak, but my throat felt like sandpaper. The fresh scent of soap and aftershave confirmed it was really him. Dad. My eyes fluttered open. He loomed over me, his eyes bloodshot and his face worn.

"It's okay. You're okay. You're home." He comforted me, wrapping his arms around me. I was sprawled out on the couch, covered in a yellow afghan. My pink toenails peeked out from the bottom of the blanket.

"Darla," I whispered. My mouth felt like I had eaten cotton balls. If anything had happened to her, I would never forgive myself.

"I'm right here, and you have a lot of explaining to do." Darla came into view from around the couch. Although boasting a series of grass stains, she appeared to be unscathed. My dad stood, allowing Darla to come into full

127

view. She crossed her arms over her chest and puckered her brows.

Dad pulled away and walked toward the stairs. "I'm going to go get you another blanket." My eyes adjusted to the dull glow of two lamps on the end tables, which confirmed it was still night. The recliner and love seat were empty. Where was everyone else?

"I'm so glad you are okay," Darla whimpered as she threw her arms around me and sobbed into my hair.

"I'm fine." My words were muffled by Darla's small body, which was pressed up against my face. Strands of her mane found their way into my mouth.

"Why are these . . . whatever they are . . . fighting over Influencing me? What even is that? What the hell is going on? Who was that lunatic with the funky eyes wearing white after Labor Day?" Darla released her kung fu grip and sat down next to me, wriggling to gain more room on the couch. She wiped away the tears from her eyes with her sleeve and sniffed her nose. Mascara lined the edges of her eyes to her hairline, giving her a wild look.

"I told you," Sammie whined from behind me. "I don't see why we can't fix her mind."

"I made a promise to Bea," Cash spoke in a low voice from somewhere behind us.

"It's not like you have to keep it," Sammie argued. "If we just Influence her, we can make her think what happened was part of the movie or something."

"Listen here, Barbie, you are not taking me back to your leader and erasing my brain like a science project," Darla snapped. She rose from the couch and perched her hands on her hips glaring over my head.

"She's so annoying," Sammie moaned.

"What will kill you—kryptonite? Because I swear, I will find it to put an end to your pretty little alien life." Darla was not backing down, and it was evident she knew they weren't human. I wondered what they had told her.

"Come on. She's threatening us now. Can I please Influence her?" Sammie begged, turning to Cash.

"No," he said with finality in his tone as he rounded the couch. He was still wearing jeans, but he'd changed his t-shirt and replaced it with a tight-fitting, long-sleeved, waffle shirt.

Cash placed two hands on Darla's shoulders and carefully moved her out of the way. The couch dipped with his body weight; his thigh pressed against my hip. My breath caught in my throat as a fission of nervous energy passed through me.

"How are you feeling?" He brushed the hair away from my face and examined me. I scooted over to make more room. His fingers traced my jawbone. Tingling vibrations sparked wherever he stroked, and the buzzing in my chest returned with the intensity of an electric chair. He cupped my cheek and warmth spread through me. "You handled a rogue bug. I'm impressed."

My body flushed from Cash's closeness, and suddenly the blanket was too warm. "I think he did most of the handling. He's a bug?"

Cash released my face. "Yes, that's what they call rogue Ferroeans who illegally roam Earth. He's been working for years as an informant for both sides. He wasn't properly assimilated, so his appearance and mobility are different on Earth than on our planet. He's pretty harmless, though."

"My throat and body beg to differ," I said and a muscle flexed in Cash's jaw.

"It could have been creepy Jon or Phil. I was happy to see Grouper knowing those two have been roaming Earth recently like little rodents," Sammie said. Then she turned to me, "I mean I hate that he threw you, of course!"

I smiled.

"Her body, my iPhone . . . we all took a beating. Now, which one of you will be reimbursing me for my phone? And would anyone like to explain to me what's going on here? I realize you," Darla said, pointing to Cash and Sammie, "are not human. I'm a complete believer in other life-forms, but that bug, as you call it, was super creepy. He would have absolutely killed us."

I pushed myself up, so my back was angled in the crook of the L-shaped sofa.

"Would he have killed us?" I swallowed, trying to get moisture to my throat. It was still rough and itchy.

"Sammie, go see what's taking Tasha so long with the tea. Darla, why don't you help her?" Cash motioned for them to go to the kitchen.

"Ha! You must be joking. I wouldn't—" Before Darla could finish her sentence, Sammie had her arm wrapped around my friend. She hauled Darla off.

Cash stared at me. He was silent.

"What?" I shifted. I couldn't get comfortable.

"What would you like us to do about Darla? Currently she thinks we are aliens who invaded hot human bodies." I rolled my eyes. Cash held his hands up. "Her words, not mine. I will leave this decision up to you. We can Influence her and send her home, give her full disclosure, or something in between . . . But you need to choose now, because we have to talk."

I nodded, knowing the responsibility he'd given me was not only a rather large one, but also a vote of faith. He was holding up the deal we'd made that first night, in my bedroom.

"Can you give me five minutes with her?" My voice still grated.

Cash nodded and placed his hand back on my leg. "You were brave at the movie theater and yesterday with the DOAA." He took a deep breath. "I know this is hard on you."

The strange thing was that I felt fine. Okay, it's not like I could run track tomorrow, but nothing appeared to be broken. Even my minor cuts and bruises were already fading.

"You healed me again, didn't you?"

Cash blinked, and in the span of a single second his expression cycled through concern, guilt, and outrage before finally settling on anger. His brows slammed down, and his forearms pulsed. "Actually, I started to, but Sammie had to take over. I didn't want to let Grouper disappear until we spoke." Cash ground his teeth. "The truth is, he wasn't trying to hurt you. He was more scared of you if you can believe that."

"Not really." I remembered how easily he tossed me through the air. That didn't feel like fear.

"I should have never let him hold onto you for so long. I just needed him to verify . . ." He looked away from me, like the memory of it pained him. Maybe it was remorse. I couldn't tell. Cash closed his eyes and exhaled heavily. "Darla drove my car here while Sammie healed you in the back seat." Staring off at the kitchen, he said, "They might not look like they get along, but I think there is potential."

"Thank you," I whispered.

Cash turned his head and looked at me, and a flicker of sadness—or possibly regret—crossed his face. Then he went rigid. Cold. Emotionless. He pulled his hand away and stood.

Darla came bounding in with tea in her hands. "Barbie and Skipper," she gestured to the kitchen with her head, "made you this. It could be poison."

"Who's Skipper?" Cash and I asked in unison.

"Barbie's sister, duh. I mean, alien boy over here has an excuse—I doubt they play with Barbies on his planet. But Bea, are you telling me you never had a Barbie doll?"

Cash shook his head and walked out of the room, grumbling something about humans and their poor senses of humor. I laughed, loving Darla for her impeccable timing.

Darla sat next to me, taking Cash's spot, and handed me the tea. I sipped it, welcoming the warm liquid cascading down my throat. It tasted like chicken noodle soup minus the noodles and chicken, with about ten spoonfuls of salt. Maybe an alien recipe?

I told Darla everything. I started with the first day I found the Kingstons and Flannerys in my house. I explained how my mother and father worked for the DOAA and how my mother had stolen something of value and put it inside me for safekeeping, and now the DOAA and the planet Ferro wanted it back. When I finished, she sat there in awe.

"Wow," Darla said. She walked over to the mantle and held up a picture of my mother, father, and me. "Your mom was like a kick-ass superhero."

I laughed. "That's one way of putting it, but she didn't have any superpowers." As the words left my mouth, a pesky memory tugged at my brain. Did she?

"You okay?" my dad asked, peering around the doorway to the hallway with two blankets in his hand. His face held more color; his eyes shone brighter.

I nodded.

"Well, I'm all caught up. Now what do we do? I think we need a plan," Darla said, sitting down in the recliner and rubbing her hands together. Great. I'd created a monster.

Tasha and Sammie emerged from behind my father. Tasha smiled at me. "You look better." She took a seat at the end of the couch.

"Can we please ask her," Sammie said, pointing to Darla, "to go home?" She plopped down between Tasha and me. I attempted to rearrange my position, so we could all fit, but Sammie caught my legs and pulled them over her lap. Okay, when did she stop hating me?

"I am not leaving. I am going to help." Darla's hands were fastened to her hips.

Sammie huffed as Cash walked into the room with a bag of pretzels in his hands.

"Hey, why did Grouper say I had a familiar smell, and who's Gabe?"

Every face except Darla's and Cash's went pale and still.

Sammie's grip tightened on my legs. "He sensed Gabe," she whispered, looking at Tasha. Her eyes enlarged, and I thought they might pop out of their sockets. She whipped her head toward Cash. "Oh my god—you used her as bait? You knew!"

Chapter Seventeen

Beatrice

My brain felt like it was on the Tilt-a-Whirl as I watched my dad launch himself at Cash. All it took was for Sammie to mention Cash had used me as bait, and my dad went wild. The two of them tumbled backward. A loud thud sounded. Several pictures and two sconces fell from the wall, shattering on the floor. Dad's fist clocked Cash straight across the jaw, but Cash didn't even block it. He took the hit, reeling back against my grandmother's piano. Notes and chords chimed to their deaths as his body crushed it to mere splinters. My dad lunged again at Cash, taking him to the ground. They rolled from the living room out into the hallway. Another smash sounded as more wall hangings crashed to the hardwood. Tasha, Sammie, Darla, and I ran after them. Shards of glass covered the floor, glistening beneath the ceiling light. I attempted to separate them, but I wasn't sure who was who as they flipped each other, tumbling over one another like in a game of leapfrog.

Tasha put her arm in front, cautioning me to stay back. "Cash deserves this."

I watched my dad strike Cash again. This time, he got it above his right eye. Instead of Cash bleeding or bruising, my father's knuckles tore open, exposing raw and reddened skin. Crimson fluid covered the beige runner in the hall, smearing like finger paint as they stumbled back down to the ground together. My father straddled Cash and repeatedly punched him in the face, the chest, and one even to the gut.

Whether Cash deserved it or not, I wasn't okay with them brawling like UFC fighters. Someone could get hurt—probably my father. We could lose a wall . . . Hell, they might even go through the floorboards, at this rate. I pushed Tasha's hand out of the way and moved forward, but another arm grabbed me.

"You do realize your dad is human and, even though he is well trained, he isn't even close to Cash's strength. Your dad needs this, and Cash knows it. That's why he's not fighting back. For once, I have the human's side. Let them go." Sammie held onto my arm, pulling me back to her side.

Before I made my argument, the front door flung open.

"What the hell is going on?" Chris held a baseball bat in his hand. He wore Eagles sweatpants and a white t-shirt. His hair was messed to one side and his eyes were bloodshot.

My dad and Cash froze on the ground, their legs tangled together. If it hadn't been such an ugly situation, I might have laughed. They looked like they were cuddling.

Dad stood up first, extending his hand to Cash, who took it and rose next to him.

"A little misunderstanding," my dad said, brushing off his pants and straightening his shirt. A little misunderstanding—that was a cute response. The hallway table was broken in two. Not a damn picture was left on the wall, and the front hall closet had a giant hole in it. When had that happened?

Chris raised one eyebrow at me. "Okay, that I don't believe. Something is going on. No—something *has* been going on." He placed the bat against the wall. "My mom was freaking out because your porch light kept flickering. She thought it was Morse code for help. I had to beg her not to call the cops. Then I got near the house and it sounded like a war zone, and I thought for once my mom might not be overreacting. What the hell is going on?"

Chris clasped his hands behind his neck. Distress rolled off his body in waves. I'm sure Peggy was freaked out. That poor woman has been through so much.

I walked over to him, looping my arm in his and dragging him away from the fight scene, toward the kitchen. He assessed the damage as we proceeded down the hall.

"Seriously, it's nothing. The Kingstons and Flannerys are family friends. My dad and Cash were just messing around." I threw a look over my shoulder, daring one of them to disagree.

"Sure. Sounds like fun," Chris said as he walked with me, clearly not believing me. He patted Darla on the head as we passed. The others followed us into the kitchen. Tasha, Cash, and my dad took seats at the breakfast bar, while Chris, Darla, Sammie, and I sat at the kitchen table. Chris hadn't taken his eyes off me. Neither had Cash. I could feel his steel-blue eyes penetrating me from across the room. He wasn't Chris's biggest fan.

"Anyone hungry? I could order Chinese food," my dad offered. It was a gesture of apology. Also, it was almost eleven—other than the Chinatown restaurant, nothing was open.

"I'm starving," Darla and Sammie said at the same time. Both looked like they wanted to kill the other for stealing her line.

"Me too," I said, turning to Chris. I was surprised he hadn't said anything—he's always hungry. I could swear he has a wooden leg, the way he ate.

Chris looked ghostly white, his hands clenched the kitchen table, and his eyes bulged from his head.

"What's wrong?" I asked.

"When did Barbie get here? And how. . .?" He shook his head. Oh shit. I'd totally forgotten about that. With everything we had been through, that little scene earlier this week at school felt like a lifetime ago. I can only imagine what he was thinking. "You guys hate each other! How is she here? In your house?"

Chris's voice cracked like an adolescent boy's, and Cash chuckled. I glared at him, warning him to behave.

"They made up," Darla said before I even breathed. She was paging through *Us Weekly* with Sammie. They had already ripped out five pages. Darla hung them on a board she'd created at home for outfits she liked or ideas for fashioning an ensemble. I swore she was going to be a designer one day.

"Could you guys stop calling me Barbie?" Sammie scowled at Chris.

"Sorry. It's just . . ." Chris threw his hands in the air. "Never mind."

Dad ordered from the hallway landline. Yeah, we still had one of those. It was Grandma's and Dad refused to toss it and upgrade. His voice was loud enough that I could hear the food choices, and my mouth salivated at the mention of dumplings, pork fried rice, vegetable spring rolls, and General Tso's chicken. Yum.

"You sure you're okay?" Chris whispered in my ear. I rested my head on his shoulder. His heart was beating loudly enough that I could hear it.

"I'm better now."

That was the truth. Chris always made me feel better. He was like a warm cup of hot chocolate with tiny marshmallows in it.

Chris leaned in closer, placing his hands on each side of my cheek and tilting my head down, like he always did before kissing it.

"You have a cut on your head." Concern filled his voice. He scooted his chair back, angling my head to get a closer look. "It's still bleeding."

"Oh yeah, I bumped it . . . getting out of my car," I rubbed my head. Moisture clung to my fingertips.

Oh man, I hoped that sounded believable. Chris stood. Guess not.

I watched as he glanced around at the room. Everyone was frozen, except Cash, who rose from his stool and moved closer to us. His arms crossed against his chest while his legs spread in a strong stance. He mirrored the protective position he'd taken that night in my bedroom, when everyone walked in on us kissing. I blushed from the suggestive memory, silently groaning.

"Were you wrestling with any of them?" Chris asked me. It wasn't a far-off guess, considering Cash had given me a bloody nose, and Sammie and I had given our vocal cords a battle in the cafeteria this week, and Chris *did* just walk in on Cash and my dad brawling.

"Of course not." I gave Chris a shy smile.

"Are you sure?" he questioned again, each word said slower than the next.

My cheeks burned. "Really? Do you think my dad would let me wrestle?"

Chris shook his head and kissed the top of mine. "You want me to help clean you up?"

I didn't even see it coming, but Cash swooped in between us and pushed Chris up against the wall. The loud crack of Chris's back against the sheetrock made me flinch.

"Why don't you get your hands off my girlfriend, Kyle?" Cash growled. His brooding testosterone was palpable.

"Whoa, you really need to calm down, Kingston." Oh no. Chris had used Cash's last name. Why do guys do that? "And it's not Kyle. It's Chris!" Chris raised his right brow, as Cash's words sunk in. "Your girlfriend?" He stared at me with a curious expression.

"Yeah, it's sorta new. We haven't even made it official on social media," I grumbled. Darla chuckled from behind me. Cash shot me a look of confusion and anger.

"Wow, Barbie and you had a fight and then became friends. Now Cash Kingston is officially your boyfriend, after being back at school for a week. And when did you get social media?" He paused and gazed to the front of the house. "Oh wait, and mysteriously you are bleeding from hitting your head on a car that isn't even in the driveway."

Protest died on my lips. Chris had made some excellent points.

"It's been quite a week," my dad said, reentering the kitchen. He eyed Cash, who was still holding Chris against the wall. "Let go of Chris. I doubt he wants to wrestle with you, too."

Cash flashed a cocky grin and backed away from Chris. "You got that right, Robert."

Chris mouthed to me, "Robert?"

I grabbed Cash's hand.

"Come on, boyfriend. Why don't you help clean my head before I give you a matching mark? Let's go."

Cash arrogantly laughed as I dragged him out of the kitchen and up the stairs, as far away from Chris as I could. Surprisingly, Cash didn't fight holding onto my hand. Instead, his grip tightened.

I pushed him into the bathroom. "What's wrong with you?" I hissed.

"He's always touching you," Cash growled.

I closed the door behind us and turned on the fan to muffle our voices. "So? It's not like you're my real boyfriend. Why do you care?"

"He doesn't know that." Cash riffled through the medicine cabinet. He found the hydrogen peroxide, cotton balls, antiseptic cream, and Band-Aids, and placed them on the counter in front of him.

"He found out like a second ago," I said while jumping up onto the sink. I watched Cash work with the medicine. When he didn't respond, I kept talking. "Why don't you just do your healing thing?'

"Lover boy would probably get suspicious if you came down and, miraculously, your cut was gone, especially since he listed several mysterious events from this past week." Cash washed his hands and dried them on the towel.

"True." Logical Cash was so infuriating. "Wait! Lover boy?" I arched a brow.

"Yeah. Tell me you don't know Chris has a crush on you." Cash smiled, slanting his head. "You had no idea, huh?"

Cash spread my knees apart and moved between my legs. A fine undercurrent of electricity permeated the room. My skin rippled from my wrist to my chest, and from my ankles to my core. My breath caught in my throat as Cash placed his hand on my knee, steadying it.

"Stop it. He does not," I countered, my voice wavering.

Cash laughed. It was a sound so genuine and real that it untangled me.

I smoothed my hair over my right shoulder, playing it into a side braid. "You're kinda bearable when you're not an arrogant jerk."

"Don't get used to it." He winked. His breath brushed against my face as his hands methodically moved over the cut with a cotton ball. I winced. The cool cotton tingled against my skin. "Hurts?"

I nodded, feeling like a child.

"There's a sliver of glass in here. I can remove it. Hold still, okay?" I blanched as he dislodged the shard. He shook his head. "I can't believe Grouper threw you," he muttered to himself.

"Why did he?" Sitting on the counter, Cash and I were level. The colors in his eyes slithered throughout one another. His black pupil pulsed.

"Because you remind him of who he used to be."

"How is that possible?" I scrunched my nose.

He looked up to the left. "You know you are part Ferroean, right?" He tapped me on the nose with the antiseptic cream, and then twisted the cap off. He rubbed a smidge on his finger and gently applied it to my cut.

"Yeah, but what does that have to do with Grouper."

A muscle in Cash's jaw jerked. "You're from the same bloodline."

Chapter Eighteen

Cash

Mark walked into the living room and sank into the love seat across from me. The room's only illumination came from the TV, which cascaded across Mark's face, shadowing his expression. The sun had retreated into the edges of this planet hours ago, but I couldn't sleep. Yesterday's meet and greet between Grouper and Beatrice was not exactly what I had anticipated. One mystery had been solved, yet more questions arose. And although I believed, eventually, we would have Grouper's help, he didn't take the news he had a niece as well as I had hoped.

"Still sleeping on the couch?" Mark kicked his legs onto the coffee table and threw his hands behind his head.

I closed my eyes and took in a deep breath. I dipped my ear toward my shoulder and then the other side, cracking my neck. Let's be honest, I barely slept these last few months. I exhaled all the air out and reopened my eyes.

"Yep. I hated that bed anyway. Sera had a hundred pillows I wasn't allowed to sleep with. Truthfully, it's easier to throw a blanket on this couch and call it a night. I don't want her to come back and haunt me because I drooled on one of her fancy decorative pillows."

A commercial brightened the screen, allowing me to see the corners of Mark's lips curve upward. Sera was his younger cousin, but he always said she acted way too mature to be around us. I agreed.

"What's up with girls and pillows anyway? I need one. It goes under my head." His mouth dipped and I knew the down-to-business Mark had taken over and our casual banter was ending. "So . . . what do you want to do?"

"That's a loaded question." I motioned for him to toss me the chips on the floor next to him. He rolled his eyes, leaned forward, and grabbed the bag. I caught it midair and popped it open at the same time. *I really am that awesome,* I said, speaking from my mind to his.

"Yeah, so awesome. Back to my question, what do you want to do about saving these planets? You can't really believe we can save both, do you?"

"Tasha thinks we can. And I do believe in the prophecy, so that means we have no choice." I popped another chip in my mouth. Human food was so much better than Ferroean food. "I know the Ferro Council is split but King Kingston is not, and he is our leader. He, too, believes in the prophecy and we follow his orders. We took an oath." I grabbed three chips and layered them into a sandwich. "Let's be serious, Earth can't afford for us not to. Billions will die."

"The prophecy could mean many things." Mark said.

"For example?"

"The prophecy says that two worlds will be risked, and if you choose to save one, they both shall perish. What if we don't choose? We try and save both but can't. If one falls, even though we tried, are we really responsible?"

I laughed. "Nice try, buddy. Thank the Council you are not in charge. If the asteroid is going to hit our planet at year's end and we pull out of Earth to get back to our planet, will we have a planet to save? Earth will inevitably fall. And we would have chosen to save our world. So according to the prophecy, we all die." I crunched down and bits spewed from the edges of my mouth. The chip sandwich sounded better in my head. Tasha was going to freak when she saw this mess. Because let's be honest, I wasn't vacuuming this crap up.

Mark leaned forward, propping his forearms on his thighs. "Well then, let's save 'em both. But to do that the source needs to be removed from Bea and implanted in Sammie. She was always Sera's backup shell like your brother was . . ."

My fingers curled, pressing my nails into my skin. "Don't finish that sentence," I snapped. "I swear to the Council I will break your Ferroean alloy if you even think the rest of that sentence."

Mark held up his palm.

"Enough said. I was only pointing out that Sammie knows. Her electric cavity will be able to handle connecting, but she might be wiped after weaponizing herself. Sera's had her whole life preparing for ultimate connection to you, going about it a little at a time. She had you down to a science. She knew how much power to give you and when to make you stop. I don't know how we can train Sammie to do that while the Blood-Light is still harboring the opposing energy source."

I jackknifed up on the couch. My teeth ground together. "Are you saying we should remove it now? We still don't know why Faye did this or if we can do this safely."

"Yes, that's exactly what I am saying. Time is the one thing we do not have. You know how to do the removal safely. Contact your father! And let the DOAA deal with Bea and Robert."

My body stiffened. Mark better pray to the Council that he has a better idea or I'm going to use my Ferroean knife and release some of his power with a cut to his wrist.

"I'm serious. Bea and Robert cannot be the priority. Explain to Zane they were manipulated by Faye and have him spare their lives. He would listen to you. He might be the biggest a-hole of all time, and I know you hate him, but he does value the opposing sources, especially yours. The planet always comes first. A request made by the Captain of the Guards, the future King of Ferro, and his son . . . that cannot go unheard."

"He'd kill Bea. He hates humans more than any Ferroean. In fact, he'd kill her just because of Faye's affair with Gabe. You know the history. My father would leap at the chance for revenge on Gabe's lineage."

"I'm not going to sit here and dispute that, but let's face it, Sammie needs time to adjust to the source and build the connection with you, or you both could blast something other than the asteroids and kill us all."

I stood. "What about Bea?"

"What about her?" he protested. "What are you holding on to? We may never know why Faye did this. What's going on with her and you?"

"Nothing," I snapped back. I threw the bag of chips across the room. Mark ruined my appetite. "I cannot be responsible for her death."

"Don't do that. I know you harbor guilt over Sera's death, but we need you to lead, protect, and fight for our kind. It cannot be about one human girl's life. Your father will be able to get the best assimilation doctor."

Mark was thinking about the mission; his head was in the right space, but I couldn't risk Bea. I know for damn sure neither could Tasha, and I was hoping maybe even Sammie. When I designed this team, there was a purpose. Sera was an obvious choice since I couldn't be without my opposing source, and I was madly in love with her. Mark was one of the best fighters I had ever seen in training, and he had a cool head about him. Paul showed no fear, no emotion, and was childish as hell. Adding levity to combat was important. Tasha was the yin to everyone's yang. Her history of our species and of the human world surpassed all, and her kindness and do-good personality would always bring balance to my emotionally reckless behavior. Sammie—hell, she was a jalapeno, a spicy firecracker, a good fighter, attractive, perfect for missions to bend the will of men, and more loyal than any bloodhound.

"You have more power than you want to admit." Mark's words interrupted my thoughts. "You are the heir to our kingdom, even if you don't want to take the throne. But regardless, you are our leader. You're the leader of the guards and the most powerful being on our planet. It's time you start acting like it."

"You're a douche, ya know that." I threw a couch pillow at him.

"Yeah, yeah, yeah, a douche you trained. You taught me to put the mission first, but Tasha has taught me to care. I do care, Cash. I don't want anything to happen to Beatrice or Robert. Contact Zane and use your power as leverage before we end up getting a human killed or losing a planet because we waited too long." Mark stood, matching my stature. "We all have family back on Ferro. We all have those we want to protect."

Mark was thinking about his little sister, his mother, and his father. Hell, I couldn't blame him. If Tasha was back in Ferro, maybe I'd be feeling a little different. But this nagging question was holding me back. "Answer me one thing," I asked. "You've known Faye as long as I have. Does it make sense she would have chosen her daughter as the Blood-Light energy womb to Sera's source, knowing full well once the source would be removed and, fingers crossed, that would be a successful extraction, Bea would be owned by the DOAA, and once associated with Gabe, possibly killed for his treason by the Ferro Council?"

Mark looked toward the floor while shaking his head. His gaze traveled back up to meet mine. The creases around his eyes softened. "Maybe she was hoping no one would find out about Gabe. The mission was always her priority. If she was trying to save both worlds, maybe she thought Bea was the safest energy womb. There're so many maybes, I could never answer that question. It's time, Cash. It's time to take it out."

I nodded. I didn't agree, but there wasn't anything I could say to convince Mark otherwise. In my deepest of all sources, I believe she must mean something else, something more. I don't believe Faye ever planned on removing the source from Bea and that's why I've been dragging my feet.

The gang gathered in the basement in combat gear with no idea why I called them together.

"Why am I in these awful clothes right now?" Sammie hissed, pulling at her olive cargo pants. It was another excuse to stare me down like she wanted to stake me with a thermo dagger.

"I think it's time to act. I will send a message to Zane Kingston . . ." Before I could finish my sentence, Tasha interrupted me.

"You're contacting Dad. Are you insane? He had our brother killed; what do you think he will do to humans?" Tasha cried.

I shook my head. "We need help. My objective is to tell Zane what we've learned, in hopes he will share information. We will be the guards on duty for the source removal from Beatrice in a remote location with an assimilations doctor we trust; and once Zane guarantees a high probability of success, I will set up new identities and a safe house for Bea and Robert to escape to. Zane won't have a choice to let them go. He will have the source. He is our king. It is his decision if we stay on Earth and complete our mission or if he summons us home. But just in case, we must fight our own rogue bugs or highly skilled DOAA agents, we need to be ready. We haven't trained in months. You lazy asses need a kick in the butt."

"Have you ever thought . . . maybe, just maybe . . . Faye intended for Bea to keep the source inside her? It could be her destiny to save both planets," Tasha pointed out. It was a thought I've had since I met Beatrice, but not one I was willing to share without proof. My feelings for the human were starting to become muddled and without hard evidence to support this theory, I couldn't indulge my sister's suspicion.

"You cannot be serious," Paul spat. "That's insane."

"Even if that were the case, we have no evidence supporting it. Blind faith in Faye cannot be reason enough." In a softer voice, I said, "We might not be able to save both planets, Tasha. I know the prophecy, and although I believe in it, at the end of the day, our alliance is to Ferro."

Tears welled in Tasha's eyes. Her lips trembled.

"Don't you want to save the planet we were born on? The planet Mom lives on?" I asked, trying to appeal to her emotional side. Not that I had spoken to my mother in years, but she was important to Tasha.

"Yes, but I can't handle knowing all these humans will die and we could have saved them. Robert and Bea will be dead, too." She gathered her emotions, took a long deep breath in through her nose. "If the prophecy is right, then it's a death sentence for all of us if we leave and go home." The air expelled from her mouth as her chest deflated.

An unexpected knot formed in my throat. "I understand. And I will do everything in my power to save both worlds." And I meant it. But Mark was right, we needed to make a move. "We must get the energy source removed from Beatrice." I turned to Sammie. "It is with great honor that I ask you to carry Ferro's opposing source. Do you accept?"

Sammie sat up straighter and responded "Of course. It would be my privilege. Thank you." Those might have been the nicest words the two of us had ever exchanged.

The next day, I got into the sedan and peeled out of the driveway, leaving all devices back at the house. I was headed to a place I had been to only once, a clandestine location. This secret could tear Tasha and I apart. I could lose the only family I had, and yet it was a secret I'd never regret keeping from her. Not one regret. I couldn't take the chance of being found, so I'd have to take a chance on my team holding down the fort until I returned. I left a note for Mark on the kitchen table next to my cell phone.

I've gone to see the King.

Chapter Nineteen

Beatrice

Darla, Sammie, Tasha, and I walked into the girls' room giggling about Darla's newest fashion idea called Pitties, a way to avoid pit stains with thin pads that attach to the inside of your shirt. She swore it was the next million-dollar idea she would pitch to *Shark Tank*. She couldn't stop talking about this blockbuster proposal. Earlier this morning in PE, she tried to sell Coach Barb on the idea, yammering a mile a minute. Coach Barb wasn't the least bit interested and instead tried to sell me on getting back on the track team. She was relentless. Every day since giving me the watch, she would be at my locker trying to convince me to meet her after school for a run. And every day, I would say no. The funny thing was she'd stay at my locker until Cash or one of the others would arrive and then flee the scene. It was becoming so obvious that Paul made a joke Coach Barb didn't even exist.

"If she doesn't exist, then why do my calves bark at me every time I am in that woman's presence. It's as if she wants everyone to join track from her PE class," Darla exclaimed in Paul's direction before we headed into the bathroom.

The door shut and Darla spoke to the group. "So, as I was saying, I legit think we could sell this. I'm not the college type. I have an entrepreneurial spirit. I'm hoping to leap from Senior year to the cover of Forbes magazine." She tossed her hair over her shoulders. "Can't you see it? 'Youngest female millionaire, Darla!' I'll have one name like Madonna or Pink." She headed to the mirror and took out her red lipstick, lathering it on her bottom lip and smacking her mouth together. "I'd slay interviews. Maybe I should reach out to *The Tonight Show*. By then, hopefully, it'll be hosted by a woman. Oh hell, I could host it!"

Tasha washed her hands as I used the lavatory. "Being an entrepreneur and going to college isn't exclusive to one another. You can do both! I'm sure *The Tonight Show* can wait until you graduate and get a degree."

I walked out and headed to the sink. Darla scrunched her nose, clearly unhappy to hear Tasha's logic.

"I don't get it," Sammie said, moving closer to Darla and taking a sniff. "Why can't you use extra deodorant?"

Darla moved her shoulder backward toward Sammie's nose. "I don't smell bad. I'm suggesting it so that there are no marks on a light-colored shirt. Everyone sweats from time to time." She glared at Sammie's armpits which were dry as a bone. "Well, at least humans do!"

Tasha and I giggled while the four of us headed to leave. Tasha pushed the door open with her hip as Darla beelined it out of there. Our laughter ceased abruptly as a knife whizzed by my head and landed in the wall behind me. The familiar hilt jutted outward. It was the same one I saw the DOAA agent use against Cash on the street, and the one Mark threw to Cash when he slit his wrist to show me the source. It was a thermo dagger, a deadly weapon used against Ferroeans.

"What the hell!" Darla screamed.

Sammie grabbed me by the arm and swung my body around back into the bathroom. My hair didn't follow as fast and ended up in my mouth. The door slammed, and Sammie dead-bolted the lock. She held her palm up melting the latch.

"No! Tasha and Darla are out there!" My heart raced. Whatever prowled the halls could hurt them. "Undo your melty power thing and go help them!"

"See, this is why you are so annoying," Sammie responded, moving toward the window. She unlatched the hook and threw it open with such force, the wood splintered at the edges. "We need to get you out of here."

I grabbed her by the arm, desperately trying to pull her back toward the exit. It was useless; she didn't even budge. Instead, she swiped her arm out of my grasp. "If you think I am leaving here without Darla and Tasha, you are nuts. What was that? Who's out there?" I asked with panic-soaked words.

Sammie barely paid attention to me. She was looking around the room and then back out the window, plotting our escape. "If YOU think I am letting whatever is out there get you and the source inside of you, you're the one who's nuts. There are millions of humans counting on you to save their lives. You are the answer to the survival of your race. If I let you out there and something happens, you are the death sentence to everyone you know. Do you still not understand your importance?"

Her eyes stopped darting around, and she focused on me. Colors whirled around her pupils—reds, yellows, and purples. The pulse in her neck was so powerful, her skin barely held it inside.

"I'm going to say this once, and then you are going to jump with me out of this window and run as fast as those stupid human legs can carry you."

Jump. Run. Is she serious? That's a three-story drop.

"If your source gets into the wrong hands, we all die. Does that hit home?"

Well, that hit something, but . . . Darla, Tasha. I couldn't leave them.

"Darla will be fine. Tasha will protect her. Like I am protecting you."

Damn, aliens can read minds. So frustrating.

"Tell me about it. Now, are you ready to jump?"

"I'm going to break a leg!" I shouted, looking down at the grass that resembled spikes rather than soft blades.

"You sure will. But then I will heal you, and we will run as fast as we can to the first fast car I can jack. Ok?"

I nodded my head and followed Sammie to the window, glancing one more time at the door behind us and internally apologizing for leaving Darla in the halls with a problem I caused. I'll never forgive myself if either of those girls are hurt because of me.

Sammie threw her legs over the windowsill and extended her hand out for mine. I closed my eyes, filled up my diaphragm with air and slid my hand into hers. When I released the oxygen, I opened my eyes. I swung my legs over the ledge. There was a small landing my toes dangled off. I made a giant mistake. I allowed my eyes to follow my feet.

"Don't look down."

I shook my head. "Too late!" I couldn't do this.

"Yes, you can! When I say three, we jump. Even though this will break your legs, try and land with a slight bend in your knees. It will help impact and injury, so I have less to heal."

I shook my head again.

"You can do this. You have to." She squeezed my hand in support "On three. One. Two. Three."

With our hands interlaced, we jumped and landed in a crouched position. Dirt and grass parted under us like the wake of a boat.

"My legs!" I screamed. But instead of pain, I could feel my bones shifting beneath my skin.

"I know," Sammie said in response. "I'll heal them. Where do you feel the most pain? I'll restore that first."

My eyes widened in complete disbelief. I don't know if it was relief or terror but there was no need to repair my bones. My voice quivered as I answered her, "I don't feel any pain. They're . . . they're fine."

Sammie wrapped her hands around my kneecaps, ignoring my response. The pressure from her fingertips sent tingling sensations throughout my veins. Heat penetrated off her hands, and then a bright white glow appeared in my peripheral vision. She was pointlessly trying to heal me.

"There's no damage," she gasped, volleying her eyes to my legs and back to my gaze. "Holy shit! There's no way this is possible unless —" But our surprised reactions were abruptly interrupted by Darla.

"Run! Run, guys! Run! And take me with you!" Darla came running down the front school steps, taking two at a time. She ran past us and toward a yellow hellcat, owned by Kathleen Butler. We followed, ignoring the revelation that my legs were fully capable of running on their own accord. Impossible!

Sammie used her powers to unlock the doors and start the car, and like a scared cheetah, we took off down the highway. The engine roared.

Darla sat in the backseat. Her arms wrapped around her waist; her eyes as big as the Beanie Boo stuffed animal I had as a kid.

"It was a woman!" she screamed.

"You saw who attacked us? Did she reengage?" Sammie asked, her eyes diverting to the rearview mirror to connect with Darla's in the backseat.

"Yeah. No. I mean, we saw her red curly hair as she ran away from us. She didn't come back after us at all. She ran so fast. Tasha ran after her and told me to run out the front doors. I think . . ." Darla shook her head. "I mean this sounds so stupid, and I know you'll never believe me, but I think . . ." Darla shook her head again like she was shaking the image into clarity.

"Spit it out, Darla," Sammie urged. Her hands clenched the steering wheel so tightly her knuckles went white.

"I think it was Coach Barb."

Sammie rolled her eyes. "You and your dumb human imagination. Your gym teacher did not attack aliens and get away with it."

I turned in my seat, my heart still racing. "It's ok. She's the only person I know with red hair, too. Don't worry. Cash will figure this out. We're ok," I said, trying to calm down my own thudding heartbeat.

I spun back in my seat only to find Sammie staring at me the same way she did the day we fought in the cafeteria, with extreme agitation. Her eyes swirled with one color, yellow. I've come to learn yellow was their source, but I've never seen it as the sole color swirling in their irises. She mouthed three words.

"What are you?"

Chapter Twenty

Cash

It was a long drive to the underground safe house in New Jersey. To get in touch with my father, I had to call on someone I had declared dead a long time ago. In fact, his existence was known only by my father and myself. He was an implant for emergency communications when traditional means were not available.

I walked up to the Victorian-style office building and punched in my code. The door clicked open. There was very little in this lobby, just a circular table with a fake plant and two end tables on each side of the elevator. I pressed the button, illuminating the switch. The doors opened, I walked in, and it shut automatically, descending ten floors below ground level.

Each floor chipped away at my heart. I had no idea if I was signing Bea's death sentence or saving her life. As the opening unveiled, a voice I never thought I would hear again greeted me.

"Well, hello, brother; it's been a while," Ashton cooed.

"Brother," I said through gritted teeth as I stepped out of the elevator into his den. He lived in a one-floor apartment created by the Ferro guards as a high-end prison. It was intended for solitude, punishment for his crimes against the high council. Only a handful of Ferroeans knew the place existed. But only my father and I knew Ashton was, in fact, alive and residing in it. Both my mother and sister were under the assumption Ashton was killed for his treason. My mother stopped speaking to us after that. The only communication she had was with Tasha, and even that in the last year had dwindled exponentially.

"Have you come to let me out of my jail cell or join me in this hellhole?" He wandered out of the darkness and came toward the light. His hair was still perfect: caramel brown with strands of strawberry blonde like our mother's, tangled throughout and flowing like a human model. But his appearance lost the flair he was known for. He looked older, worn out. His skin was pale and chalky, and dark circles lay under his blue eyes.

"Get me in touch with father," I said, getting straight to the point.

Ashton took a seat in a chair with wheels and rolled back and forth. The plastic groaned against the tiles. "What do you want with that man? He's almost as boring as you." The chair settled to a stop, and he crossed his arms over his chest. "What's in it for me?"

I growled. "You know you don't have a choice. Why are you being an ass about it?"

"I've spent a year in solitude, and you want to know why I'm toying with you? Don't be foolish. I need entertainment." Time was very different on Ferro and even though this safe house was on Earth, my brother didn't know that. He was banished from Ferro exactly four human years ago at the age of twenty after attempting to dethrone my father and the other council members under the rule of the rebel leader, Sayor. The rest of his Ferroean gang were killed for this crime. I had no idea why Zane let him live; his punishment was to guard the in-between galaxy space—something we kept from him. In fact, he knew very little about his exile. It was one of the only things my father and I ever agreed on.

"I don't have time for your games. Let me speak with father."

Ashton snapped his fingers and the brick wall behind me turned into a screen. My father appeared. He looked oddly content; no traces of panic or sense of urgency outlined his features. In fact, the muscles in his jaw were more relaxed than I had seen in years.

"Captain Cash," my father acknowledged me. God forbid he called me son. "Ashton," he growled.

"King," I said respectfully and bowed.

"What's up Papa Bear? Miss me?" Ashton cooed. I kicked the chair he was in, and it rolled halfway across the room. Ashton threw his arms up like he was on a human roller coaster ride at an amusement park.

"The opposing source. I've found it," I said. His eyes illuminated. I held my pointer finger in the air, pausing his excitement. "It showed up in a Blood-Light: Faye Walker's daughter's chest cavity."

"Where's Sera?" Ashton interjected from behind me. His tone was void of derision and wit and replaced by genuine concern and gravity. I gritted my teeth and ignored my brother who was now standing.

"Amazing!" Zane exclaimed, doing something I've never seen my father do before . . . smile. "And what have you learned about this energy womb? Anything different about this womb than you've been taught during your schooling about a human host?"

Zane always knew everything. There was no use in lying or concealing disgrace. "She's able to invoke the source," I proceeded to tell him. "Alloy runs through her human veins, mixing with her blood. I was able to feed from her."

As if the smile wasn't scary enough, my father placed his palms together and clapped. Only once, but still, by definition of a clap, an action of applause. "Wonderful, dear boy. You've done an excellent job."

A compliment? Where the hell was my father and who the hell was this man on the other end of our communication wall. "King, I do not understand. What's so wonderful? Why is this good news? Shouldn't we remove the source and have it surgically placed in a Ferroean?"

"Absolutely not! Faye Walker is a very special human, and her offspring is a very powerful ally for our planet. She's also a very important weapon for Earth. Your mission is dissolved. You are no longer observing humans at Cartwright High School. You are in charge of protecting Beatrice Walker at all costs. Never leave her side and keep her far away from the DOAA."

"Father, you can't be serious." I exclaimed. Why the hell would he want a Blood-Light harboring the most powerful energy source of our time? Unless . . .

"I've never been more serious. Jesting is not my forté. That is for your inept brother who's inherited traits from your mother's side." He glared at Ashton. "This isn't any energy womb. She will need to be protected here on Earth and never leave your side. Because the Ferro Council is split in their beliefs, and the fate of two planets hang in the balance, this is a secret even from them. Do you understand? Your mission is to keep her safe and a secret!" His eyes darkened and the smooth skin of his forehead furrowed with deep penetrating wrinkles. "Or do I need to request the presence of another special team and have you thrown off this mission and return to the California office immediately? I'd be happy to have you hand her over to another guard if you feel unsuited for the new assignment. Although my disappointment will fall harshly upon you and each of your unit. It will not go unpunished."

Threats. Now that sounded like the father I knew.

I would never hand Bea over to another team, but I also couldn't let my father know I had emotions for a human. Hell, I didn't even know what my feelings were, but I cared for Bea, and I wouldn't let just anyone protect her. What was nagging at me was why my father, the council, and the DOAA were no longer communicating and working together.

"My team will protect the human girl at all costs."

And with that the screen went dark. A brick wall had replaced my father's face. No goodbye. I turned back toward the elevator with no regard to my brother, but his words stopped me in my tracks.

"Tell me what happened to Seraphina. Tell me, or I swear to the Council I will find a way out of here and let mother and sister know I'm alive." His voiced quivered with animosity as he stalked over to me. His shoulders grew in size as he moved. Ashton loved Sera like everyone who ever met her. I didn't think about how the news would affect him.

"She was killed."

Ashton pounded his fist against the kitchen table. "Father. Father killed her!"

"What? No! Of course not!" My brows furrowed. "Why do you blame father for everything?" Sure, I wasn't a Zane Kingston fan, either, but I took an oath to my planet and the leader of it. Great leaders are not always well-liked but Ashton held our father responsible for all wrongdoings and held himself liable for nothing, even breaking up our family.

"Because daddy dearest is normally the reason. You're just too thickheaded to see it. Are you sure he had nothing to do with Sera's death? A highly trained combat guard, an opposing source, and the girlfriend of the head of the guards—Sera was overthrown and killed? There must have been some epic attack for her not to survive." He crossed his arms over his chest. His eyes narrowed in on me. "I've never seen Dad so happy to hear of a human harboring a source let alone an opposing source. He hates Blood-Lights. And he doesn't want to remove it from this energy womb. Tell me you haven't turned into an errand boy and that you still have a damn brain inside that thick human shell."

I pounded my fist into the brick wall behind me; red and brown pieces flung around my hand, littering the floor. "I have a brain. It's you that's lost it. Going against father under Sayor's rule! Are you nuts? He's a damn rebel. A bloodline going against the council to take it over and insist on being equals with the humans. Now who's an errand boy?"

"All we wanted was peace. To live on Earth openly instead of shamefully hiding our existence. You think that's going against our planet? You have no idea what Dad really does. He uses humans as experiments—pets and projects. He doesn't want to coexist with them. He wants to rule them!" Ashton raged.

Shock coursed through my veins. Rule humans? Father always said it wouldn't be worth our time. How could Ashton even suggest that? He was delusional. Sayor convinced him of these things. The brother I adored, admired, worshiped even, was killed the day Sayor and his band of rebels tried to take my father into captivity. Sayor ruined his bloodline's name and tried to take mine down with it by aligning with a Kingston.

"Sayor was in love with a human and for that he was dissolved of his rightful spot in the council. Love shouldn't be a punishment."

"There are rules, Ash!"

He laughed. "Rules? I've never known you to follow those, baby brother." He stood and walked over to the kitchen. "You don't even pick up on things Daddy says. For example, I never heard you mention Faye Walker's daughter's first name, but somehow, he knew it. When it comes to Dad, you're a robot." He opened the fridge and grabbed a beer. "No, you are a puppet. That's right. Daddy moves you on strings. You're a damn puppet and Dad's the puppeteer."

My teeth ground against one another; my jaw pulsed with rage. Zane knew about her. He knew Beatrice's name. There wasn't an explanation on how and my dumb ass didn't even ask. Because no matter how much I hated my brother for breaking up my family, he was right about one thing. When it came to Zane Kingston, I always had blind faith for my King.

"Zane has always been all knowing. I'm sure Faye been forthcoming with him." I had no idea if that was true, but it had to be.

Ashton shook his head. "You don't really believe that, do you? Who would confide their Blood-Light daughter to a man who hates Blood-Lights? Now you are stretching the facts to fit your convenient story. Thank the Council

Tasha's smart. Maybe she can knock some sense into you. That's unless Dad has her conditioned as well. Could you imagine if she knew I am alive, and Daddy and you are hiding me? Who would she believe then?" He turned his back to me. I gritted my teeth. "I'd be more worried about this Blood-Light's survival. She must be pretty important to be liked by Daddy dearest this much. Who's her father anyhow? Some stupid, low level Ferroean guard or something?"

He grabbed a glass and poured beer into it. The foam bubbled at the top, settling before it flowed over the rim. I headed to the elevator and pressed the button. I stepped inside and without thinking, I answered my brother out loud as the doors shut.

"Her father is Gabe Sayor, Rebel Leader of Ferro."

Chapter Twenty-One

Beatrice

As Tasha and I approached the front door, I sucked in a deep, courageous breath. Cash ordered me to the safe house after he found out about the school attack. I don't know where he went and why the team couldn't get in touch with him, but when they finally did, he threatened to move me out of Cartwright all together and Dad didn't disagree. It took the whole team, with an emphasis on Tasha, to calm him down and make him rethink his decision. I wasn't safe anywhere and to move me now without knowledge of who our new attacker was might be even more dangerous.

Tasha twisted the knob and let me in.

"I'm going to run back to your house and meet up with Sammie. Plus, I'm sure my brother would like to speak with you alone. Don't tell him what Darla said. I don't want him torturing a poor human just because she has red hair."

I nodded.

"Thanks for walking with me," I said, slightly embarrassed that I wasn't allowed to do anything on my own anymore.

She smiled sympathetically as she retreated back across the street.

The house was set up exactly like ours. Identical. The room to the left was a dining room with the same furniture from our house. A pillow and blanket lay across the couch as if someone had been sleeping on it. The room directly to the right was a sitting area, but in our house my dad used this as a work area. The hallway led to the kitchen on the right, opposite the living room, which was on the left. The stairs to the second level were right off the kitchen, and the basement steps adjacent. Everything was the same. Déja-freakin'-vu.

A smacking noise and the low hum of music came from the basement. I opened the door, and the sounds grew. Smack. Crack. Thwack. Someone or something was taking a beating. I tip-toed down the stairs and froze at the landing.

I bit back a gasp.

Cash was going face to face with a punching bag. The ripples on his bare back danced with each jab, tightening and swelling with his movements. He pulled back, letting his chest rise and fall, and delivered another right hook to the bag, then a left, an uppercut, and a roundhouse kick.

Sweat cascaded down his body, gliding over his taut skin. Every lithe muscle popped, creating a mountainous valley of flesh and bone. All Cash wore were olive cargo pants and black boots. I stared at the wet, dark curls clinging to his forehead and immediately wanted to brush them back. God, my priorities were in the toilet lately.

His body tensed. "You going to stand there ogling me all day, or are you going to say something?" Cash said in between jabs to the bag.

"Glad you haven't lost your humor." I sighed. I didn't like the idea of obeying all of Cash's demands, but I didn't want to leave Cartwright again, either. "I'll be smarter. Don't make me leave." It was a plea but also the truth. I knew the dangers. Cash delivered two more right hooks. Damn, he was fast.

"This is the second attack," he said calmly. "You are not a secret anymore. It's not safe."

Cash steadied the bag and then grabbed a towel and water from the bench behind him. I surveyed the room. They had turned the whole basement into a gym. It was impressive. I didn't know what half of the equipment was, but I wanted to find out. Tasha urged me to come over here and work out since I couldn't run any more.

"What is all this stuff?" I motioned to the band-like weapons hanging from the equipment wall.

"We are training," he said. He wiped his face with the towel and wrapped it around his neck. Sweat dripped from his dark brown waves, absorbing into the cloth. "We have no idea who we are up against. Tasha never saw the attacker from the front. All she could see was a tall woman with curly red hair who moved faster than a human could. We are making a list of all Ferroeans we think could be responsible and then investigating on where they have been traveling to lately to see if they could have been able to get to Cartwright. Red hair is pretty common in assimilated Ferroeans since we all have reddish hair on Ferro, but it's important for us to blend in on Earth, thus ruling out Ferro Guards." When he eventually turned around and looked at me for the first time, surprise flickered over his face.

I tilted my head, trying to piece together his reaction. "What?"

Cash stilled. His intense eyes trailed the length of my body. The silence was awkward. I felt compelled to move, as if I could physically push it away. His body tensed and the thick cords protruding from his neck and shoulders jumped as the distance between us diminished.

Cash took a long, deep breath. "Did you wear that outside? In public?" His voice was a deep, husky sound. I glanced down at my outfit, running shorts, a sports bra, and sneakers.

"Um. Yeah."

"It's not even warm out, and you're practically naked." Cash thrust his hands through his hair and grunted. "Do you remember when I said to keep a low profile? You were attacked on the street. Attacked at school! Do you care at all about your safety? Running around town in the buff is the opposite of a low profile. And how did you get here? By yourself?"

Anger flared inside of me like a fireplace coming to life.

"Okay, Dad." I let the sarcasm seep out of my tone. "First of all, I was escorted by Tasha the whole fifty feet it took us to get here, which was embarrassing enough. Second, I feel like a prisoner and an out of shape one at that, so I was going to work out, like you were just doing, hence the clothes. And third, how dare you try and tell me what I can wear. Get with the times buddy!" I started back up the steps, but before I even hit the first landing, Cash was in front of me. Damn extraterrestrial speed. "What?"

"I'm going to ask you nicely. Please put on more clothes when you leave the house." His voice was low and precise.

"Are you serious? I really think you need your head examined. I am not changing my clothes, especially because you are ordering me to. You can't make me."

"Oh, but I could," he said with a hint of a smile.

I groaned. I couldn't believe we were even having this conversation.

Cash flashed a wry grin. "Fine. How about we make a deal? You wear more clothes and . . ." He motioned for me to finish the sentence.

"Fine. I will wear more clothes if I can stay in Cartwright."

"No!"

"Why?"

"It's not safe."

"It's not safe anywhere for me," I spat. I tapped my bottom lip. There must be a way to convince Cash to let me stay and maybe a way I could protect myself against these threats.

"Train me!" I practically yelled. The idea flowed out of my mouth. I hadn't even realized that training was something I was interested in until I said it. But now, more than ever, I wanted to control a portion of my life, to learn my own strength, and to feel power like Cash and the others did. Plus, time wasn't on my side. At the rate I was being attacked, eventually someone would overthrow my protectors, and I'd rather not be a sitting duck.

"You want me to train you?" He ran his hand through his hair, pinning it back with moisture. "To fight?"

"Yes. This way I can defend myself and not be so helpless. It could come in handy." I smiled wide. "And we could stay in Cartwright."

"Hmmm. That's a deal I might be able to live with. I will have to get another bag, though. This one is made from a material for our strength. We can start with basics until then."

I nodded feverishly. It felt as if Cash was giving me a piece of myself back. It felt liberating.

I jumped up and down like a pogo stick, clapping crazily, and then jumped on Cash, hugging the crap out of him.

My breath hitched in my throat as my arms froze. Cash lifted his hands to my back and guided his fingertips down my spine. Goose bumps trailed his touch while the blood in my veins turned to molten lava. I lowered my arms and attempted to step back, but Cash moved along my waistband until he rounded the front and tugged on the dangling string from my shorts. Our bodies were flush against each other. My chest pressed against his, heaving from my ragged breaths. Each pulse felt like a magnet pulling together and breaking apart.

Cash leaned in. His hard body pressed up against mine. His damp cheek brushed mine as his lips breathed in my ear. "Don't make me regret this deal." He released me and turned.

I didn't move, breathe, or speak. The hum in my chest reached out to him like an invisible cord. My body was unable to sync correctly with my mind as my legs walked on their own accord. I placed my hand on his shoulder and unconsciously turned him around.

I wanted him more than anything in this world . . . or any other world, for that matter. Without thought, I moved closer toward him, and I closed my eyes, falling into a trance. The energy in my body increased, buzzing with pure intoxication.

I closed the distance to a sliver of space and pressed my lips to his. As the hum inside of me intensified, I sunk my fingers into his flesh, gripping at his hard biceps. Responding to me, he coaxed my lips open, but instead of kissing me, he breathed me in. My senses whirled as my fingers traveled up and around his neck, pulling him in closer. Desire fluttered in my stomach while his hands gripped my hips tighter. A small whimper of pleasure escaped from my mouth as Cash caught my lower lip between his teeth. He lifted me up. My legs wrapped around his waist while my thighs tightened above his hips. His hands gripped my back, pulling me closer to his body.

Our faces pulled apart as our eyes locked. Something between us changed, had been changing.

I slid down Cash's body never breaking eye contact. As my feet landed on the ground, Cash attempted to back away. His eyes were intense and searing. His irises changed into a hundred colors, more than I've ever seen before. Then, as if all the colors had melded into one, all I saw was purple. The color called to me. *Touch him*, a voice inside me said. *Touch him. Become one.*

My pointer and middle finger reached for his chest and pressed into his diamond-shaped scar. I don't know why I did it. But what I felt next would change my life for eternity. Energy coursed through my veins bubbling to my fingers, melting their tips into Cash's flesh. I couldn't release them, nor did I want to. I was adjoined to him; my flesh was his with no beginning or end to either of us. And then, as if lightning had struck me, my wrists and ankles felt like they were on fire, and I screamed. Bloodcurdling screams.

Chapter Twenty-Two

Cash

Beatrice's screams vibrated throughout my throat, elevating into my temples as if they were my own. The pain was so intense that bile crawled up my esophagus. She had somehow evoked our connection, a power only fully simulated Ferroeans could do on Earth. It was a power she shouldn't have, and a power I feared Faye, Tasha, and Zane knew about. My hands clutched my chest, and I fell to my knees, bringing her down with me. My ankles and wrists scorched as if they were being held over a flame. Bea was pushing too much power into me, too forcefully. At this rate, she would kill me. I tried to back away. Her eyes pleaded with me. She wanted the same, but the source had taken over. Torment ridiculed her face. She winced. *Visualize breaking free from me.* I pushed those thoughts into her head. *Visualize our bodies separating. You can do this.* I was too weak to speak, the blood around my joints boiled, including my face muscles.

Slowly she drew away. Sweat cascaded down her red cheeks. The pain dulled as soon as she stopped touching me, but the vacancy of her connection left me yearning for the agony. Our predecessors had warned Sera and I about the downfalls of the connection, which was why she and I had spent long hours in effort to take it slowly. Even in our most connected state, Sera and I had never joined flesh. We had been warned: 'For the Flesh craves what is contrary to the Source, and the Source what is contrary to the Flesh. They are opposed to one another so that you do not do what you want, but what you are intended.' It never made sense to me before. Honestly, I wasn't getting the whole picture now, either. But while we were connected flesh to flesh, Bea's source had more power than mine, and that was not supposed to be the case. Sera and I were each other's checks and balances.

"What the hell was that?" she said breathlessly, looking at her wrists then bending down to soothe her ankles—the four points of connection on a Ferroean that exerts from our energy source to our whole body and pools in our joints.

I stared at her as I tried to conceal my expression. I had no idea how she did it. I looked at my extremities. Other than the dulling pain, my wrists and ankles were unscathed. She could have killed me. She didn't know it yet, but her power alone was the only other way we as a species could die, other than the thermo daggers. She's not only my Achilles heel, but our race's.

I cleared my throat. "Are you okay?"

"I think so," she answered, still eyeing her body for damage.

I walked away not saying a word and headed for the stairs.

"Wait! Where are you going?" Bea ran after me. "What happened to us?"

"Dinner. I'm hungry. You hungry?" I kept my voice even, showing no emotion. This was a game changer. I now knew why the DOAA wanted her. They would use her against our kind. With the energy running through Bea's veins, her Ferroean veins, I wasn't sure how much humanity she would have left in her, but I knew removing it could never be an option. Zane was right. We had to protect her at all costs and never let the DOAA get ahold of her.

"Mark, Paul, you hungry?" I asked, holding the basement door open for Bea to walk through. The look on her face was pure confusion. I hoped my lack of reaction kept her calm and quiet, but with Bea, I never knew. Any second, she could have diarrhea of the mouth and start spouting questions. If Mark and Paul knew she was a threat to our kind, I'm not sure they would protect her. Which brought up an even more disturbing question: why was Zane protecting her?

"Hell yeah," Paul said, jumping over the side of the couch and landing horizontally. He grabbed the remote and powered the TV on. It blared as he yelled, "Mexican?" over the *Game of Throne's* finale in the background. They've watched that episode a hundred times, rewriting the ending out loud each time.

"Sure. Bea, why don't you order and set up the table? My credit card is on the counter by the phone for these idiots to use for food. You might as well use it, too. I'm going to run back to your place and get the girls. Sound good?"

She nodded, still dazed and confused but kept mute heading toward the kitchen.

I dashed across the street and walked right into the house. I had no intention of talking to the girls, but I had every intention of grabbing Robert and shaking the shit of him. There was something about Beatrice he was hiding, and I was going to strangle him for withholding it from me when I found out.

He was in his study, focusing on the computer while his fingers tapped away at the keyboard. The screen lit up his face, accentuating the creases around his eyes.

"We have a problem," I growled. No use beating around the bush. Bea was able to melt flesh into flesh.

Robert looked up from his computer. He removed his reading glasses.

"Other than the already existing problems?" His right brow lifted.

I nodded. He waved toward the chair in front of him, and I took a seat.

"Bea connected to me. Fully connected. Flesh to flesh," I said as I gripped the chair handles so hard, I broke one off. I tossed it to the other side of the room.

"That's impossible," he choked. "She'd be dead if she had fully accessed the source."

"She's been turning it on. I've been feeding from her since the night you found us on her floor." Robert stood in fury. I matched his motion. "Don't! I know you've been hiding something." I took a deep breath. "I'm not here to argue. I'm trying to understand without killing you, so don't turn this around on me. Feeding off my opposing source is like breathing. I need to do it to stay alive. This isn't news to you. I already feel guilty as hell for doing it without her knowing. I didn't know her body was absorbing the source. I didn't even know that was possible."

Robert's face went white—ghost white.

"How is she doing this?" I growled. My fists pounded onto his desk. What the hell was going on?

Robert slouched into his chair.

"What the hell was Faye?" I thundered.

"Faye was human," Robert answered. "But she was also an experiment. Faye had traces of Ferroean lineage from long ago. So miniscule, she didn't have enough to be a Blood-Light. But Dr. X thought she might be a candidate for an experimental procedure."

"Dr. X experimented on her?"

"Yes. He combined the alloy that flows through your veins with her own blood, and like a dialysis machine, it was resynthesized and put back into her veins."

"That's a thing?" I scratched my head. This was the first time I was hearing about this, and it was my job to regulate the scientists. "Why? Why would he do that?"

"Faye was recruited at the age of ten and trained up until she was eighteen. She was part of the experiments that involved placing sources inside humans, but after all of the failures and deaths, Dr. X didn't want to take his chances on her. He erased her records as part of the trial. He told her to go live a normal life. She even attempted college, but the DOAA sucked her back in. I don't know how or why. She never talked about it."

"What the hell does that have to do with Bea?"

"The experiments started before Faye went through adolescence. As she matured, the alloy adapted to her veins. When she was pregnant, she passed the composite onto Bea. Since Bea's father is one of the five original Ferroean descendants, Bea is more Ferroean than human. She just wasn't born with a source."

It was like an avalanche of information caving in as recognition took hold. "Gabe was part of the council bloodline. Bea's a descendant of opposing energy sources. Goddamn it, Robert. What the hell am I going to do? There's no safe way out of this for Bea. She will have to connect to my source." I slammed my fists again, cracking the desk down the middle. It splintered but didn't split in half. "Faye knew this and let this happen to her daughter anyway?" I questioned. I didn't dare tell him Bea's power could kill our kind. To protect Ferroeans and Bea, it would be a secret I'd take to the grave, which seemed likely each day I spent in her presence.

"I don't know what to do. I don't." Robert looked down. "Maybe she thought that if Earth was annihilated, this was her way to protect Bea from being killed. She'd have to go to Ferro to save your planet. I honestly have no idea."

My temper got the best of me, and for the third time, I slammed my hands on the desk breaking it into two. The computer crashed and all the items on it slid to the ground. The door flung open and the girls gasped.

"What the hell is going on?" Sammie asked, her hands pressed into her curves.

Robert's eyes pleaded with me. Yeah, like I'm going to tell anyone else about this mess. He didn't need to beg.

"Nothing," I snarled through gritted teeth, glaring at Robert. I twisted back toward the girls. "Bea's ordering food across the street. You hungry?"

"Really?" Sammie crossed her arms over her chest, pointing with her eyes to the mess on the ground. Tasha walked over to Robert and helped pick up the fallen desk objects. Her eyes were soft as she held my gaze.

"You hungry or not?" I avoided my sister and barked at Sammie.

She threw her hands into the air. "Whatever! Yeah, we are hungry."

"Good. Grab Bea a sweatshirt and meet me over at the safe house. Close the door."

"But . . .," Sammie argued. I turned to Tasha. "Leave."

Robert was on the floor, picking up papers and placing them on the shelf beside him. The computer was not salvageable, but I didn't give a rat's ass. Robert should have told me about Faye's past. I'm not sure what it would have changed, but having this mystery piecemealed didn't help either. Like an onion that went on forever, each layer added more questions as I peeled it back, and the stench of this debacle was growing odorous.

"What the hell are we going to do?" I asked.

"Faye left me something. Maybe it will make more sense to you. Hell, maybe it was for you to find." He reached into his pocket and grabbed a set of keys. I followed him to a locked cabinet. He opened the drawer and handed me a manila envelope. Inside were three things: a picture of Dr. X, Faye, and Beatrice, a blank key card, and something I couldn't believe Robert had in his possession—a necklace. Sera's necklace.

I draped the chain over my hand and held the dagger pendant in my palm. The hilt was silver, and the blade was black stone. The second it touched my skin, the charm turned from black onyx to a colored tornado of hunter green, midnight blue, and blood red, swirling around each other.

"I gave this to Sera the day we left for Earth," I whispered.

"What is it?" Robert asked, leaning to get a better view. "It wasn't like that in my safe." He motioned to the dark colors intertwining each other.

"It's a tool. It's like a thermometer for the source." I remembered it around Sera's neck when she left for California. How did Faye end up with it? "The necklace helped us evaluate our sources and what we needed. The elders gave it to me."

"Why would Faye have it?"

"Good question. Faye's done a nice job leaving a lot of those," I growled.

Robert sighed. "I'm guessing you don't understand the picture or key?"

I grabbed the rectangular flat key with an encryption code on the back and flipped it in between my fingers. Didn't have any significance to me. I shook my head. Robert handed me the picture.

"You might as well keep all three. She seemed to have trusted you more than me, anyway. I can't believe she took a picture with Bea and Dr. X when she left me," Robert said.

"How do you know that?" I asked.

Robert pointed to the time stamp. It was during the days Faye and Bea were missing. I searched the picture for clues. Not much was visible. Faye had her arm around Bea, and Dr. X had his arm around Faye. The background was black. Nothing to see. It looked more like a family portrait than a clue.

That's when it hit me. Their eyes. Dr. X had the exact prism-like hazel eyes. Like Faye's. Like Beatrice's.

Chapter Twenty-Three

Beatrice

After dinner, we played an archaic video game that Mark and Paul were obsessed with, while I called Darla and asked her to drive to school tomorrow. Obviously, Betsey was out of commission due to Grouper's grand entrance at the movie theater. Darla said she'd spoken with Chris, and he offered to take my carpool day. Cash fought me on this, reminding me how dangerous my world had become and that I needed constant supervision. I argued like a criminal defense attorney, but it was Tasha that came up with a compromise. Sammie and she would trail behind us, keeping watch. And Paul and Mark would drive in front of us. I warned that if I stopped acting normal around Chris, it would add to his already growing suspicion. Cash didn't seem to want to deal with that and ended up conceding.

The next day, when I jumped into the backseat, Chris shot me a strange look. Darla sat in the front with her arms crossed over her chest. The tension between them was thick and icy. Total buzzkill.

"What's up with you two?"

"Oh, nothing much. Except Chris thinks you and I are lying to him, and he accused me of being fake. Can you believe that? He called me fake." Darla flicked her seatbelt off and shot up in her seat. Her hand wrapped around the headrest while her eyes said, *What do we tell him?*

I nodded, knowing this conversation was bound to happen. "Chris, Darla is not fake. I'm assuming you are talking about her and I being friends with Sammie, right?"

Chris shrugged like he couldn't care less, but his tense grip on the wheel told me otherwise. Chris's suspicions had been piling up like a four-car collision since Cash and I started to pretend to date. Each doubt was another hit to his proverbial bumper.

"Listen, Sammie didn't like me at first because Cash and she used to date, but it's been over between them for a while."

"That brings up a good point," Chris said, meeting my eyes with his in the rearview mirror. "You don't think it's strange that Cash dated Seraphina, Sammie's best friend, for most of high school? Seraphina visited her aunt, died in a freak accident, and then he started dating her best friend. That doesn't scream douchebag to you?"

My mouth dropped as my heart sank. My chest hummed in response, almost as if it was happy to hear Chris's words. "Who's Seraphina?"

Darla immediately dropped in her seat. I shot in between them, hovering over the center console. My eyes darted back and forth between Chris and Darla, while my nails sank into the leather seats. They obviously knew something.

"Who is she?" As my voice grew, so did the buzzing in my rib cage. It was like bees in a beehive.

Darla glared at Chris, and then softened her gaze when she looked at me. "Listen, this whole Cash thing just happened. I didn't mention it because it didn't seem right. I mean, she's dead." Darla's eyes seared Chris's head, like she wanted to burn him alive for blurting out the truth.

I sat back, my body sinking into the plush leather. No one had ever mentioned her before. Not once. My hand rubbed my scar, trying to calm my awakened insides. It's not that I was jealous. Well, maybe a little. But it just felt like another secret.

"How did she die?" I asked.

Darla sighed. "The rumors are that she and her aunt were in a car accident and died."

I didn't respond. What would I say? The three of us sat in silence the rest of the ride to school.

Darla and I were caught at our lockers again by Coach Barb. The tips of her lips rose as she stared at my watch.

"Are you enjoying the watch I gave you?" she asked.

I feigned a smile. "Yes, thank you."

"Have you given any more thought to coming back to track?" It was like Groundhog Day with her. Every morning!

Darla moved in front of me, her small frame was an ironic bodyguard. "Have you given more thought to supporting my Pitties idea? Because I really think this is a winner and I need financial backing!"

Coach Barb shook her head, dismissing Darla and lasering in on me. "Think about it. A one-on-one session with me would be good for you. A little fresh air couldn't hurt and would maybe help these family issues you've been having. A good distraction!" She held up her finger like she was going to add to her plea, but her head twisted to the right. Not even looking back at me, she said, "It's important we meet one-on-one soon. Just the two of us." Then she darted down the hall to the left.

Tasha rounded the bend.

"Ready for English?" she questioned.

When Darla, Tasha, and I walked into class, I immediately searched the room for Cash, ready to confront him about his ex-girlfriend. Was she human, an alien, a cover story? I needed to know the details. He was already in his seat, leaning back on two legs of his chair and twirling his pen in between his fingers. But he wasn't alone. A girl with curly blonde hair had propped her butt on his desk. She giggled repetitively, touching Cash's arm as he spoke.

"Why does that girl have her nose in everything?" I asked Darla from the back of the classroom. A different kind of jealousy squeezed at my insides.

"Kathleen Butler is so annoying. She's such a nosy busy-body," Darla responded. "I'm sure she wants Cash's attention. But don't worry—he doesn't look interested."

"I don't care," I lied, shrugging. Darla smiled an oh-yes-you-do grin. Damn her.

In passing Cash's desk, I bumped Kathleen, causing her to falter backward.

"Oops! Sorry," I said with a voice so phony it sounded foreign, even to me. "Didn't see you there." I smiled. Kathleen shot me a death stare and continued speaking to Cash.

I took my seat, my blood boiling. Thoughts of Seraphina drifted away and were replaced by real-time possessiveness. I know he'd said that ours was a forged relationship, but hell, shouldn't that be even more reason for him to tell her he had a girlfriend? And what about our kiss yesterday! That had to mean something. Ok, I was starting to sound crazy. I took out my book and homework, trying not to hear their conversation.

Cash interrupted her. "Kathleen, have you met my girl-friend, Bea?" Cash tapped me on the shoulder. I turned around with probably the goofiest grin, half elated and half startled.

"Girlfriend?" Kathleen stammered. "But I thought . . . I thought Sammie and you broke up."

"They did, and now he's with me," I said with much more coolness than I knew I had in me. I guess being attacked multiple times can give one new confidence.

He winked at me and I blushed. Kathleen's nose crinkled and she gave an insincere smile.

"Like I was saying, my parents are away and I'm having the biggest, baddest party of all time this weekend. You should come."

"I have plans. But thanks."

She glared at me, then sighed. "You can bring your plans. Think about it." And with that, she finally took her seat.

About ten minutes into class, I felt the heat of Cash's breath on my neck. My lips spread into a ridiculous smile, and I turned slowly.

"Can I help you?" I said with a laugh.

"What are you doing tonight?" Cash asked. He twirled his pen in between his fingers like a baton. His blue eyes sparkled with mischief.

"Nothing. Why?"

"Come watch training. It will be good for you to ob-serve."

"Mr. Kingston and Miss Walker, is there something you would like to share with the class?" Mr. Mack asked. My gaze darted back and forth from Mr. Mack to Cash. I couldn't afford detention.

Cash leaned back in his chair, resting on two legs. How was it that he was never intimidated by anyone or anything?

"Not especially. I was asking my girlfriend if she wanted to hang out tonight. I doubt the class would be interested in that."

The students around us snickered. My face burned with humiliation, although, deep down inside, butterfly wings fluttered wildly at the sound of being called Cash's girl-friend.

"No, that doesn't seem to have anything to do with our English lesson. Does this mean that, because of your new-found relationship—one about which, if I remember correctly, you were unhappy with several days ago—you haven't read the homework due today?"

"Nope, I finished," Cash said with ease. There was no way he completed *The Catcher in the Rye*. He'd been training nonstop. Even I was only halfway through the book, and I was a fast reader.

"Great. Then could you please share with the class your favorite part of the book and how it affected you?" Mr. Mack leaned against his desk and crossed his arms, waiting for Cash to falter.

"Well, my favorite quote from the book was, 'Life is a game, boy. Life is a game that one plays according to the rules.' It's probably the most powerful quote within the novel. It sums up exactly what Holden is going through. At the beginning of the novel, he tries to play the game of life by his own rules and is unsuccessful by doing so. Through-out the story, however, he learns that, in order to succeed in life, he needs to be more responsible. I believe he finally realizes that when his sister wishes to move out west with him. He realizes his actions set a bad example for her. As for how it affected me . . ." Cash tapped his bottom lip, drawing my eyes to his mouth. God, his lips were full. And the perfect fit for mine. Cash stared at me. My heart flipped in my chest while the source buzzed like I had stuck my hand in an electrical outlet. Could he control the energy source inside of me? Was that what was going on?

He must have read my thought, because sadness crept into his eyes. When he finally answered Mr. Mack, it almost felt like he was answering me. "I think it just reminds me that no matter how much we want to live by our own rules, to effectively succeed, we have to work within the rules we are given, because our decisions affect not only ourselves, but those we love."

Strangely, part of me wanted to cry. I bit my lower lip in fear that I might. His words were beautiful, too flawless, and yet they tugged painfully at my heart. It felt like he was letting me know something I didn't want to hear. Panic stirred inside of me.

Mr. Mack cleared his throat. "Unexpected but very good, Cash. Anyone else?"

After school, I went over to the yellow house. I dressed in more clothes, as Cash had requested: sweatpants, sneakers, and a white sports bra covered by a white tank top. I braided my hair back and out of my face. Even if I didn't get to punch the bag, I might be able to mirror their moves, to get the feel of it. I also wanted to recreate that highly charged moment from the day before. But not the part that had lit my extremities on fire. I planned on asking Cash about it, but he was so dismissive yesterday, it felt awkward to bring it up.

I walked down to the basement. Tasha, Sammie, Mark, Paul, and Cash all wore the same gear: olive cargo pants, black tanks or t-shirts, and black boots. The five of them looked ready for a fight.

Everyone sat on the mats facing Cash, who sat on the bench. His pulsating forearms rested on his knees while his hands played with the cap of his water bottle. Sweat already darkened his black shirt clinging to his body. Clearly, he had started training solo.

He nodded when I joined them. "Okay, let's train. Tasha, partner off with Sammie, Mark with Paul, and Bea, you're with me. An hour of hand-to-hand combat, an hour with weapons, and then we all run. Got it?" Cash said. His smile reached his eyes. He loved this. Everyone else groaned and got into position.

Cash walked over to me and placed his hand on my lower back. Gently he pushed me forward, toward Tasha and Sammie's mat. He spoke softly in my ear; the heat of his breath tingled across my skin with sweet pleasure. I concentrated on breathing, and not thinking.

"I want you to watch how the girls fight. Notice their stances, their precision, their moves, and their techniques. Watch their feet, their hips, and how they balance." He pointed to the girls as they moved gracefully around each other. "The fight between you and your opponent will always be different from one another. They might be faster than you, more offensive or defensive, more skilled with hand-to-hand combat, or might maneuver better on the ground. Each adversary will be better at something than you, but they will also be weaker at something, too. A good fighter finds her opponent's weakness while hiding their own. Always be prepared and use your surroundings to your advantage."

I nodded and watched the girls take their stance on the mats.

Sammie launched herself at Tasha first, but Tasha was prepared for it and dodged to the left. She threw a right hook at Sammie's face, but Sammie deflected it and recovered fast with a punch to Tasha's gut. Ow—that looked like it hurt. But Tasha bounced back. She feigned to the left and drove in a kick on the right, swiping Sammie's legs out from underneath her.

"If she had thermo daggers, you'd be halfway to deadsville," Cash said. Sammie stood back up, glaring suspiciously at Cash. What I thought was going to be a smartass answer turned out to be a roundhouse kick to Cash's face. He caught her foot in midair and, with a flick of his wrist, flipped her over. He never broke eye contact with me. *Holy shit.*

"Try it again, and I will break your leg," he said, smiling.

"Oh my god, Cash!" My hands flew to my mouth.

Sammie laughed from the floor.

"Bea, its fine. We are always trying to take him out. It doesn't happen often," Sammie said, blowing Cash a kiss from the ground. "One day, baby, I will get you." She stood and winked.

"In your dreams, Sammie, in your dreams." Cash's lips twitched, fighting back his smile.

I watched them practice every day for the next week, after school for three hours. The five of them moved lightning fast—so fast that I missed some of the moves. Punches to the jaw, deflected. Roundhouse kicks, deflected. Punch after punch, hit after hit, kick after kick. One out of twenty actually made contact. They were so good.

Cash only sparred with them occasionally, and his actions were always defensive instead of offensive. At the house one night, I asked Sammie why he didn't attack, and she explained that he was too skilled. He anticipated most of their moves. Apparently, he'd run the guard program on their planet. Cash was a badass fighting machine and, as crazy as it sounded, I totally crushed on him harder because of it.

I alternated from staring at the group to ogling Cash. His arms were so defined that it looked as if a painter had carved them. His movements were as fluid as a dancer's. And he taught as if it was his purpose in life to be a soldier. I was pretty much a blob of goo around him.

As for me, I watched, absorbed, and practiced with the air. Cash helped me with my stances and taught me some basic boxing combinations. The jab, straight right, left hook. This was the classic 1-2-3 combination.

While everyone ran, Cash stayed behind and worked on self-defense moves with me. He said he would rather I learn how to evade a fight than attempt to dominate my opponent. So, as much as I loved the fight moves, Cash was more focused on the escape plan for me.

We never spoke about the moment in the basement when our flesh joined. Part of me was starting to think I made it up. Cash hadn't touched me . . . other than to help with training sessions. The heat between us was still there, burning brightly and infecting my soul, but Cash ignored it. If I advanced closer to him, he would subtly move away. If I pretended to brush against him, he would distract himself. It was beyond frustrating.

On the following Monday, Cash texted me to say my punching bag had arrived. I was amped. I literally bounced down the steps to the basement.

"Look at the jumping jellybean over there," Mark said as the others warmed up. My bag was already hung, waiting for me. I flew over and wrapped my arms around it.

"You're not supposed to make love to the enemy," Paul said, laughing at my ridiculousness. I didn't care. I was so excited.

"Since you and the bag are now acquainted," Cash said, smiling. His eyes were bright blue and clear. His face void of derision. I wished I could freeze-frame Cash in moments like this and replay them. In school, he pretended to be my boyfriend, and I loved every second of it. After school, we watched the others train and conversed like old friends. We never kissed or really touched—clearly, he was avoiding me in that way. But he had wriggled his way into my heart, and I knew I couldn't let him go.

"Let's get started." Cash went over the basics again while my eyes kept darting to the bag.

"Bea, pay attention. What did I just say?"

"You were reminding me how to fall from a hit. Can I please, please, please give it a go with the bag?"

Cash laughed. "All right. Get into your stance," he ordered. "Let's try a simple combination: jab, straight right, left hook." Cash threw out commands as I hit the bag. "Get your range with the jab, then throw out the straight right to get your opponent to cover up in front of his face. As you throw the straight right, shift toward your opponent while moving your weight onto your lead foot. Then you should be able to land a left hook to the side of his head while both your opponent's hands are still in front of his face.

"No, no. It's a mistake to try to land the left hook from the same distance that you can land the straight right. You need to be closer to land a proper left hook," Cash said, moving my body in closer to the bag. His hands gripped my hips and my heart squeezed. "The right hand is just a setup punch. It's not thrown with knockout power; rather, it's just there to get his hands out of position and to allow you to shift your weight in preparation for throwing the left hook. Again, Bea, keep going."

I continued pounding away, but the bag never moved. Depressing.

"Watch your hips. Remember, the power comes from the whole body. Again," Cash said, watching, critiquing, guiding me. Every time he spoke, I tried harder. At least if we were attacked again, I wanted to hold my own.

"Put your feelings into it. Anger. Sadness. Hate. Regret. Let the bag symbolize everything you feel and fear." Cash's voice held passion for teaching.

I attacked the bag as if it represented all the secrets my parents kept from me: my mom for putting the energy source in me, my pent-up desire for Cash, and the fear of the unknown bottled within me. I hit the bag for an hour every day for three days. Sweat poured off me, drenching my shirt until it clung to my skin and stray hairs stuck to the back of my neck. My undergarments latched to my body like suction cups. By Thursday, every part of my body hurt—really hurt. I was sore in places I didn't know I had. My body felt like death, but my energy level soared. Sadly, the bag never moved an inch.

"It's okay. It was your first week. You did great," Cash said in a low voice behind me.

"It was pathetic," I muttered. "Nothing compared to you guys."

Paul threw his arm around me. "You were great! Think of it this way, when we neutralize the situation and leave, you'll be able to ward off asshats like Cash."

Paul's eyes were emerald green, caring and kind. Every word he said was meant to comfort me, but all I could focus on was one word: leave. A dull pang shot across my chest, and I stumbled back out of Paul's hold.

"You're going to leave?" The words strangled out of my mouth. Unease swirled in the pit of my stomach and spread like a weed up to my throat, closing off my breath. The others still practiced in the background.

Cash lowered his head and dragged his fingers through his hair. He looked everywhere but at me. Mark answered, "Yes, when this is over, we are leaving."

"Why?" My voice faltered. A flare of panic twisted my insides into raw knots.

Cash's jaw hardened as he lifted his chin. His eyes turned into a thousand thunderous blues and grays. His shoulders tensed but he said nothing.

My eyes darted to Sammie, to Tasha, then back to Cash. The three of them were very quiet. And then back to Mark and Paul. I felt like the floor was moving under my feet. "You are all leaving after this? Just remove the source, and that's it?" I asked, sucking in a shallow breath.

Tasha stepped forward. "Our mission is to be here until we are called back to Ferro, but you never know what could happen. There's been a lot of changes since we were given our first orders by the King and Council."

Pressing my lips together, I shook my head. Sammie moved forward in line with Tasha. I put my hand up, wordlessly telling them to back off. Each breath I took hurt. Hell, my insides were on fire. Never once in the last month had any of them mentioned leaving. Tears threatened my eyes, but I forced them back.

"It's fine." My voice was raspy.

"Bea," Sammie said, her tone pleading.

I put my hand up, and she backed away. "I said it's fine." I pivoted around to the punching bag suspended behind me and rammed it once more with my fist. I hadn't even realized what I'd done until the audible gasp filled the room. Not once had this bag moved when I pummeled my fists against it, and yet . . . there was a hole the size of my hand in the center of it. The threads had splintered where my knuckles made contact. I stared at it, feeling the anger inside me give way to a burning numbness, and then I turned around and walked up the stairs.

After a hot, draining shower, I melted into bed. My body hurt everywhere, but it was nothing compared to the ache in my heart. I couldn't believe they would be leaving after this. My whole life revolved around leaving, it seemed; I was always parting from people and places I could never get attached to. I had finally found a place to call home, and now, five out of my seven friends were going. It just didn't seem fair. It never did.

I rolled onto my side. Every muscle in my back groaned with the movement; my arms felt like spaghetti, and my thighs burned like licking flames.

A soft knock rapped at the door.

"Come in," I said, with my head facing the wall.

"Hey," two sweet female voices said. I rolled over.

Tasha and Sammie stood in the doorframe. They looked afraid to come in. I sat up slowly, trying to ignore the sharp, shooting pangs. Damn, my muscles throbbed.

"Training sucks, huh?" Sammie said, watching me struggle. "We could heal you," she offered.

I shook my head.

Tasha took a seat at my desk chair while Sammie plopped on my bed.

"You are special," Sammie said. "You are not who I thought you were when we first met. I don't know what you are . . . in fact, could you tell us what that was back there?"

I looked at Sammie, confused. "What do you mean?"

"Uh . . . you annihilated that bag," she said cautiously, shaking her head.

The two of them sat with blank expressions and eyebrows raised. I gave a shrug. "I guess I got a little angry."

Sammie drew a long sigh just then. "If I am being honest, Tasha and I have agreed we don't think our time on Earth is done."

"What does that mean?"

"It means until we are given a new order, we stay on the path Mark and Paul shared earlier, but it doesn't mean that is final. And even if we do leave, it doesn't mean we can't visit or stay in touch."

"Why didn't Cash say anything?"

"Cash is an asshat," Sammie said through gritted teeth.

Sammie and Tasha exchanged a strange expression, and then stared at me. "Listen, it's obvious to us he has feelings for you. What they are, I don't know. My brother isn't good at emotions or communication."

"That's an understatement," I muttered, reminding myself that touchy-feely Cash had been completely absent for the last two weeks.

Tasha, Sammie, and I ended up chatting about nails, hair, boys, shopping, all while avoiding the subject of their unavoidable departure. We talked about how nosy Kathleen Butler was, and how she asked a hundred questions all the time, which Sammie hated. Tasha spilled the beans that she and Mark liked each other, but they were taking it slow. Also, Mark didn't want Cash to know—for obvious reasons. We spoke for hours. My dad finally came in and broke up the party, claiming that 1:00 a.m. was too late to be gossiping on a school night.

I fell asleep with a mild headache but when I woke, my head hurt like someone had clocked me with a club and my pj's were soaked with sweat clinging to my skin. A vision of my mother popped into my head, like it had three weeks ago. This time it was clearer, more detailed.

"Our planets do not have long. You need to listen to me." *My mom's brows were lined with moisture. Her long hair was tied in a ponytail, with loose strands clinging to her damp face. She was wearing combat gear. Behind her, the walls looked like black marble.* "Oh baby, I love you. You are more than you will ever understand. You can save us all. The connection will release your memories. You need to connect to find the answers. Crede Mihi."

And then the vision cut out. I blinked frantically, willing the image back . . . but there was nothing.

Chapter Twenty-Four

Beatrice

As Darla and I walked into English class, I rehashed the events from the last week to her, leaving out my meltdown during training and my strange hallucination from earlier that morning. The last thing I needed was for her to mention I might be going insane. I could see it now—my arms in a white straitjacket.

"Is it cool if I come to practice?" Darla asked as she opened her notebook. Lace material littered the floor from her pages. "Oops, my latest fashion fabric. I'm over the Pitties idea. I need a sexier fashion legacy." She winked.

I picked up the tulle and handed it back to her. We hadn't hung out in forever. I didn't see why it would be a problem if she came to the training center in the basement, but I knew I needed Cash's approval.

My chair skidded backward. My back smacked into the front of Cash's desk. Damn alien powers. I waited a moment before turning around. My face red.

"Why can't you tap me on the shoulder instead of giving me whiplash?"

"Where's the fun in that?" Cash winked. "Oh, and Darla can come to practice." He paused just then, his eyes holding

198 ~ DANA CLAIRE

a strange cocktail of awe and confusion. "As long as you don't punch a hole through her."

"You're really annoying," I retorted.

Cash sported a lopsided grin. "Annoying. Sexy as hell. I don't really see a difference."

I turned back around and scooted my chair up. For the rest of the class, Cash didn't prod me again. Slight disappointment settled in my stomach. His jabs had become part of our relationship. The lack of them only reminded me of the emptiness I would feel after he left. A huge knot formed at my throat, and I feared it would never dissipate.

At lunch, Chris sat across from me and next to Sammie. They got along surprisingly well. Both loved baseball and, since Chris played for Cartwright, they had a lot to talk about.

"Are you kidding? The Yankees are so much better than the Phillies. What's wrong with you?" Sammie said while opening her sandwich. Chris shook his head.

"You have much better taste in clothes than sports," Chris cracked back. The tips of his mouth lifted.

Sammie chucked a mayonnaise-soaked tomato at him. It landed on his face painting it white then continued on its journey to the lunch table. Chris picked it up and ate it, then licked the mayo off his face.

"Ewww," Sammie and I said in unison.

"You are so gross," Sammie added before going back to her food.

"Got you your favorite chocolate chip cookie from that bakery in town," Mark said, sliding a cookie bigger than my hand onto Tasha's plate. She lit up like a Christmas tree. Ok, now that I knew about their mutual crushes. How adorable!

Darla and Cash flanked me, and Paul sat next to Cash. We took up the whole table in the middle of the cafeteria. "What's the plan for tonight? It's Friday. We should do something fun," Chris asked. I looked with pleading eyes at Cash. He responded with a stern, I-don't-think-so look. Whatever. This was my life and I felt like a prisoner. I was so over it.

"I'm going to Kathleen Butler's party. Wanna come?" I asked before taking a bite of my sandwich.

Cash spit out his soda, spraying the table in brown substance. Mark and Paul started laughing hysterically. Tasha, Darla, and Sammie stared at me like I had lost my mind.

Chris sat up straighter. "Really? I'm totally in. It's about time we go to a senior party. This year's been pretty lame so far. We need a little action!"

I nodded. Be careful what you wish for, I thought to myself. Excitement isn't exactly what I was looking for, but normalcy was. I was tired of living in a prison. I knew there were threats. I remembered Claude's death vividly, being thrown by a bug into a bed of glass, and jumping out of a window while chased by who knows what. But it was senior year, and I was still a human girl. Chris would eventually wonder what we were doing if we kept training all the time and never hanging out. And if these guys were just going to leave me after it was all said and done, then I'd better make memories with my human friends.

After lunch, Darla and I headed back to our lockers, and Cash followed. His loud footsteps sounded behind me. Every sigh blew hot hair on my neck. He wasn't happy.

"What was that?" Cash said, leaning against the locker next to mine. His tone was colored with disbelief. Some guy with red hair, pimples, and green eyes—I think his name was Sean—tried to get in the locker that Cash was blocking.

"Tell your teacher that your dog ate your homework, buddy. I'm not moving," Cash responded to the poor kid, who just wanted to get his books. The kid's eyes darted between Cash and me before his body ran away, scared.

"Was that necessary?" I huffed.

Cash raised his brow. "You tell me. What's gotten into you? You can't go to a high school party."

When I didn't answer, he put his hands on my shoulders and spun me toward him. Sparks flew from the weight of his touch, sending that persistent hum through my veins. My blood turned to liquid lava, and I flinched. I sucked in a deep breath and removed his hands, finger by finger.

"You can't tell me what to do. You guys are leaving soon. It'll be good for me to make new friends. Come to the party and guard me there." I slammed my locker.

"Umm, see you guys after school," Darla said, scurrying away from us. Can't say I blamed her.

"That's what this is about." He ran his hand through his hair, and frustration rolled off him like thunderclouds, "You know how you sound?"

I crossed my arms over my chest. "Like a girl who's tired of being locked up in her own house," I huffed.

"No. Like a child." As if that was a physical blow, I reeled back. But he didn't stop there. "You think this is a joke? You think I like knowing people want you captured or dead?"

Anger ignited in my core. "I don't know," I yelled, releasing my hands down by my sides and curling my fingers into balls of anger.

Cash's jaw popped. "Do you think I want bad things to happen to you? That I want you to be upset with me?"

The bell rang and I started toward class. Cash was in front of me before I took my second step. His body was so close, I could feel his breath on my nose. "You don't understand."

"No, I don't but it's not like you guys tell me anything," I shouted. The empty halls carried my voice louder than I intended.

"What do you want me to say, do? What will make you feel better?" Cash said. His tone softened, but his face didn't.

I turned away. Tears pricked my eyes. Cash caught my wrist and whirled me around. A single sob released, and I knew if I didn't pull away now, I wouldn't be able to stop. The look in Cash's eyes said he understood, so he tugged me in closer, crushing me against him. Without warning, I burst into tears.

"I'm sorry. I never wanted to hurt you," he whispered.

I should have broken our embrace, protected my emotions, but I couldn't. Being in his arms felt like coming home. I rested my head against his chest and wrapped my arms around his waist. Through my tears, I felt his heart beating against my cheek. I memorized its rhythm. I didn't want him to leave. Or the rest of them, for that matter. These five aliens had squirmed their way into my heart; it was breaking into little pieces, knowing I would have to let them go.

Finally, I lifted my head, leaving my hands resting on Cash's chest. The gentle drum of his heartbeat pulsated under my palms, filling me with warmth. With tear-ridden eyes and a moist face, I asked, "Do you want to leave?"

Cash sighed, pulling me back into his embrace. His hand smoothed down my back while his chin rested on my head.

His pulse danced frantically, but he never answered my question.

Practice was rougher than I had imagined. Cash worked me so hard that I actually wanted to quit at one point. He showed me how to get out of a chokehold like the one Grouper had me in, how to use my surroundings as weapons, and how to take advantage of my opponent's weaknesses.

"No quitting," he barked.

I sent a roundhouse kick to his head, which he effort-lessly blocked. "You think you can take me?" Cash asked. His voice held the air of confidence I wanted to beat out of him.

"Ya know what, maybe one day I will be able to. And what will you do then, Mr. Show-off?" I said through pant-ing breaths. I threw a left jab at his face, and he spun around, ending up behind me. He dropped to the ground and swiped my legs out from underneath me, sending me straight to the mats and knocking the air out of my lungs. Jumping to his feet in one quick, fluid motion, Cash ex-tended his hand. "You never know! One day you may."

I put my hand in his and accepted his help to stand.

"And if it ever does, I will be the first to commend you."

I got back into my stance "Yeah, yeah, stop patronizing me."

We went again and again. I groaned and he smiled, a pattern we repeated for the next three hours while sweat dripped around me on the mat, pooling in rain-like puddles. Cash hardly perspired, which I found incredibly annoying.

Finally, around eight, practice ended, and I went home to shower and get ready for the party.

Kathleen's house was on several acres on top of a hill. From the outside it looked like a Victorian mansion with pointed peaks, bay windows, and a wraparound porch. But in the back, where the party was in full swing, it was modern. Trees lined the walkway to the heated inground pool. Cabanas with trays of food were set up for guests, and an outdoor bar area with a dozen stools was manned by two bartenders making mocktails. She had a donut wall, chocolate-tiered fondue waterfall, and two women in cupcake skirts. It was the oddest high school party I'd ever been to, but also the coolest.

Chris, Darla, Sammie, Tasha, Mark, Paul, Cash, and I showed up to the party together taking an Uber XL, but most of the kids drove their own cars, pulling them onto the grass. We hadn't been there for five minutes when I heard metal crushing.

Grouper landed on top of the car right in front of me, and I screamed. Glass shattered from the window. Cash ran to my side, his body protectively blocking mine. Sammie grabbed Chris. Tasha seized Darla. Mark and Paul flanked them.

Cash's right hand swallowed mine while his other hand was held up toward the party. Everyone was frozen. I hadn't seen him do this since the day we first met.

"Ah, fancy party trick, Cash," Grouper said, motioning toward the other kids. "A trick I'm sure you are glad to have back?" He smiled.

Back? Cash lost this power once? Or this specific power?

"Didn't know you liked human parties, or have you come back to fondle me some more? I told you I wasn't interested. What is it with bugs? When a guy says no, he means no," Cash said wickedly.

A distracted Grouper stood stock-still, staring at me as he ignored Cash's digs. It was as if he was looking at me for the first time, and not like we'd met before. Something about his gaze was different, almost empathetic. I wondered if he knew how we were related.

For a second, he closed his eyes and the night sky darkened. When he opened them, he said, "Your pretty shell is something I would consider, if this wasn't a professional visit. I have some information worth sharing." Grouper raised one of his bulb eyes and it flickered like a strobe light as he eyed Chris and Darla like prey. If his tongue wasn't split, he probably would have licked his lips. "Ohhhh, how many human pets are you playing with tonight?" Grouper said rubbing his pale and scaly skin hands together. Goo dripped onto the car he stood on.

"What the hell is that?" Chris muttered in the background. One of the others shushed him.

A rich, hearty noise, possibly a laugh, escaped Grouper's mouth. Web-like slime shot across the grass. Ewww.

"Have you learned anything child?" Grouper pointed to me. I scrunched my brows and inched to the side. I wouldn't give him access to my neck again, but I was curious . . . and Cash did call him an ally.

When I didn't answer, Grouper continued. "Do you know who you are?"

"Grouper, enough. What's your intel?" Cash said, leaning his weight to the right, where I stood. "I've been polite, but you're trying my patience."

Out of the corner of my eyes, I watched the others get into position. Behind them, Darla and Chris huddled together, Chris appearing on edge as if ready to jump to my rescue in a heartbeat. My own heart pumped so fast I was afraid it would burst from my chest. Wasn't Grouper a friend? It didn't feel that way.

"No need to get sassy with me. I come bearing gifts of information."

"I can't wait," Cash said. Even from where I stood, I could see the edges of his mouth form his notorious, cocky grin. I had those lips memorized. It was the same smug expression he flashed at me when I dared him. Funny, how opposition excited Cash. He was like an adrenaline junky or something.

Grouper stared at me again. The silence was getting awkward.

"You are testing my tolerance. Either spit it out or leave," Cash demanded, bringing Grouper's eye contact back to him.

"Calm down. We all know the mighty Cash Kingston loves a good fight. From what I hear, your father is extremely disappointed in your lack of enthusiasm to take the throne. You would think that being the leader of a planet would be so much more fitting for that huge ego of yours." Grouper's nostrils flared, and moisture leaked out. His skin shimmered from the goo that cloaked his fake human flesh. Ick. Bugs were so gross, but this one took vulgar to a whole nother level.

"That's not the only huge thing I have." Cash snorted.

"Seriously," I whispered. "Are you flirting with him?"

Cash turned his head and winked at me. I rolled my eyes. Only Cash could make this into a joke.

"What do you call the child?" Grouper asked. His curious eyes landed back on me. He wouldn't stop staring. It was like he was memorizing my features. He started at my hair and moved to my eyes, ears, nose, lips, chin . . . not in a perverted way, but curiously.

"I doubt she wants you calling her at all." Cash responded more smugly than before, if that was even possible.

Grouper's eyes burned a bright yellow orange, like flames. Whoa, not what I was expecting. "You think you are so cute." His voice grew with anger. "Does she know what Faye did? Does she know who she is?"

"What?" I shouted. My mother—it always went back to my mother. What had she done other than surgically implant an alien's energy source in my chest? The others inched closer to me, caging me in. Cash squeezed my hand for comfort. A foreboding feeling crept up my spine.

Grouper smiled—well, I thought it was a smile. "I didn't think so. Anyway, about that news." The calm had returned to his voice. "The energy source's mother is in town. She's not happy about *her*. Although I am positive she doesn't know everything," Grouper said, seeming almost relieved.

Cash nodded, as if they shared some private thought.

"Gertrude is here?" Tasha asked, stepping forward. The others seemed to relax as well, except for Sammie, who was still attached to Chris's body. For reasons other than guarding him, I was sure. But Chris seemed more focused on me. I could almost feel the tension rolling off of him in waves. If I turned around, I'd surely see his eyes bugging out of his head in confusion over what was going on.

"Yes," Grouper said, plopping down from the car's roof. His legs dangled. His periwinkle socks peeked out from under his barely-fitting navy blue corduroy pants. Who wore corduroy anymore?

"With or without the DOAA's knowledge?" Mark asked, positioning himself next to Tasha.

"With, but they think she's here for planetary relations meetings, not for her daughter's source. She thinks the council is up to no good. Gertrude wants her daughter's energy source back . . . as, I'm sure, so do you, Cash."

Cash slightly winced while his hand tightened around mine. My stomach twisted into a knot as my fingers trembled in Cash's grip. Why did Grouper say it like that? Why would Cash want the energy source? Was it personal to him?

"Gertrude only asked to extract the energy source and bring it home to Ferro. Unlike the council, who would probably kill the child to obtain the source, Gertrude is willing to do it without harm to the girl," Grouper said. "Quite simple, really."

I moved around Cash. When he didn't stop me, I assumed I was safe. My hand stayed inside of his, of course. My bravery only went so far.

"Do you know why my mother would implant an energy source in me?" My voice wavered.

"You sweet, little thing." Grouper shook his head. His focus left me for a second to gaze at Cash. They shared a thought and Cash nodded, as if he understood. Their relationship was bizarre. Like frenemies. "I have my theories, but they would just create more questions—a string of useless queries that none alive could answer. And the pain those questions would cause would outweigh the truth of why she did what she did."

"I don't understand." I never did.

Grouper snorted. "Does she know whose energy source she harbors?"

Cash gave a slight shake of his head and said, his voice dark and dangerous, "Tell Gertrude no."

"Don't be a fool. Gertrude will do right by the girl. She will return to Ferro with the source and will not reveal where it was hidden. The DOAA will have no proof once the source is extracted and Ferro will not have any reason to harm the child," Grouper said, shaking his head like a slobbery dog. Gook flew across the car. "Her terms are reasonable." His always-playful voice turned cold.

"I said no, and you can tell her she'll have to go through me to get it," Cash said.

"I don't understand. We are running out of time. The DOAA knows the source is in Cartwright. The Ferroan Council has been alerted to the news, as well, and has given a short timeline for the source's return with specific instructions to use force if necessary. If you want to keep the child alive, Gertrude may be your only hope." There was a long pause. "Unless you have already spoken to Zane, and there's something I don't know," Grouper said with a raised brow.

"Gertrude cannot have the source. And do me the favor of telling her the source belongs to our planet, not to one being," Cash challenged.

Grouper matched Cash's stare. "If you were being honest with yourself, I'd say those words are meant for you." He sighed. "If you love her, and I mean both of them, you will set them free. For neither is yours to have as well."

I had no idea what Grouper meant, but my throat knotted, and I fought back tears. The hum inside of me vibrated like a plucked guitar string.

"Cash," Mark said, his voice rose. "I thought we were to remove the source."

Cash avoided Mark's eye contact. "Zane wants us to keep Bea and the source safe. There will be no removal. Beatrice will harbor the opposing source. It's already running through her veins. She is intended to connect to the opposing source to destroy the asteroids."

"I knew it!" Sammie said shaking her head back and forth.

"Are you serious?" Mark moved closer toward his sister.

Cash ignored them all.

Grouper stood. His eyes flared as his fist curled. Ooze dripped from his knuckles to the floor. This guy needed to be wrapped in gauze. Then I remembered that the stinky substance raining from Grouper reminded me of something. It was from the first day I met Cash and the others, when ooze trickled from my car like sap from a tree. Had that been from him? Or was there another rogue bug?

"I will take your message back, but do not be fooled, this isn't over. Gertrude will come for her regardless of Zane's command. And unless Zane has shared his objectives with the Ferro Council, they too will come for her. The DOAA might not be a threat to you but they have a naughty list, and you are at the top. Remember what the child means to me, as well. I cannot let anything happen to her. Igniting the source . . ." Grouper shook his head. "It's dangerous!"

"I know. We will take care of her. Neither I, nor my team, will fail. It is at the request of King Kingston and Faye Walker to keep the source inside of Beatrice and to keep her safe. I will obey it as I have taken an oath to protect my kingdom, my people, and our sources."

Grouper shook his head. "Your flame may have turned to coal, but no one forgets what you are. One day you will have to become what you were created for. It is not a choice—it is your destiny. I hope you can live with these decisions."

Cash's entire body stiffened. His neck and shoulders appeared to have grown. The only movement came from the clenching and unclenching of his fists, which were thrust down by his sides.

"It is her bloodline that cursed her, not my decisions."

Grouper growled. His Adam's apple pulsated against his creped skin where secretion ran down, absorbing into his collar.

"Be that as it may. Your decisions define you. Gertrude will come after you, dear boy. The child is all but a weapon of war!"

"I'll be ready!"

Chapter Twenty-Five

Beatrice

The wake of Grouper's visit was no less tense than his presence. Cash started spewing out orders. Sammie was in charge of the humans. Chris's face paled with a tint of green at the mention of being human. He looked like he might puke as Darla and Sammie ushered him into the car. Cash agreed to let them update Chris on what had been going on, but Chris and Darla needed to be returned home. Sammie was told to expedite the trip and her explanation. Cash figured it would be easier than Influencing Chris, since his mind was filled with solid doubt.

Paul and Mark were in charge of finding Robert.

Tasha and I were escorted back to my house where I had strict instructions to stay seated on the couch and refrain from talking, which was fine by me. My entire body, mind, and mouth were numb.

Cash paced in front of the fireplace.

"Cash," Tasha said in a low voice. Her eyes closed briefly.

"Not until Robert is back," Cash said, answering whatever Tasha must have asked him in their minds. She sighed, releasing not only air, but her shoulders.

I sat paralyzed, staring into space. I had so many questions, and yet I had no idea where to start. It was as if my body was there, but my mind was drifting somewhere else. It wasn't until my dad walked in that I snapped back into reality.

"Beatrice, honey, are you okay?" my dad asked, kneeling down in front of me. His face was strained and colorless.

Everything came into focus, as if the clouds had parted to a clear, blue sky. "Sure, Dad, just peachy. The DOAA knows where we are. The Ferroean Council does as well. And I'm pretty sure that, according to the bug who drooled slime on some poor rando's car, the energy source's mommy wants to perform god knows what surgery on me to get it back. Yeppers, I'm just great." I stood and everything started to snowball at once. "Their leader, father, whatever he is"—I pointed toward Cash and Tasha—"wants this alien organ to stay inside of me and 'ignite' it against an asteroid that pretty much threatens to kill everybody in the world and apparently another planet. I mean, this is my body and yet I'm sharing it with something—no, someone—else." I started to pace. My breathing picked up, causing me to take desperate sips of air just to speak. "I mean, what the hell is actually inside of me, and how is it running through my veins? Oh my god, can the alien kill me from within?" I started to scratch my body.

"No," Cash said, looking at me cross-eyed. "It's not like that. The alien, as you call it, died. Her energy source is what Faye saved, not her being. She was murdered."

My fingers furled into my palms, pressing into my skin. I sucked in a deep, calming breath and ordered myself to keep it together. "I'm sorry for her, I really am, but can someone please explain in more detail? I want to know whose energy source I have inside me so when I run into her mom, I can be a little more prepared. I don't blame the mom for being mad and wanting her daughter's alien part back."

Mark and Paul walked through the door and quietly seated themselves on the couch. Tension flowed through the air, weighing on my chest like stacked bricks. My gaze darted back and forth between Cash and my father.

"You want details? Fine. No one told you whose energy source you harbor because I asked them not to," Cash said, shoving his hands into his jeans.

"Okay, why?" I asked.

Cash's beautiful face paled and grimaced. Uneasiness slithered in my stomach and I felt nauseous. The hum inside of me hissed violently, like a bug zapper.

"Seraphina, a guard who originally came with us to Earth—"

"Wait a minute," I cut him off. That name sounded familiar. *Oh my god, oh my god.* "Your ex-girlfriend, who supposedly died in a car accident in California?"

"How do you know that?" my dad asked.

"Chris and Darla." I waved off my father and continued. "I have your ex-girlfriend's energy source floating in my chest? Is she an ex-girlfriend, or a pretend girlfriend like Sammie?"

Cash thrust his hands through his hair. He sighed so loudly that I doubted any air lingered in his lungs. "Yes, she was my girlfriend, my *real* girlfriend." Cash pinched the arch of his nose and closed his eyes. My heart bottomed out. His real girlfriend?

His voice wavered as he spoke the next words. "Why didn't you say anything about her if you knew from Darla and Chris?" he asked.

"Well, I was going to, but I got distracted. I never really had the chance to bring her up again. Plus, it's not like we sat down and had the "ex" conversation. I figured she was like Sammie, a cover story for your mission. I mean, I never told you about my first kiss with Troy."

"Troy? Who's Troy?" Cash asked. His eyes narrowed.

I groaned. "Does that matter? All I am saying is we never talked about it. Why do I happen to have your ex-girl-friend's energy source? And how did she die? Since clearly it wasn't in a car accident with her aunt in California." I crossed my arms in disgust of the lie my friends knew about.

"I have no idea how she died, or how Faye took her energy source and planted it in you. None of us do. I have a thousand questions for your mother."

I barely heard Cash talk about my mother. The light in my head went off. His real girlfriend had one of the two opposing sources, which meant . . . I glared at Cash—like really glared. Son of a . . . I didn't even have to say anything. He knew I knew. His gaze lifted, his eyes meeting mine.

My voice was swallowed up by the current of air as I shot out of the recliner. "You." My voice grew louder as I forced my vocal cords to obey. "It's you," I yelled. A dense dread assembled within me, a slow simmer of foreboding alongside the rapid boil of anger rising inside my core. I had been lied to. Again. My heart pounded in my chest, almost deafening my own voice. "You are the opposing source."

"Yes. I am," Cash said as he walked closer to me, his shoulders tense. "The bond is caused by the electrostatic force of attraction between opposite charges. Together, our sources can sustain a planet."

"You kept this from me. Why?" I shouted at him.

"Faye sent me a message to protect her daughter. She never said why or explained anything else. She didn't even tell me your name. We had no idea that Seraphina's energy source was implanted in you. All we knew was that it was missing. Our entire planet could be destroyed without it—so could yours," Cash continued. With each word, he stepped closer to me. The others followed, caging me like an animal about to run out of the gate. They all knew this whole time, and no one had told me. Anger rose inside of me.

"Why did my mom do this to me?" I breathed, not even sure if the words came out of my mouth. Blood rushed through my veins at a violent speed, making my heart falter.

"I'm not sure, other than the fact she was trying to protect the source and the planets. When I saw you by your locker the first day we were back at Cartwright, I knew Seraphina's source was inside you. We are connected. It's why your body reacts to me like an electric charge. The closer we are, the stronger the bond. The more powerful we become."

Cash grabbed my wrist, pulling me forward. The prickly humming hovered over my skin, piercing me like a series of tiny needles. An invisible thread wrapped around me, connecting me to him. And then veins by my ankles and wrists elevated. What the . . .

"Oh my god, is that what this is?" I looked down at his hand, which enveloped mine. The torrent of blood swelled where his fingers curled. "What I'm feeling? Is that why, when you touch me, my whole body stirs with energy? It's her energy source connecting with yours, isn't it?" The horror of my realization sent bile to my throat. I thought I might puke all over the carpet.

"Yes and no," Cash said, flustered, releasing his grip. He eyed his hand with anger.

"Yes and no? Which is it?"

I looked at my father. What kind of father—no, forget that—what type of mother used her daughter as a human incubator for an alien life-form? I didn't care that its power could break a planet in two. What mattered was that my own mother had done this to me. A strange sensation trickled down my arms toward my fingers, causing them to warm uncontrollably. It matched the heat building in my chest, and when I tried to clench my fists together, the sensation only grew in intensity. The room started to rumble. The knick-knacks on the mantle, the tables—shaking and rattling as if by an unseen vibration.

"Bea," my father said, moving parallel to Cash. His eyes were wide with fear as a framed family photo toppled over.

"You!" I pointed at my father. "That's why you gave Cash so much control. You felt guilty for what Mom did to him. I'm still your daughter, and yet you let him"—I pointed to Cash—"dictate my life!"

"I did feel guilty. I still do. Cash has to fight his natural instincts to not feed from you. But that's not why I let Cash be so involved. Protecting you is our number one concern. And the source. Cash is the most powerful Ferroean other than Sera." My father's voice was stern, but his face revealed his pain. "You need to listen."

I waved him off. "Listen to what?" I eyed the group of people standing before me, whom I had regarded as friends. "Cash's ex-girlfriend is inside of me. You all knew about this, and no one had the decency to tell me. My whole body responds to Cash like it's under some magic love spell, or recently, like I'm being struck by lightning." I stared around the room.

Cash grabbed my arm and the buzzing inside of me shot up from my toes to my head. I keeled over in pain. "Great! And now your ex is trying to blow up my head." I wrapped my arm around my waist as I bent over. Cash knelt down next to me as my stomach jerked back, and I heaved all over the floor.

The buzzing in my head was so powerful that it took me with it. The edges of my vision darkened as I crumbled to the floor.

"Mark, your dagger!" Cash demanded.

The last thing I remembered was Cash slicing my wrist. The cold knife tore my skin apart. My eyes closed. Moist lips covered the cut, gently suctioning at the open skin until it all went dark.

Chapter Twenty-Six

Beatrice

Monday at school, I was a mess. Books fell out of my locker, tumbling to the ground, while I pressed my palms into the sides of my head. The pain sliced through my temples. I've never had a migraine before, but I imagined this is what it felt like.

"You okay?" Darla asked while wincing in my direction.

"No," I snapped as I shook my head. Sammie bent down with me to retrieve my stuff. I could feel the weight of her apprehensive stare as she eyed my new necklace. The colors had been a tornado of swirling hues.

"Cash give you that?" Sammie asked.

"Yes, he said it would monitor the source inside me." I picked up my books and shoved them back into the locker. Every bone in my body ached. I reached for my notebook.

Sammie placed her hand over mine and whispered, "Take deep breaths, okay?" I nodded and concentrated on my breathing. In through the nose, out through the nose.

I stuffed the notebook into my satchel and twisted toward Darla. "Sorry! I know you are trying to help."

"It's okay," she answered with a meek smile. "Hey, at least no Coach Barb sneaking up on you this morning since we have an assembly instead of English. That's a nice relief. That woman is like a fly at a picnic!"

I forced a laugh while fixing the picture of my mother in my locker. The tape had been adjusted and a honey-colored glue residue coated the ends of photograph. I took the picture off and rubbed the substance between my fingers. I'd felt this before. Wait a minute. The first day the aliens came to town! This was the substance on my car. And Grouper. It was the goo that dripped from his limbs.

"Grouper," I whispered.

"What?" Sammie said, whirling around.

Darla and Sammie crowded me into my locker. "What?" Darla exclaimed. I showed them the picture and the ooze on the ends of it. Sammie held it to her nose and inhaled.

"Damn it," she hissed, handing me back the photograph. "It's not Grouper's smell. It's another rogue Ferroean."

"Darla, don't let her out of your sight in the auditorium. I'm going to get the others." Sammie turned to me. "You okay?" she asked, cupping my shoulders. "If not, I will take you home right now. Just say the word."

"I'm fine," I said, breathing deeply.

Her eyes searched mine. "Are you sure? Whoever it is won't come into the school during sessions. It's too risky. Like Grouper, they aren't fully assimilated, and we could take them out instantly. You are safe here."

I nodded, swallowing the lump of fear in my throat. Darla looped her arm through mine. "I won't let anything happen to her," she said with resolve. Not that I thought Darla could take on an alien even with limited powers, but that girl would go down trying.

Darla guided me down the hall and around the corridor to the auditorium. We were already late, and everyone was seated inside. About three feet away from the door, a tall, dark figure blocked our path. It was most likely a teacher ready to ream us out for being late, but . . .

I did a double take as my heart pounded in my chest. The buzzing inside electrified, and I felt like my insides were on fire. The low hum in the right side of my chest spread like tendrils of an octopus throughout my body, encircling my rib cage. It snapped like a whip, wrapping itself around my organs in a big hug. Only one person, one being, could cause such a hypnotic reaction.

Cash.

Without thinking, I ran, throwing myself into his arms. He was caught off guard and stumbled backward but was able to keep me in his grip while balancing us both. His source beat against my chest, filling me with warmth and, for the first time, I understood how the source worked. Chest to chest, I could feel the connection to him. It was almost unexplainable. Like a magnet, we forged together. When pulled apart, it was like an uncompleted puzzle; a picture missing its other half. Uncontrollable tears cascaded down my face.

"I'm sorry," I said. His strong, capable hands held me tighter.

"Hey," Cash said, letting my feet gently touch the ground. He looked over my head at Darla. "I have her. Go ahead in." I didn't even turn to see her leave. The world around me disappeared, and there was only us.

"I'm so sorry. I . . ." I couldn't finish my sentence. I pressed my cheek against his chest, allowing the hum of his source calm my sprinting pulse.

His hands ran through my hair while his chin rested on my head. We stayed in that position for several seconds. Finally, he pulled my face back, and our eyes met. His red, purple, and green hurricane irises swirled around his pupils. His hands cupped my cheeks while his thumbs brushed away my tears. Each warm stroke sent shivers to my skin.

"Why are you sorry? You have nothing to apologize for." The soft, smooth sound of his voice undid me.

"How I acted . . . it was stupid. And childish." I looked up and into his eyes. "I understand why you kept Sera from me. I wish you hadn't, but I do understand."

His eyes dipped from mine and found my necklace. Words echoed from his mind. *For the Flesh craves what is contrary to the Source, and the Source what is contrary to the Flesh.*

He flinched and dropped his hands from my face. The withdrawal of his touch chilled my insides, and I reached out. But he stepped back and said, "It's the energy source. I've never seen anything so strong before."

"What does it mean?"

He thought the words again as if he didn't know they were loud enough for me to hear. *For the Flesh craves what is contrary to the Source, and the Source what is contrary to the Flesh.*

Out loud, he said, "It means if your source was removed, the magnetic pull between us would be gone."

I shook my head. "I know we are drawn together by these alien parts but it's not just that."

Cash ran his hand through his hair, looking everywhere but at me.

My heartbeat accelerated as the electricity ran like a current through my limbs. I could actually visualize the light mixing into the blood in my veins. My body was changing. Seraphina's energy source was flooding throughout me, yet my mind and body were still under my control. Every emotion I had weaved in and out of my insides, threading together into three words. I sucked in a breath.

"I love—"

Cash cut me off.

"Don't," he warned. Cash's body tensed. The veins and muscles in his neck throbbed. He stared at me for what seemed like forever. I had never wished to hear thoughts more in my entire life than at that moment. What was Cash thinking? And, just as quickly as I was about to ask, he blurted out, "You don't feel that way. It's the energy sources pulling us together. It's fake. Like our relationship." His voice was low and dangerous—angry, almost.

I jerked my head back. The buzzing in my veins retracted, slipping from my limbs into my very center. "No, it's not," I argued, hating the withdrawal of the source. "It can't be. I don't just feel it running through me. I feel it here." I grabbed his hand and held it over my heart. My pulse beat wildly. It was true. I did feel the energy source within me, but I also felt my own heart and soul. Both were on the same page. Both loved Cash.

He closed his eyes for the longest time, but when they opened, they were void of any emotion. The colors had disappeared, leaving a human blue iris in their wake. The lines around his mouth tightened as he grabbed my shoulders.

"Listen to me. Seraphina's energy source is in you, and that is what has created this pull. Beatrice Walker does not love me and never will. Do you understand?" His venomous tone stung like a scorpion. My hand fell away as I swallowed back emotions.

"You're telling me you don't feel anything for me? Nothing?" I pulled out of his grip and wrapped my arm around my stomach. The ache of his words reached deep. The electricity wasn't even present. It had recoiled into my chest, like a retreating dog that's misbehaved.

A muscle in his jaw twitched. "This is not love. It's the source. The sooner you accept that, the easier it will be. We have a mission." The coldness in his tone turned my blood to ice. My heart broke into a thousand pieces. I'm not sure I was even breathing. I just stared at him.

"Then why did you kiss me?" A sharp ache twisted inside my chest.

Cash closed his eyes as if trying to erase the memories. "I was feeding." He paused, clearing his throat. "I need to feed."

Pain and white-hot anger sliced through me. "Wow. Are you serious right now?"

"I never lie." He deadpanned. It's true. He never outright lied to me. Yes, he used me. Yes, he withheld the truth at times. Yes, he was an arrogant asshat. But he never lied to my face.

"This feeling is the source," Cash repeated. "Even now you have no idea. That necklace is a tool indicating the truth. Before I walked up to you, I bet it was black onyx but look at it now."

My gaze traveled down. The blade had turned into a thousand colors like Cash's eyes when he felt emotion.

"What does that mean?"

"The source is yearning for a connection. It wants what the flesh does not. Your source wants me."

"What?"

Cash grabbed my hand with a little more force than normal. "Watch!" he said and I stared as the colors melted into one another and turned into a reddish purple. "The source is violently trying to get to me."

He flipped my arm over and held it in his grasp. With the other hand he reached into this boot and pulled out a thermo dagger. "The pain must be from excess source inside of you. If we don't release some of it, you'll die." He muttered what I thought sounded like, *or kill someone.*

"This won't hurt. It will help with your pain." He sliced my wrist. I watched as my human blood and a yellow gooey substance released together and pooled onto the floor. I staggered back, almost unable to keep my balance. Pain flickered in Cash's eyes as he lowered his mouth to my wrist and gently pressed his lips around the cut. I shut my lids and inhaled deep breaths, expanding my rib cage with air. Warmth crept slowly in, soothing my skin and releasing tension in my head. The pain was gone.

He grabbed the bottom of his shirt and wiped away the remnants of moisture on my skin. He then interlaced his fingers through mine; heat penetrated my palm while a soft white glow appeared in between our hands. The deep cut receded but wasn't completely healed.

"It takes longer for you to heal when you are cut from a thermo dagger."

He let out a long sigh.

"I think it's in your best interest to be protected by my team while I work closer with the King on the next steps. They will watch the necklace and proceed like I did to relieve your pain while I go back to California and work with the Ferro Council and DOAA on a plan for your connection to my source."

"How will you feed?" I asked.

"I'll manage." He shoved his hands in his pockets.

"Do you want to leave?" I prayed he didn't answer.

"I do," he said, his face stoic.

He turned toward the main door and made it about five steps before hearing the words I threw into his head.

I hate you!

He pivoted around, yet his hand held onto the door handle.

"You need to start blocking your thoughts. Think the word 'blank', imagine a white or black canvas, or hum a tune in your head. These mind tricks will keep your thoughts blocked from any Ferroean. It'll take practice but in time it will be second nature. Your mother was exceptional at the craft of blocking her feelings and her words. I can only imagine you will follow in her footsteps since I believe you are extraordinary as well."

His eyes softened a bit, then he pushed the door open and was swallowed up by the outside.

I was left alone in the hallway with an emptiness so deep it stabbed my soul. I forced my body to move as I ran in the other direction, toward the gym doors. They were open and led to the sports ground.

In a daze, I sprinted through the parking lot, out to the empty field behind school. Running and running. The air chilled my skin. Raw pain overwhelmed me, and I doubled over. The headache was back not two minutes after Cash released the pain. I gazed down at the pendant. It was bright purple. I didn't understand. I thought when Cash fed, it would make this go away.

If I could just lie down . . . I staggered to a tree and curled into a ball at its roots. The dirt, branches, and stones provided a bed of comfort. I closed my eyes and a vision of my mother popped into my head, like all the other times but stronger.

"Bea, I don't have long. You need to listen to me." My mom's brows were lined with sweat and dipped with worry. *Oh god, sweetheart, I love you. There's so much I want to tell you. I wish I had more time. But remember this—I love you with all my heart. You are the most amazing gift life has given me. By now, you've met Cash. He's difficult but he's the only one who will help see this through. He's the only one who will understand. The key to our survival is to connect the sources. The prophecy is real. I know this is confusing, and I wish I could implant more into your memories, but we don't even know what you'll recall until you break these walls of salvation. The pain you feel is coming from fighting complete connection. You must connect flesh to flesh. Do not be afraid, be strong, and never forget . . . Crede Mihi."*

The vision cut out.

I blinked, frantically willing the image back, but nothing happened. Instead, a sharp pain carved through me like a butcher's knife, and I cried out. My head felt like it had split into two pieces, as if the skin on my scalp had ripped at the edges of my hairline. With the heel of my hand, I pressed into my temples, but nothing subsided. I curled into a ball and covered my eyes, drifting into darkness.

Chapter Twenty-Seven

Beatrice

My head felt heavy as I was lifted off the ground. Masculine arms wrapped around my limp body as I drifted in and out of consciousness. Warm breath stirred my hair, but my eyes stayed fastened.

When I finally woke, my lids stuck together as if someone had glued them shut. I struggled to pry them open. At first, shapes blurred together, plaguing my mind with a slight case of amnesia. Where was I? How did I get here? Who brought me here?

The floor was cold and the room dark. I pushed my hair from my face and found chucks of tresses tangled together in a honey-like goo. What the hell was I covered in? As my eyes adjusted to my surroundings, I gasped in horror. *Oh shit!*

"It's not so bad, child." It was a voice so familiar that the hairs on my arms stood at attention. Panic clawed at my throat as my scream died between my clenched teeth.

"Grouper," I finally managed to whisper. I flattened my hands against the concrete bottom, pushing myself upright. My eyes focused on my surroundings.

"The one and only," he admitted from the large, rusted cage that was imprisoning him. It mirrored the one I was in. The silver crossbars were painted yellow and set just far enough apart that I could fit my hand and arm through, but not enough to escape past my shoulder. I looked up. The cage appeared to have been recently extended to the ceiling, with the top three feet bearing new material.

"Where are we? Why are we in cages?" I asked, pressing my back against the cold bars. The small room was empty, damp, and windowless. Layers of dust coated the floor. A lamp sat next to Grouper, illuminating him in a dingy glow. He rested on a folding chair inside his cell.

"Pennsylvania," he answered, chuckling.

"Not very informative," I grumbled. My heart flipped around in my chest like a fish out of water. This was *so* not good. I hoped someone would realize I was missing, and soon.

I forced a calming breath and attempted a different approach. "Why are you here?"

"Gertrude." He shrugged, flipping through a magazine. "She's kind of a bitch."

Gertrude? Seraphina's mother? "But I thought she was trying to help?" I pulled my knees into my chest. My jeans were covered in mud and gook.

"You and me both, little one. You and me both." He kicked his feet up onto the stool in front of him, and his periwinkle socks stuck out from his brown corduroy pants. What was up with his fashion sense?

I shook my head. "I really don't understand you."

"Sounds about right," Grouper said, folding his arms over his chest. Ooze dripped from his elbows, falling like the pitter-patter of raindrops against the floor.

"And what's with Cash and you? You are enemies, allies?"

Grouper kicked the stool, and it flung against his cage door. His dull eyes lit up like the Fourth of July. I scuttled back up against the bars, wishing for more space.

"We have a history," he snarled. "He's such a pissant that one. Gets my feathers ruffled, if you know what I mean?"

I folded my arms around myself. "Yeah, he's something," I sighed. "What's your history?"

Grouper shook his head. What might look like drool on a dog flung from his mouth, landing on the ground beside him.

"Love is so precarious," he said, returning to his seat. His bulbous eyes softened while his shoulders relaxed.

"You love him?" I asked. Not what I was expecting.

"No, sweet little half human. I do not love him, but love is why we are all in this mess," Grouper said in a singsong tone. God, I wished he would work on his communication. Could he give me one straight answer? Getting information from him was like parallel parking. It could take a million times before getting it right. Sometimes I'd just give up and find an easier spot. Wish I had that option with Grouper and his logic.

I slouched against the silver bars, reminiscing over my love confession to Cash earlier. The sharp ache of our last conversation carved through me, scraping away at my insides. He's going to be so pissed now that I had been captured. All of his hard work to keep me safe, and I had to go and muck it up.

Grouper's bulb eyes turned to a soft yellow glow, as if he had a dimmer switch on them. He leaned his elbows on his knees, bringing his head nearer as if he wanted to tell me a secret.

"Your love is mutual child. Do not listen with your ears, listen with your heart. Cash might say he doesn't love you, but his actions are those of a man who hungers for your love as much as he hungers for the source."

My eyes widened and, although this was not the time for a lesson on love, I couldn't help but wonder what Grouper was talking about. "I really don't know what you mean. I think you have me confused with someone," I said.

"The sacrifice Cash made for you was the utmost sacrifice; one of a man in love."

"What sacrifice?" I lifted myself up, clenching the bars so tightly that my knuckles whitened. My body was weakened from the headaches, but I didn't want to miss one word of whatever Grouper was about to tell me.

"To protect you, Cash had to return to the one person he hates the most and the one person who broke his heart. That pain is grief I know too well, and one I would never want my kind to experience."

My heart dropped into my chest as I slid down the cage, thudding to the floor. "Who? Who does he hate and who broke his heart?"

"His brother."

My brows shot up. "He doesn't have a brother." I went through all the times Tasha and he discussed their family. They spoke about their dad. I even heard Tasha mention her mother once, but not a brother. "Are you sure? How do you know this?" How could they have a sibling no one spoke about. I didn't believe Grouper.

"I'm an informant. I know almost everything." Grouper smiled.

Why would Cash conceal having a brother? And what would that have to do with loving me? To save myself from a Grouper riddle, I'd put this one on the back burner.

"We have to get out of here. We need a plan."

"No can do, child," he said. "No power can break these bars. They are designed to block our energy. That's what the yellow painted color is for. Smart move on the old bat's part!"

"Where is Gertrude?" But before Grouper could answer, a door opened, shedding a sliver of light into the dark, square room. My heart pounded, matching the clickety-clack of heels behind me.

"Right here," a raspy female voice said.

I spun in my suspended yellow birdcage, staring down at the most stunning woman I had ever seen. She was tall, with long legs like mine, but hers led up to curvaceous hips, a tiny waist, and a large bust like that of a 1950s pinup girl. Her eyes were bright blue, the color of turquoise, and her lips a luscious red, plump and full. Her sooty lashes fanned her eyes, while red, curly hair fell to her backside. She wore a formfitting, cream dress that dipped into her cleavage and matching cream stiletto heels. She was drop-dead gorgeous and she was . . .

"No," I whispered. My hand covered my mouth. It couldn't be. My voice faltered as I met her gaze. "How is this possible?" Coach Barb? Darla will piss herself when she finds out she was right! And if she saw her without her tracksuit and running sneakers, she would be impressed. This woman was a goddess, barely recognizable as my track coach.

"I'm flattered by the compliment. I hated having to dress down my pretty shell to wear a whistle, striped sweats, and a baseball cap. How revolting! It's nice getting all dolled up and being my fiery self. Some heels, a dress, a little makeup and . . . ta-da," she said, gesturing to her sexy body.

She was a Ferroean! Holy shit balls!

"You seem to have acquired my daughter's energy source, and your time keeping it is up," she chuckled, rounding the cage. Her long fingernails flicked each bar as she passed. My eyes and body followed her movements. I can't believe she had been under my nose this whole time. No wonder she avoided the gang. They would have known who she was.

Gertrude was Coach Barb.

As Seraphina's mother stood in front of me, I wondered what type of relationship she had with Cash. Probably not significant now, but I was still curious. It seemed so surreal to meet an adult from Ferro, especially the mother of Cash's ex-girlfriend.

"We hated each other, if you really must know," Gertrude said while examining her nails. She appeared bored with our conversation.

Damn, she read minds as annoyingly as the others did. "Why?" I asked.

"Well, for one thing, Cash doesn't appreciate power, and I find that rather a poor use of a good position. Not to mention, I blame him for my daughter's death, so of course I don't like him."

"Cash didn't have anything to do with your daughter's death," I snapped.

She laughed darkly. "Is that what you think? Oh, dear child, Seraphina would still be alive had it not been for Cash. They were never supposed to be apart. So, truthfully, Cash's actions killed her. The plan was to kidnap them both, but when my men showed up, Cash wasn't there, and Sera was dead. They delivered her to the DOAA and retreated to our safe house. There was no DOAA meeting for her to attend. It was all a setup."

I felt my blood boil in my veins, but Grouper was the first to fire a response. "You were going to kidnap Cash? And do what with him?" Grouper stood from his chair. More ooze dripped from his appendages. *Oh hell!* Even bugs didn't like when their frenemies had been betrayed.

"Yes, I just said that. Are you hard of hearing, Bug?" Gertrude asked with an exasperated tone. "I needed both of their energy sources. I wouldn't have harmed my daughter or your dear Cash, but I would have brought their celestial butts back to Ferro and held them captive until it was time to weaponize them." She held up her pointer finger, tapping the air. "But you see, someone found out about my plan and, instead, killed my daughter." Gertrude came closer to my cage. Her approach sent me skittering backward. Her skin was a golden hue—beautiful—as if she'd rolled around in gold dust. Coach Barb always looked dull and tired. But her eyes were a blistering blue, singeing into me like she would on the track when she yelled at us to hustle faster.

"Now . . ." Her finger-tapping migrated to her chin. Her red, pointed nails flashed like a stoplight off the ceiling illumination. "Who has the power and the means to kill a highly trained guard and make it look like an accident?"

"You think Cash?" I quipped.

"No. That boy was lovestruck when it came to my Sera. But same family . . . higher on the food chain." She hummed.

"The King?" Grouper questioned.

Gertrude winked. "Sounds about right. Don't you think?"

"You're mad," Grouper hollered.

"Just the opposite, Bug. I'm rational and driven by power. The only thing the King and I have in common is that we want supremacy. The oncoming asteroid gives me the perfect opportunity to rule within Ferro. But to do that, Ferro cannot fall. I can't have Earth being a priority over my own planet. You are nothing but inferior beings."

My jaw dropped to the floor. She accused Cash's father of murder and now wanted to rule his planet? What a crazy bitch!

"I don't understand you," I shook my head.

"I'm not really surprised," she said blandly. "You don't seem very perceptive. Although, you were my favorite runner." A bored sigh escaped her lips. "Not that you had much competition. Sad track program at your school." She continued walking around my cage, eyeing me like a child peering into a candy shop. "It does amaze me that none of your friends have figured it out. They really should be thanking me for this."

"I'm sure they will show their thanks when they end you," Grouper responded. His fists clenched and unclenched at his sides. Excretion trickled to the floor and echoed. "And how are you planning on getting the energy source out of Beatrice now?"

"I'm going to kill her," she said with a look so devoid of emotion that even I didn't believe it.

Grouper roared and gook flung from his mouth. I swallowed, unable to speak. This crazy woman was serious.

"Calm down," Gertrude said, waving off Grouper. "I don't know why you really care. She's nothing to you, right?" She poked at him with her words and a devilish smile. "I mean, it's not like she's flesh and blood, as these humans call it."

Grouper shook his head. "How long have you known?"

"Like many, I had a theory about Faye's past, but it wasn't until you showed your cards that it was confirmed. A bug caring for a human girl," she laughed. "That's absurd." Her one eyebrow rose incredibly high, almost touching her hairline. "Unless he has a reason."

Gertrude's focus returned to me. Her red hair flung over her shoulder, and her eyes narrowed. The air was sucked out of the room. I couldn't breathe.

"Your mother wasn't as smart as she thought. Oh, thinking back to the days we sparred, and I never won. If I only knew they were experimenting on her, and she held some of our powers, I wouldn't have been so pissed. She thought you'd be the answer. Do you know you were designed for this?"

"Designed for what?" I slid back, away from Coach Barb. My shoulders pressed against the cage. The cool metal bit at my exposed skin.

"Designed to save Earth," she snickered. "A Blood-Light prophesized for greatness."

I frowned. Her words were like a game, random and ridiculous.

"Your mother had small traces of Ferroean lineage from long ago. So miniscule, she didn't have enough to be a Blood-Light, but she was a candidate for an experimental procedure. They combined the alloy flowing in our Ferroean veins with her blood, and like a dialysis machine, they resynthesized it and put it back into her veins. The experiments started before Faye was pregnant. The alloy was already flowing in her blood stream when she found out about you. And since your father is one of the five original Ferroean descendants, you my dear, sweet, pathetic girl, are more Ferroean than human. You just weren't born with a source." She continued to stalk my cage, never taking her eyes off me. "So, your mother and father had a theory, a very farfetched theory based on rubbish from an elder. You'd be the key to saving Earth regardless of your opposing source. But you won't be able to save Ferro after all, and that's all I care about."

"I don't understand." It was a response I had said a lot these last couple of months.

Gertrude pressed her face up to the bars and seethed. "Something as disgusting as you should never have been created. It's a disrespect to our kind. You are nothing but a shell, designed by nature to store an energy source, not to ignite one. The thought of you is repulsive."

Heaviness clamped down on my chest as her words sunk in. My mother designed me to save one planet and let another be destroyed. That didn't add up. I might not know my mother as a DOAA agent, but I knew her as a person. She wouldn't sacrifice an entire world.

"I'd like to say it's been a pleasure, Beatrice, but I hate pretentious babble." She smiled. "Oh and thank you for keeping the Think Watch on. I knew it would pay off one day." With that, a splinter of light from the door appeared and disappeared, swallowing Gertrude up.

I gazed at Coach Barb's gift realizing it was how she tracked me. I removed it and threw it against the wall. I crawled closer to Grouper's cage and clung to the bars. My chest fluttered so fast my breath wheezed. "Is it true? I'm to save Earth, but not Ferro?" My voice was pleading.

Grouper scratched his bald head and swore under his breath. "I don't have the slightest idea, but if it is, you were designed as a weapon not a gift."

Chapter Twenty-Eight

Cash

Mark and Paul joined me back at the house to pack for California. We decided to keep the girls at Robert's and leave the safe house entirely, then destroy it before we left in the morning. I had questions and wanted answers. I also needed to stay away from Beatrice. Being around her made me want to feed without stopping. The yearning was unbearable. Until I learned the extent of her powers and why she was in pain so often, it wasn't safe.

I walked down the stairs with my suitcase, passing Mark and Paul on the way. Mark nodded in my direction.

"You keeping my knife?"

I reached for my boot as the door flung open. I crouched, ready for an attack.

"Cash! Cash!" Sammie screamed. "Where the hell are you? Bea is gone!" Sammie rounded the bend. "She's gone, Cash. Gone!"

I grabbed her by the shoulders, steadying her. "Calm down. What do you mean she's gone?"

Through panted breaths, she said, "There was a rogue Ferroean at Cartwright. I think it was Jon. I left to find the others, and when I came back to class, Darla said Bea never returned." Sammie pleaded, her eyes bloodshot red. "Don't be mad."

"I'm not mad at you." I released her shoulders. "I'm furious with myself. I should have walked her back to class." I pounded my fist into the wall, leaving a crater-sized dent. "Hell, I should have stayed with her."

"If Jon is here, that means he's with a council member," Mark said as he grabbed the car keys from the wall hook and pressed the car button twice, unlocking it. We all rushed out the door and into the sedan. "There's no memo of a council member traveling to Earth this month due to the high priority asteroids. Who is he here with?"

Jon used to be part of the guards until I kicked him out, but my dad said he could do private security for the council. Jon had a bad attitude and was an idiot. He had a brother, Phil, who followed him everywhere he went. Knuckleheads and morons if you asked me.

"I have no idea." But did I? I thought back to what my brother had said, *'You have no idea what Dad really does. He uses humans as experiments; pets and projects. He doesn't want to coexist with them. He wants to rule them!'* Was there any truth to that? And if there was, could Beatrice be an experiment like her mother?

I threw Mark's dagger back to him and asked, "How did you track Jon?"

He caught it in one hand and tilted his head. "You don't want it?"

"If I have it, I'll use it."

Mark slid the knife back into his boot.

"He was in Bea's locker. His scent was on the picture hanging up."

His scent? My nosed scrunched. "He's not assimilated? He's working as a bug outside the council's knowledge. Get me the picture. Let's track this asshole and hope he has answers to where Beatrice is, or so help me Council, today will be the day I intentionally kill my own."

Chapter Twenty-Nine

Beatrice

Grouper closed his eyes and announced he needed a nap. At a time like this? What the hell? Hours passed as I paced my prison. I came up with a hundred and one ideas to escape, and a hundred and one reasons why they wouldn't work, all while Grouper snored. With a loud sigh, I sank to the floor.

"I can't believe this is how I'm going to die," I huffed. The headaches had subsided, and my brain felt a little more at ease, even though I knew I had only hours until I met my fate. The buzzing in my chest had ceased as well, giving my pulse a break.

"Wake up. Wake up!" I yelled.

Grouper picked his head up and slowly unstuck his lids.

"Talk to me. I'm going crazy in this coop. Tell me about the first time you met Cash," I asked, wrapping my arms around my knees. I picked at the frayed rip in my jeans.

"Why?" he replied, raising one of his thick, hairy brows.

"Because I can't have the last memory of my life be you snoring. I want to talk about him. He's never really told me anything about his past. Have you known him a long time?"

"Yes, many years now. Our families used to be close before I went over to the dark side and became an informant on Earth." His bulb eyes dimmed. "Cash helped me with my brother. With his . . . mistake."

Ah, so *he* had a brother. Interesting! "What mistake?" I asked.

"My brother was much older than me. He was on the council. Our bloodline carried matching energy sources a long time ago. We have a very well-respected last name: Sayor." Grouper paused and looked at me, as though his name should mean something to me. Maybe on his planet, but I had never heard of it, so I smiled and let him continue. "My brother Gabe fell in love with a human girl on his first trip to Earth. At the time, her father worked for the DOAA as an assimilation scientist. She was in college and, although she knew about the DOAA, she had plans to be a doctor and live a normal life. She and my brother had a brief romance—well, brief compared to what my brother wanted. They concealed their relationship for years, until the Ferro Council and DOAA caught wind of it and threatened them both. Gabe was asked to step down, which shamed our family. We lost our status, and our bloodline was forever tarnished. Cash's father had been trying to push Gabe out of the council for years. He leveraged the affair to win leadership and power."

"What happened to the girl?" I asked.

"The girl was given a choice: show her loyalty to the DOAA or cut ties with her father and the DOAA completely. She chose the DOAA and became a guard."

"That's awful," I said, biting on my nail.

"Which part?" Grouper raised a brow.

I thought the tragedy was obvious, but I answered anyway. "How your brother and the girl he loved had to deny their feelings, all because of where they came from. It sounds very Romeo and Juliet—it's not their fault they fell in love. And who is the DOAA or the Ferro Council to sit back and tear two people apart like that? They are the ones who should be asking forgiveness."

Grouper chuckled.

"That's funny to you?" I asked, crossing my arms over my chest.

"More than you know, child. More than you know."

"What does that have to do with Cash and you?"

"I'm getting there. Several years later, my brother was asked to travel to Earth as a favor to the council. He had been so many times that they knew he would be able to navigate quicker than any of their own researchers. It was the first time he had been back on Earth since saying good-bye to the human girl. Of course, my stupid brother wouldn't give up the chance to see her again. They saw each other for one night —a night that would change everything."

"Really, you—a rogue alien—couldn't be associated with your brother, your own flesh blood and whatever else you aliens have inside of you?" Sarcasm soaked my words as I repeated Gertrude. "Sounds to me like you're a pretty big hypocrite." I couldn't believe Grouper would be such an ass to his own brother because of a group of aliens who made rules and laws that were unjust.

"At the time, little one, I was not a rogue. I was young. He was much older than me."

I huffed. "I still don't see what this has to do with Cash and you."

"Patience—I'm getting there. I saw my brother one other time. After I went rogue, Gabe came to Earth, seeking me out. He had a favor to ask. He needed me to find his human love. He feared she was in danger. I refused, of course, but Gabe was desperate. I caved and called Cash in on the job and made my brother swear to never seek me out again once we found her. Cash and the others had just gone through assimilation and were to be admitted as freshmen at Cartwright High School. I had been working with Cash as an informant for the last two years during his frequent travels back and forth between Ferro and Earth as he prepared to lead his team. He paid me for information. We trusted each other. Maybe it was our mutual dislike for his father, or maybe it was the mutual pain our brothers had caused us, but the truth was that Cash and I were friends."

My ears perked up. "Did Cash ever find her?" I asked, scooting closer to Grouper.

"Ay, he didn't have to. He had already been working with her. In fact, this was a human he was very close to. Her name was Faye Walker, your mother."

I gulped at this revelation. Mom dated a Ferroean before Dad.

"No way," I gasped.

"She didn't only date Gabe. She was at one time madly in love with him." Damn alien powers. Clearly Grouper was reading my mind. "Gabe started a rebellion over your mother and the fact that humans and Ferroeans could not be together. I had already gone rogue myself and was a bug on Earth. Rumor has it, the Ferroean council found Gabe, killed him and his followers. Not much of a surprise there. I think Cash felt guilty for the damnation his father caused to my family. Recently, Cash brought me information that a part of Gabe still lives."

"A part of him is still alive? How is that possible?" I asked, unsure I was following the logic. "Gabe is dead, right?"

"And that, my dear, is why this is so funny."

"I don't think it's funny, more like confusing."

Grouper smirked with the information he held. "Gabe has a daughter. The girl is a Blood-Light."

Chapter Thirty

Beatrice

My hands flew to my mouth. Butterflies fluttered in my stomach. I couldn't believe what he was saying. "That would m-mean . . ." I stuttered.

"Gabe was a father," Grouper finished for me.

I shook my head. Words were having a hard time connecting to my tongue. "Yes but . . ." I took another deep breath. "If what you are saying is correct, Gabe's daughter was illegal, and no one knew about her." I swallowed before asking the question I would never be able to take back. "Are you talking about me?"

Grouper yawned while rubbing his eyes. He balled up his jacket against the wall behind him and rested his head against it. "Get some sleep, little one. It's going to be a long day tomorrow." Then the light in his eyes dimmed as he started to breathe heavily.

Sleep was the last thing on my mind. My head swirled with the truth. Gabe was my father. My mom created me as a weapon, and the idea of death wove itself around all of it. I tried to focus on Grouper. He appeared calm and unfazed, not a bit disturbed that I was his niece. Niece? Could that really be true? But my dad . . .Robert. He had been there for my first *everything* from scraped knees, to homework questions, to teaching me how to drive. How could I be anyone else's daughter? And yet . . . Dad and I looked nothing alike. He had dark brown hair and brown eyes and caramel-colored skin. I was the spitting image of my mother.

Grouper's soft snores sounded in the background. At least I don't look like Grouper. Eventually his snores coaxed me into dreamland.

I woke to muffled voices in the pitch-black room. Several sets of feet paced near the birdcage, but my eyes couldn't make out the figures. A piercing, heart-stopping shrill broke through the darkness, and I shot up to my feet. Shivers of terror burrowed into the pit of my stomach as the screaming intensified in pitch. Then, with a thud, there was silence. What the hell was that? Where was Grouper?

"Gertrude's gonna kill us if she finds out," a foreign voice spoke.

More footsteps joined the room as light grew. "What the hell are you doing?" Grouper's groggy voice spoke out. I spun in my cage to see two males I'd never seen before. The light illuminated from Grouper's bulb eyes. My gaze dropped to the floor, where a dead girl lay in a pool of blood. I gasped in horror.

"She's awake," the male with blond hair said, turning to me with hungry eyes. Goo dripped from his limbs.

"Maybe it's because you killed a human several feet away from her and she heard the damn thing squeal to death, you idiots," Grouper said, leaning up against his cage. His body slouched against the cage, but his eyes were filled with fire.

"The human saw us use our powers," the blond male admitted. "We had no choice. She was snooping around this place and opened the door. She saw you locked up."

As they stepped away, I recognized the girl.

"Oh my god. It's Kathleen Butler!"

"Do all humans know each other?" the black-haired male asked, turning to his friend.

"You good-for-nothing idiots! Why wouldn't you use Influence?" Grouper asked, throwing his scaly hands up in the air.

"You killed an innocent human!" I shouted, throwing my hands to my face in disbelief. My heart kicked up a notch, sending my pulse into overdrive. I was one beat away from a heart attack.

"Get this cleaned up. Now!" Gertrude roared from the doorway.

The buzzing in my chest had returned, sending me into a rhythmic overload. I wanted to tell Seraphina's source to knock it off, but even I didn't blame it. We were going to die, and it would look something like Kathleen Butler.

Gertrude shook her head. "You morons can't get anything right. Forget it. What's done is done." Gertrude growled. Her blue eyes flashed completely white before slamming the door shut.

"Where's the key, Phil?" the black-haired guy asked.

"Damn it, I left it upstairs by the back door. Go get it, Jon."

"No, you," Jon said, backing away from the door like it was on fire. They were probably afraid of what lay behind it—Gertrude and her anger.

Grouper crossed his arms over his chest. More goo oozed through his limbs to the floor. "Why don't you both go get it, so I don't have to listen to you?"

The two guys huffed but left together.

Grouper rushed toward the edge of his imprisonment. "Listen to me. When they open your cage, you run. Get away from the edges painted in yellow. It's blocking your strength. When they follow and you are away from the power paralyzer, you fight. They aren't assimilated and are much weaker on Earth than they are on Ferro. We have a fighting chance."

I shook my head as tears streamed down my face. I had no idea what was going on. Could I even take on these two aliens?

"You are much stronger and more capable than you think. When a Ferroean is young, part of our training is visualization. If you focus on something like a kick or a punch and imagine the power you want to achieve, it will assist your actual power. Try to get the key to my cage and toss it to me. We will hold them off together."

"Grouper," my voice was shaky. Tears poured out of my eyes. "I don't know if I can do this. I'm not like you, or Cash, or the others."

"You are more like us than you think," he sighed. "Trust me."

I wiped away my tears with my sleeve. I nodded. I'd have to try. There was no other choice.

The doors opened and the two males appeared with the key. Grouper stood back as they opened my cage.

"Come out, little human," Jon said, reaching in for me like an owner calling his pet. His fingers were abnormally long, and his nails pointed and sharp. Goo dripped from his wrist, plopping to the ground with a sickening splatter.

I shook my head and pressed my back up against the bars farthest away from him. If I could get him in the cage with me, I'd have a better chance at the exit.

"Well, go in and get her," Phil said, laughing at the hesitant Jon.

Jon glanced at him, then back at me, accepting his partner's challenge. He slowly walked into the cage. Each step was as if he was walking on unstable ground. I wondered why he feared me at all. I was the human. He had much more strength as a Ferroean, yet the creases around his eyes and his slow gait told a different story. I had to act. Before he could move another inch, I kicked him in the groin. I visualized hitting him so hard that his balls would land in his stomach. The contact was fast but furious, and it felt more powerful than I ever imagined. He went down in the cage clutching at his crotch.

"You bitch!" he screamed, rolling around on the floor leaving goo marks in his wake. His knees curled high into his chest. My toes tingled from the hit, but I managed to jump over him. I turned and delivered another blow to his gut.

"That's for calling me a bitch!" I grabbed the key dangling from the hook across from my cage and flung it at Grouper. He didn't exactly catch it, but it latched onto his wrist, sticking to the goo oozing from his skin.

Phil ran toward me. My eyes darted to each side. There was nowhere to go. All dead ends.

"Where do you think you are going, human pet?" he called out.

I was toast until Grouper came around the side, holding his metal folding chair. He whacked Phil across his skull, bringing him to his knees. Goo flung across the room like Nickelodeon slime. I ran past him, but he reached up and grabbed my ankle. A sticky substance from his finers wetted my socks. He tugged and I collapsed to the ground, my face connecting with the cement. Blood dripped from my mouth and pooled under my face.

"Not so fast. Payback time," Jon said, having recovered from the cage. He was coming at me. Grouper moved toward us. I watched the wheels turn as he weighed his options. He could only take one down, and then the other would still have me.

Just then, the door swung open, and Cash, Mark, and Tasha appeared. Grouper's eyes were fully vibrant, lighting the room up for everyone to see.

"Stay back, Cash," Jon said, bringing me to my feet without much consideration for my injuries. I groaned as he jerked me back by my hair. Blood dripped off my face onto the floor. I could taste the copper.

Cash's eyes went wild, colors swirling frantically in all directions, as he watched Jon wrap one hand around my throat and the other around my stomach. His thumb pressed under my bra and I sucked in a breath. Cash seemed to notice where his finger brushed, and a terrifying look flashed across his face.

"One more step and your girlfriend dies," Jon threatened.

"Are you that hard up for a girl?" Cash said, sporting a wicked grin. But his strong stance and bulging biceps were anything but playful.

"Ha! You really screwed up this time. Your dad is going to kill you when he finds out you're into pets. How would Sera feel about your obsession with human chicks? Or the fact you fell for someone else so quickly? Maybe you are only obsessed with whoever possesses your matching energy source?"

Tasha moved forward, rounding the cage. Her steps were slow, her gaze permanently fixed on me. Mark paralleled her actions in the other direction, toward Grouper. His eyes stayed on Cash.

"Is that jealousy?" Cash asked, taking slow, precise steps toward us. He captured my gaze with his and gave me a slight nod. *You okay?* he thought to me.

Been better. A little help with the guy who is cutting off my oxygen flow would be nice.

Cash's lips tipped up from my response. It was the first time I'd spoken to Cash in my head. It was natural—like I had done it a million times before.

Cash refocused on Jon. "Sera never liked you much, but I heard you had a thing for her, and now you're practically fondling Bea. Dude, ever think of trying to get your own girl? Humans have these apps I can show you. It's the new dating craze. You'll love it. Now let Bea go, and you and I can talk outside where I'll show you what I'm really into."

"Ha. You think you are something else, don't you? I may not have had your first bitch, but I could definitely have this one if I wanted." Jon's hand tightened on my throat as he licked my cheek with his tongue. It was forked, like Grouper's. Cash's jaw twitched. The slick, wet sandpaper sensation on my skin undid me. Rage filled my insides. With every ounce of strength, I lifted my high-heeled boot and impaled it into Jon's foot, envisioning the spike going through his toes.

Jon reared back, howling. Holy crap! My boot had gone through his foot. The sight and sound of his pain filled me with a sense of accomplishment. His hand loosened from under my chest, and I took the opportunity to lunge for-ward. But before I was in the clear, he caught the bottom of my top, tearing it in the process. Jon growled and lashed out, trying to recapture me, but Cash was quicker. He grabbed me around the waist and swung me into Grouper's sticky, yet safe, arms. I had never been happier to have his glue-like matter cover me.

"You okay?" Grouper said quietly. I nodded, clutching tighter to his chest.

I watched as Cash's legs rounded in the air, connecting with Jon's face and bringing him to the ground. Honey-colored goo sprayed wildly like a sprinkler from Jon's mouth. But he shook his head and immediately stood back up, launching forward with a punch. Cash evaded the strike with a quick duck, and came back up with a full, powerful swing that connected to Jon's jaw. Crack. Pop. Bones broke.

"Just like old times, huh, Jon?" Cash jested. Jon stumbled back, but quickly recovered and released a right hook. Cash blocked it and gave an uppercut to his chin. The awful snapping sounds echoed in the empty room. Tasha's voice broke my trance.

"Follow me." She pointed toward a now opened door. Grouper lowered me to the floor and grabbed my hand, leading me to the exit. I glanced back. Mark was going toe to toe with Phil in the opposite corner, exchanging blows.

"What about Cash and Mark? We can't leave them," I said through heavy breaths as Grouper jerked me out the door behind Tasha. The last sound I heard was an unmistakable hard slam to the concrete. I prayed the person on the receiving end was Jon or Phil.

"They will meet us at another safe house. They know where to go," Tasha said. She looked right and left to make sure the coast was clear. I wiped the blood off my face as I stepped into light. I couldn't believe where we were. I had been stashed in the old equipment room at Cartwright. The building was scheduled to be knocked down next week. I'd never left school grounds this entire time.

The three of us rounded the building only to come to a screeching halt. Gertrude was standing in our path. She threw her hands to her hips and tapped the ground with the toes of her stilettos. Her cheeks were crimson with fury.

Tasha stepped forward to speak, but before she breathed a word, Gertrude grabbed her by the throat. Her red-painted nails dug into Tasha's skin, and yellow goo dripped down her neck. I didn't even have time to process what was happening. Gertrude launched her clear across the field as if she were a Frisbee. Her body soared through trees, hitting and breaking limbs out in the distance. The snap and popping of branches were the only sounds. And then her figure was gone. I had no idea where or how she landed, or if she was still alive. Within seconds, Gertrude twisted and grabbed Grouper by his arm. She flipped him over. As he landed, I heard the awful sound of bone cracking. Because he wasn't properly assimilated, he didn't have all of his powers or strength. She stood over him, smirking. Lifting her heel above his throat, she violently pressed down. Even the hairs on my arms pricked in utter fear.

"You are just like your brother—in love with the humans. And now you will die just like he did, for misplaced loyalty," she spat, and then sank her heel further through his flittering pulse. Brown liquid dripped from his mouth and his punctured neck, dotting the ground.

"No," I screamed, lowering myself to the grass and crawling to him. "Grouper," I whispered next to his head. Something wet and warm streaked my face, dripping onto him. I didn't even realize they were tears until I wiped them away from my eyes.

Grouper lifted his arm and cupped my face. The sticky goo around his hand stuck to my cheek. "You look so much like him," he garbled.

"W-who?" I whispered between soft sobs.

Grouper coughed and more liquid seeped from his neck. "Your father." His hand fell from my face. "Gabe," he croaked, and then his bulb eyes went dark. I clung to him, weeping into his chest. Gertrude kicked Grouper in his side. His lifeless body jerked. My head shot up.

"You ruthless bitch," I cried, pulling Grouper closer to me. "What did he ever do to you? Are you that cruel and heartless?"

"He's dead. Stop blubbering—it's pathetic. Now, get up before I make you." She glowered at me. I kissed Grouper's cheek and silently thanked him for trying to save me. I stood up slowly, never taking my eyes off of Gertrude. My fingers curled into a fist and, without thinking, I sent a right hook to her jaw. Gertrude stepped back, stunned by the force. Even I was shocked my hit had such an impact. I examined my hand, wondering where the power came from and why there was no damage to my knuckles. But my surprise was momentary. Gertrude advanced and clocked me across the skull, splitting the skin on my forehead. I hit the ground hard, falling to my knees, face-planting into the dirt. The wind was knocked out of me. I gasped for air, inhaling soil into my lungs. This time, the wet and warm substance dripping from my face was blood.

In my peripheral vision, I saw Cash and Mark appear from the equipment room. I was too weak to call out for them. Cash's eyes narrowed on me and then fixed on Gertrude. At an inhuman speed, he launched himself at Gertrude, knocking her to the ground and skidding several feet. Grass buckled up, exposing raw earth. An orange haze surrounded them and fogged my vision as Mark helped me to my feet. Every muscle groaned with each movement. I sagged forward, allowing Mark to support me. I watched as Cash attacked Gertrude from every angle. She was fast, but he was faster. She was strong, but he was stronger. Their strength was mesmerizing, unnatural. I had never imagined myself promoting an attack on a woman, but this bitch was nuts, and I wanted her to pay for the death of my friends. I wanted Cash to end her.

With one unmatched blow, Cash was able to pin a very tired and beaten Gertrude to the ground. He waved his hand at Mark.

"Your dagger," Cash called out. Mark shifted me to the side while he slipped his free hand into his waist sheath and drew out a dagger which glowed in a bluish yellow light. He tossed it at Cash. In one swift movement, Cash caught it in his grip and slit Gertrude in three places: her wrists and her right ankle. Instead of blood pouring out of her puncture wounds, a bright white light spilled into the ground, glowing like a radioactive chemical.

Tasha rounded the bend. Her face was scratched in countless places and her limbs bloody. Her shirt and pants were torn and dirtied, and her hair stuck to her wet, sweaty skin. Relief washed though me. She was alive.

"Hold her down," Cash said, motioning to the ankle he hadn't sliced. Gertrude lay practically lifeless on the floor.

"Cash, no, not like this," Tasha said, holding Gertrude to the dirt. She wasn't struggling. I wasn't even sure she could.

Cash's cold, menacing stare brought an abrupt halt to Tasha's words.

"Aren't you even a bit curious as to why the council wasn't in a hurry to find Sera's energy source and bring it back to Ferro? Or about your father working independently from the council?" Gertrude coughed. "Or how about how easy your dear old dad reacted to Bea as the opposing source's energy womb and insisted on keeping her safe? I wonder what his reaction to Sera's death was? It couldn't have been surprise," Gertrude taunted through tortured breaths, and Cash stiffened in response. "Ah, you have wondered, haven't you, boy?" She laughed, but it caught in her throat. Goo and blood bubbled out of her mouth.

Taking the bait, Cash asked, "What are you suggesting?"

Gertrude's brow rose. "I didn't kill my daughter. No matter how evil you think I am."

Cash's Adam's apple pulsed erratically in his throat. "Then who killed her?"

"Don't ask yourself *who*, boy. Ask why? What's the advantage to her death?" She glared in my direction. "Beatrice Walker was a plan. A very well thought out plan. Doesn't it seem odd that Ferro's leaders would leave their two most powerful energy sources on another planet when their own was in danger?"

"We have to save both planets. It's the prophecy," Tasha interjected with restrained curiosity.

Gertrude gurgled. "There is no prophecy. It's a fabricated story the council created to keep the opposing energy sources on Earth, guaranteeing Earth's safety. Ask yourself—what does the council treasure most?"

Tasha stared at Mark as if they shared a thought, then redirected her gaze to Gertrude. "Power. The council thrives on power," Tasha answered, looking at her brother as she continued. "They value power and those they rule. Cash,

I believe her," Tasha practically whispered. "They want to rule Earth."

"They used you and killed my daughter. Kidnapping the energy sources and bringing them back to Ferro was my only option to save my planet, my people," Gertrude gurgled, her breaths shorter and faster. "I had no choice. I would have never harmed my daughter. I only wanted to protect what is rightfully ours, Planet Ferro."

"You always have a choice," Cash said.

He took the glowing dagger and held it above Gertrude. "For the lives you've taken without cause, and for the disgrace to my people, may your hell be forever." And with that, he slit the remaining ankle. Her veins rose unbelievably high against her skin, slithering like black worms from her wrists and ankles toward her chest and slinking down into her energy source. Gertrude's body bucked up once, and then settled like a corpse. Within seconds, she turned into a yellow gem-shaped Gertrude and the light in her cobalt eyes went out. Cash punched Gertrude's lifeless body, and she shattered into a thousand pieces. Glass shards scattered over the ground. All that was left was the energy source burning brightly where her chest had once lain. Tasha pulled out a velvet black case, and the yellow light stone was swallowed up inside.

I could barely stand. Dizzy and nauseous, I stumbled toward him. He recognized my pain and handed the dagger back to Mark, catching me before I collapsed to the ground. He gently lifted me up into his strong arms. My head fell against his chiseled chest as if it was molded for me to nuzzle into, while my legs lay limply over the crease in his elbow. Anguish consumed me, spilling out in the form of tears. All this death . . . all for what?

"You're okay. I won't let anything happen to you. Crede Mihi." Cash's voice was soft and low, whispering in my ear until I fell into a deep, dark sleep.

Chapter Thirty-One

Beatrice

I woke up, staring at the soft glow of fluorescent ceiling lights. My eyes blinked rapidly, adjusting to the illumination. I breathed in through my nose, inhaling the scent of bleach and antiseptic. My hands fumbled over the thick bandages encasing my arm and trailed up to find several tubes running from my elbow, tangled together like mating snakes. The skin below them itched and burned.

I was in a hospital room.

I straightened up to get a better look at my surroundings. The walls were a cool white. A cart with unfamiliar instruments pushed up against my bedside and a loud, repetitive beeping noise came from the heart monitor beside me. My eyes darted across the room, and that's when I saw him.

Cash.

His face was worn and worried. His hair was disheveled. Even from this angle, I could see shadows blooming beneath his eyes. He hadn't bothered to heal himself and stared aimlessly at the window, unaware that I was awake and watching him.

"No, I'm completely aware," he said in a cool voice, but continued to gaze outside like he was watching something.

The sun was setting and a peaceful glow from the dipping rays cascaded over his complexion, shadowing his chiseled jawline and high cheekbones. His lips were a dark, pouty pink—probably from biting them out of anger. He looked beautiful. Breathtaking. And I knew I was in—

"If Gertrude was right about the council, about the prophecy, about my father," Cash whispered, cutting off my thoughts, "I think I know someone who can help us."

"Who?" I said as Cash turned and looked in my direction.

"Someone who I . . . I thought betrayed me. Someone who I once adored."

A female moan interrupted Cash, breaking our conversation. I turned to find Darla repositioning her knees higher to her chest in a hospital chair, her eyes closed. Another groan sounded, and she slumped. Her head fell back against the top of the cushion, and her arms hung over the sides. Black smudges smeared under her lower lashes, while her hair lay wildly around her shoulders, as if she hadn't combed it in days.

Cash gestured with his head toward her. "That one might not wake up for some time. They gave her quite a few sedatives." I was about to ask why but shook the thought away. With Darla it could have been anything. Sedating her was probably for the best.

My throat felt raw as I cleared it to speak. "Where is everyone?" I asked.

Cash walked slowly to my bed and sat on its edge. He leaned over. The mattress dipped with his weight. Speaking softly, he said, "Robert is outside with the doctor. Tasha is with him using Influence, since you are healing at an unnatural rate. Sammie and Chris are getting food in the cafeteria. Mark and Paul are at the house packing."

"Why packing?"

"We need to leave Cartwright as soon as possible. I'm sorry."

I nodded. After what happened to Grouper, I wanted to leave, too. Cartwright would never be the same.

"Why am I in a hospital?" My hand clutched at my throat and I motioned for the pitcher on the cart next to me. Cash grabbed the plastic cup and filled it with water. He moved the tray closer and handed me the cup. I took small sips, feeling the soothing liquid coat my throat and slither down to my empty stomach. Cash placed the cup back down on the tray table and pushed it out of his way before scooting closer to me on the bed.

"Someone called 911 when they discovered Kathleen's blood behind the school. I was carrying you out when the police and ambulance arrived. They thought it was yours, since you had cuts and scrapes along your limbs and face." Cash reached out and traced the curve of my cheek with his finger, like he was touching my wounds. I placed my hand over his. I didn't feel any abrasions. "There were too many people with varied thoughts to use Influence. It would take forever to work on each mind, and we didn't have the time or the manpower."

"Are the police going to interrogate me?" I asked. I wasn't sure if I could pull that off. I'm a terrible liar, especially to authority figures. Telling the truth—that I was kidnapped by aliens who wanted the matching energy source inside of me—would probably land me in a mental institution.

"Tasha Influenced your doctor to explain that you have retrograde amnesia, a loss of memory-access to events that occurred during a time of stress. They are under the as-sumption you were attacked and robbed, since your belong-

ings were nowhere to be found. That's what the file says."
Cash pointed to a manila folder at the end of my bed. It
barely peeked out of a plastic case. Retrograde amnesia. A
fake cover story. Well, this wouldn't be the first time. "They
won't be bothering you," Cash continued.

I stared at him, keeping my thoughts quiet and trying to
hear his. After what felt like a decade of silence between us
both, I whispered, "You saved me."

He brushed his fingers over the curve of my jaw, lingering
on my chin and lifting it so our eyes matched. He didn't say
anything.

I shook my head. "It's my fault he's dead," I said.

"It is *not* your fault. None of this has been. Not what
happened to Seraphina, Faye, Dominic, Claude, Kathleen,
Grouper, Gertrude. None of these deaths are on your hands.
Do you understand?" His voice was harsh, but his face was
fixed with concern. "Grouper knew the risks. He was willing
to die for you."

"If I had listened to you more—"

Cash placed his finger over my lips. "We could all play
that game. If I hadn't let Seraphina leave and go to California; if I had told you about her energy source from the start;
if I had trained you from the day we met; if I had told you
how I . . ." He shook his head. "There are so many ifs that I'm
drowning in them, but I won't let you harbor the same guilt.
I won't, and it's not up for discussion. You are not at fault."
His voice was firm, demanding. "If anything, you never had
a choice."

"We all have a choice," I said, remembering what he'd
told Gertrude. It was true. No matter what I said, he needed
to carry the weight of what had happened. Being account-
able was part of who he was and, even though I knew he

wasn't to blame, my protest would be wasted breath on him. He'd never allow anyone else to take responsibility away from him. I inhaled deeply and slowly exhaled, releasing the need to argue. "Now what?" *Where do we go from here?* I spoke to him in my head.

Cash sighed. "Out west. We need to find Dr. X. We cannot trust anyone but our team." He shook his head. "For now, you need to rest." Cash went to stand but I gripped his hand, pulling him back down. Sparks flew between our fingers like little electric shocks, but I didn't let go and neither did he.

An odd ache pierced my heart and the buzzing resumed at an accelerated rate. It was like I had two hearts—one mine and the other the source—and they both responded to Cash with infinite intensity.

A muscle popped in his jaw, and his fist clenched the blanket that covered me. Anger flared behind his eyes. "I can't explain what I felt when I walked into the equipment room and saw Jon with his hands on you. But when he licked you . . ." The lights in the room flickered and the metal bed below me started to shake. I squeezed his hand, and then rubbed my thumb idly across his knuckles in a circular motion. His breathing seemed to calm, and the room went back to normal. Did I have some type of soothing effect on him, or had he calmed himself? "I don't kill my kind; it's not my preferred means to an end. But I would do it again. Goddamn it. If I was faced with the same situation, I would do it again to those maggots for touching you, caging you, threatening you. I would murder all of my people if that's what it took to keep you safe. Do you understand?"

Tears cascaded down my cheeks. I did understand, and I didn't need him to say it because, like Grouper said, words can be used to hide behind, but actions are truths unable to be disguised. I clamped down on the sudden pressure on the back of my throat, hoping to obstruct my threatening sobs. Everything about us wasn't normal—it wasn't how ordinary teenagers acted or loved—but no one could mistake the desperate look in our eyes. I was happy with this life—more than happy. This was my destiny, and it felt right.

"What does this all mean?" I asked, my voice barely audible. I shifted closer, brushing my leg against his hand. Heat penetrated through the sheet, warming my skin and sending a flush to my face. I picked all the wrong moments to want him—I'd have to say that wanting Cash while in a hospital gown and probably stinking from not showering for two days was definitely the wrong time.

Drawing in a deep breath, Cash said, "I'm not sure." He wove his fingers through mine.

"What about the asteroids?"

Cash leaned in so close that our breaths mingled into one. His forehead rested against mine. The mere touch sent my heart into overdrive. "We will figure it out." He pressed a barely-there kiss to my nose and whispered against them, "Together."

My heart flipped in my chest. A strange need took over inside of me, and I sat up straighter. I wrapped my hands around his neck, drawing him into me. A tingling burn started at my lips as my body singed with pleasurable tremors and shocks. I felt the gentle pressure of his hands gripping my lower back, pulling our bodies closer.

I placed one hand over his energy source. It beat thunderously under my palm. And then I was zapped. His energy source jolted me. I moved my hand to the opposite side of his chest and felt, for the first time, our sources pair up completely. It was unlike anything I had ever experienced. The reaction was so intense. I could feel everything in him as if it were in me—power, anger, lust, heat, sadness, regret, guilt—all bottled up and spilling out into this moment. It was as if we were one, moving in rhythm rather than of our own accord. These strong sensations froze my veins, then lit my skin on fire, melting the blood flowing within me. I didn't know what was happening, but I couldn't pull away. My body wouldn't let me. Cash, hearing my thoughts, put his hands on my shoulders and tried to gently push us apart, but my body wouldn't let him. I drew him closer, running my fingers through his hair and clutching onto it. I heard Cash talk to me in my thoughts. *Bea, tell me what's going on.* And that's when it hit me. Pain exploded in my head, sharp and piercing. It felt like my scalp was being sawed off. My head jerked back, and my eyes slammed shut. Memories flooded my veins—each image soared to my brain, crashing into each other, and I screamed a blood-curdling scream.

"What is it? What's wrong?" Cash demanded. I couldn't see him, but I could hear the sheer panic threaded in his voice.

Connect. Connect to your scar.

I grabbed his hand and used it to pull the gown down exposing my scar. Forcefully, without even thinking, I pressed his two pointer fingers into my scar and that's when it all happened.

The volume of recall overpowered my ability to respond as the day my mom and I had gone hiking returned to the forefront. It was her idea to take the trip. She made me leave my cell phone at home. I fought her at first but, of course, she won. As we walked along the rocks, she asked me strange questions about Dad, my childhood, if I liked living in California, if I missed Cartwright. At the time, I thought she was being chatty, but now, seeing the day replay itself, she had asked me these questions because she wanted solace in her decision. She was also saying goodbye. She told me how much she loved me, my dad, and our life together. She said if she had to do it all over again, she would do it exactly the same way. She had no regrets when it came to her family. The scenes played out like a movie reel, up to the moment she took out a needle, said two words, "Crede Mihi", and I collapsed.

"Mom!" I croaked. I rubbed my chest. My fingers stilled over my skin. I pulled down my tank top revealing a raised diamond-shaped scar, the size of a silver dollar. The flesh felt hardened, almost bone-like. My eyes scanned the rest of my appearance. My clothes were tattered and torn. Dried blood clung to the hem of my shirt. Blood? My heart pulsated, practically bursting out of my chest.

Lying next to me was a girl about my age. She had long black pin-straight hair. She appeared to be unconscious. Her chest barely rose. I worried she wasn't breathing. I reached out to touch her arm when I heard my mother's voice.

"Run, Bea. Run!"

The words got louder, closer. "Run, Bea! Get out of here! Now!" Mom yelled as she entered from the opening diagonally from me. She held two long, silver daggers, one in each hand. The blades glinted off the lights above me, projecting dancing reflections on the walls. That was not something you see every day. Her hands usually held cookware or cleaning supplies, not weapons.

I jumped to my feet. "Mom, what's happening?" My head buzzed loudly, throwing me off-balance. I grabbed the metal table to steady myself. "Whoa!" My gaze traveled to the girl next to me. "What about her? Who is she?"

"Run, Bea—that way." She pointed down a dark, narrowing tunnel, opposite the way she'd come. My gaze darted from her to the exit, and back to the girl on the table. "She will be fine. You need to run now!" Sweat glistened on her forehead and dripped down her neck, mixed with blood that trailed from a gash above her brow. Her always-perfect hair clung to her face. She was wearing olive cargo pants, black army boots, and a black tank top. Her muscles were flexed and tensed—I saw another gash in her arm, more blood dotted her body. She looked like a version of G.I Jane rather than the Martha Stewart I knew.

"No, I'm not leaving without you. What's going on? What happened to you" My gaze traveled her body from toe to head. "Where are we? Why do I feel like someone hit me with a brick? Mom, say something!" My questions blurted out into one sentence. This didn't feel real.

My mother placed both daggers in one hand and used her other hand to brush my face with the pad of her thumb. Her hazel eyes filled with moisture. "Four cuts, each wrist and ankle. That's how you kill them," she said, her voice lowered with a trace of empathy. I could tell she was trying to keep it together. She reached into her boot and pulled out a dagger that matched the others she held. A diamond-shaped symbol was etched in its hilt with the name Gabe Sayor in the middle. My eyes fixed on each letter. Gabe Sayor. I was drawn to it. She thrust it in my hand and, in an instant, a jolt ran through my body. I gasped at the shock.

"It was your father's. It's yours now," Mom said, ignoring my reaction. The hilt felt like hot lava in the palm of my hand. Fire raced through my veins. My breath seized. I could hardly focus.

"Four cuts, each wrist and ankle. That's how you kill them. Repeat that back to me. Now Beatrice Ann, repeat it back to me so I know you've heard me." I looked up. Mom's face held fear, but also determination. My gut twisted.

I sucked in a deep breath and felt the air rush in and out. My head cleared, and I repeated her words. "Four cuts, each wrist and ankle. That's how I kill them," I said, my voice cracking. My fingers flexed around the handle. A surge of energy passed through my palm like an electric current as my grip tightened automatically. "Kill who?" I whispered, barely recognizing what she was saying.

"You can do this," she said, kissing me on the forehead. Her lips were dry and brittle, void of gloss or lipstick. "Find Cash." She placed her hand on my new scar. "Tell him Sera is alive. She asked me to meet her at the cave, and when I arrived with you, she was barely breathing. I removed her source and hid it in you. She needs to be awakened. She will teach you how to control your power." She removed her fingers from my chest and cupped my face. "Tell him there's a second prophecy. One day a Blood-Light with an opposing source will lead The Reprisal. You must connect sources. The clues to our survival lie in your connection. Your humanity is what makes you different. There's no other in this universe like you." My heart swelled. We were in danger, and nothing Mom was saying made any sense. Mom spoke, "Now go, baby. I need you to run." My eyes flooded with tears—it pooled over my cheeks.

"Mom," I croaked, but before I could finish my plea, a gust of air whirled around me. Something grabbed my tank top and hurled me across the room. My back slammed against the wall, knocking the air out of my lungs. I crumbled to the floor, face-planting onto the cold surface. My cheek lay in the crevice of the tiled floor as blood dripped from the corner of my mouth, darkening the grout. The dagger flew from my hand and skidded away from me. Spots blurred my vision as I tried to sit up.

A large man with long, black hair, bulging biceps, and glowing white eyes towered over me.

"And where do you think you are going?" he growled. His white eyes brightened. No pupils. Oh my god.

I scooted backward until my back slammed against the cold wall. The man followed with slow, precise steps, taunting me with his pace. His lips curled into an eerie grin. If he was trying to intimidate me, it was working. He wore military gear, like my mother, but was armed with much more than daggers. He had two guns strapped to shoulder holsters, as well as one around his thigh, connecting to his waist. Two grenades dangled off his belt. His smile grew as he watched me eye each weapon. My heart slammed against my chest while my pulse spiked. My eyes flitted behind him to my mother.

"I wouldn't do anything you'll regret, Arron," she said. She knew him! Her stance was strong and unwavering. Her foreboding eyes narrowed in on the man's backside. All I could think of was Dad. I wished he was here. He'd help us.

In one quick motion, Mom raised her hands and waved them forward. The metal table I had been laying on soared into the air and crashed down onto my attacker. A look of surprise flickered across his face at the impact. My jaw dropped.

"Run, Bea!" Mom shouted. Her deadly gaze never left him. I scrambled to my feet, using the wall to stand, but couldn't move forward. I wanted to run. Hell, anything to get away from the freak in front of me, but I couldn't. I watched the man pull his legs under him and lift suddenly, throwing the table out of his way. It landed against the opposite wall. He grunted and lunged for my mother.

"Mom!" I yelled helplessly.

She twisted, evading his grasp, and landed a right hook to the side of his head. He stumbled backward while she rolled onto the ground and picked up my dagger. She charged him and with two quick motions, sliced his wrists. Then she spun around and slammed her foot into his stomach, sending him to the ground. Another two quick slits to his ankles.

The man looked from one cut to the next. His veins rose under his skin, slinking like snakes from his wrists and ankles toward his chest, as black as tattooed ink. Within seconds, he morphed into a faint yellow outline of his body. Mom stepped on him, and he shattered into a thousand pieces. Glass shards pierced the air like raindrops sprinkling to the ground around his arsenal. Other than my rapidly fluttering eyes, I was paralyzed. Frozen. Completely unable to grasp what I just witnessed. Mom bent down and scooped up a glowing yellow gem from within his ashes. It sparkled like crystal as she placed it in the satchel around her waist.

A high-pitched shrill echoed behind me, and I spun around. Two male forms stood stock-still in the opening. Their outfits mirrored my mother's and my attacker's. Each wore a belt with two visible sheaths, but no guns or grenades. Their wide, white eyes darted from the broken pieces scattered on the floor like sea glass to my mother, to me, then back to my mother. Pain and rage were etched in their fea-

tures. Mom threw the dagger back at me and, without even blinking, I caught it and wrapped my fingers tightly around the hilt. The same electric pulse shot through my palm as if the dagger was molded to me. But this time I didn't react with surprise. I welcomed the feeling. A surge of energy ran through my limbs, tingling down to my toes and out to my fingertips.

"Goddamn it, baby, run!" Mom yelled.

She gave me one last glance. A mixture of love and sadness filled her eyes. My heart crumbled with confusion and despair. She nodded slowly. My chest rose sharply as I nodded back. I did as I was told no matter how much it hurt. I pivoted on my heels and darted down the tunnel. My hiking boots pounded against the rock and dirt, dust trailing in plumes in my wake. I ignored the pain in my back and limbs as well as the combined moisture of torrent sweat and blood trickling down my body. I focused on the far-off spot of light, which grew brighter as I ran. Adrenaline spiked, and my legs churned at an unearthly speed. I sprinted until I saw the outside world.

That was the last time I saw my mother alive.

When I opened my eyes, Dad, Cash, and the others were in the room, staring at me with wide eyes. Darla had woken from her sedative and was gripping the side of my hospital bed so tightly her knuckles were white.

Cash held my hand in his. His thumb glided over my skin. The small gesture seemed to quiet my rioting pulse. Then I looked into his eyes. They were bright with realization. The color was clear blue.

"Oh my god," I said. My voice shook as I spoke.

He nodded and turned to the others, but never let go of my hand. "Our connection is the answer, but we need Sera's help. We need an Awakening!"

The End

Acknowledgement

First, I'd like to thank my college advisor. My freshman year she sat me down and pointed out all of my electives were English classes and thought it might be in my best interest to major in a subject I was clearly passionate about. It's been a journey since then to align myself with writing. I'd like to thank all my friends and family who have read my work and motivated me to move forward on a writing career path. A special thank you must go out to my designer, my co-pilot, and my younger but wiser cousin, Erin Foster. Over the years you have supported all my harebrained ideas, stayed up way passed our bedtimes to collaborate, and shared your honest opinions to make me a better writer, friend, and family member. I also want to thank Tara Lewis, my editor. In the eleventh hour, she closed the circle on the trilogy name for me, The Blood-Light series, and she has been a pillar of information and advice since I met her. The biggest thank you goes to my father. He has filled in as the role of my mother for so many years, and although his editing skills are nowhere near hers, his unconditional love is. Love is really all a book ever needs and certainly all a daughter ever requires. He's my confidant, my cheerleader, and my idol. I am who I am because of you. And finally, a big thanks to my husband. Thank you for playing *Call of Duty* so I can write in my office undisturbed, for putting up with my late hours, and for loving me for exactly who I am. You and I will always be the best love story of all.

About Dana
Claire

Author Dana Claire believes that the beauty of reading is that one can live a hundred lives within the stories of books. A shared dream of hers and her mother's, she promised her dying mother that she would become a published author and that dream has been realized with *The Connection*.

Made in the USA
Columbia, SC
06 January 2021

30385494R00154